THE
HURTING
CIRCUS

THE HURTING CIRCUS

Blood Red Turns Dollar Green Volume 3

PAUL O'BRIEN

Skyhorse Publishing

Skyhorse Publishing books may be purchased in bulk at special discounts for sales promotion, corporate gifts, fund-raising, or educational purposes. Special editions can also be created to specifications. For details, contact the Special Sales Department, Skyhorse Publishing, 307 West 36th Street, 11th Floor, New York, NY 10018 or info@skyhorsepublishing.com.

Skyhorse® and Skyhorse Publishing® are registered trademarks of Skyhorse Publishing, Inc.®, a Delaware corporation.

Visit our website at www.skyhorsepublishing.com.

10 9 8 7 6 5 4 3 2 1

Library of Congress Cataloging-in-Publication Data is available on file.

Cover design by Brian Peterson

Print ISBN: 978-1-5107-0935-5
Ebook ISBN: 978-1-5107-0938-6

Printed in the United States of America

For Niamh. I thank every day
whatever random lottery put us together.

CHAPTER ONE

October 12, 1972.
New York.

Lenny knew he was dying. He knew the shrieking siren was for him. His boss was dead. Lenny didn't know if his children were okay—he couldn't speak to ask. His mouth was full of blood. His throat too.

He was lifted into the waiting ambulance, a single bullet in his chest. Lenny could feel himself dying. He wanted to see his wife, hear his kids. The emergency responders worked on his body while his mind drifted home.

Five days later.
London, England.

Joe Lapine walked behind the bellhop. The carpet under their feet was soft and the place was quiet.

"How long is your stay in London, sir?" the bellhop asked.

"Forty-eight hours," Joe replied.

"A flying visit, then?"

Joe didn't want to talk. He particularly didn't want small talk. "Listen," Joe said as he removed a fifty-pound note from his pocket. "There's a Mister Tanner Blackwell staying here, too. You need to go wake him and tell him his meeting is about to start."

"Yes, sir," the bellhop said as he took the money and walked quickly away.

Once inside his room, Joe took a seat at the desk. He laid out his watch and a slip of paper that had a couple of phone numbers written on it. Those numbers were all Joe had to make everything right again. The watch was to make sure he did it in time. Danno's death had made the spotlight on the wrestling business too bright. It had dragged an operation that thrived on secrecy into the public eye. The wrestling world was being turned over and it was up to Joe, as chairman of the National Wrestling Council, to change it back to the way it had been.

Since 1948, all of the bosses of all the wrestling territories had met under the umbrella of the NWC. They used their monopoly to crush any likely competitors, discuss wrestler trades and match endings, and, most importantly, decide who was going to be their world champion. Now, the NWC's most prestigious territory had a dead boss—and an investigation that was getting too close for comfort. Joe wasn't directly responsible for any of the incidents that had set the law onto them—he wasn't the one who had broken the wrestling business —but Joe was sure going to try to fix it. The sooner he could drag the wrestling business back into the dark rooms it thrived in, the sooner they could all start making real money again.

On the ground, the NYPD didn't give a fuck about wrestling, or the fact that some wrestling guys were taking each other out. What really got the law animated was the fact that a New York senator had been attacked on their streets, under their noses. Senator Hilary J. Tenenbaum was working on a bill to ban professional wrestling in New York State. He had been assaulted and stabbed in both legs the night before the hearings began. This had left the wrestling business looking more than a little suspect. Such a high-profile and shocking event wasn't beneficial for anyone—not the wrestling bosses nor the police chiefs who ran the city. And now the main suspect, Danno Garland, had been murdered. Too much bloodshed and too many column inches provoked every badge and uniform in New York to grab the wrestling business by the throat. In all their years of existence, the National Wrestling Council had never faced anything like this before. New York, their crown jewel, was now a toxic city to them, and a scandal like this was very bad for business across the country.

The only thing that saved the entire wrestling business from being exposed was that Danno's right-hand man, Ricky Plick, had burned Danno's office to the ground before anyone in uniform got to it.

But someone like Joe just couldn't risk assuming that Ricky had destroyed everything.

That's why he was sitting in front of a couple of phone numbers and a watch. He was going to use the Royal Horseguards Hotel in London to try to stem the rot that was spreading in New York. Before he could begin, though, he had to get his fellow bosses in order. And he needed to do it as far away from the growing chaos as possible.

The phone rang, and Joe answered it to hear the receptionist: "They're ready for you downstairs, sir."

About four thousand miles away, Joe had already set another pillar of his plan in place. He didn't know the details—and didn't want to—but was safe in the knowledge that a large part of his problem was about to be dealt with.

The same day.
Atlanta.

Donta Veal was the kind of man that the wrestling bosses loved: he was loyal, he was tough, and he enjoyed hurting people. He had grown up with Joe, which meant he could be trusted when the call needed to be made. Joe couldn't think of a time in his career when he more needed Donta to do what Donta did best.

Joe had tried Donta in the ring about a decade before, but had quickly had to rethink his decision. Donta didn't seem to grasp the *collaborative* nature of professional wrestling. Joe doubled Donta's salary and retired him from competition. If Donta was going to hurt people, then he might as well hurt the people that Joe *wanted* hurt. Donta would happily bite, break, or maim anyone who tried him—and some people who didn't. He never really gave a fuck who it was.

Joe had had to hide Donta for a couple of years after Donta pulled out the eyeball of a bar patron in Joe's hometown. To someone who didn't know Donta, such a thing might sound like the act of a frenzied man. But Donta didn't do frenzy, or any emotion for that matter. The eyeball came out as calmly as one could do that sort of thing. Joe made some calls, protected his friend, and Donta went on a long vacation, which he was happy to end when Joe made another call to put him back in the game.

Joe usually only called if someone had stiffed him on a payment. Sometimes venues would try to pay as little as possible, or some local TV guy would move Joe's TV time. They would get a visit from Donta. This time, it was going to be Donta's highest profile job. Joe knew Donta could be a liability in delicate matters, but he didn't have any choice. Joe's problem needed to be dealt with, and the NWC chairman didn't have the luxury of time to meticulously plan it out.

"Mister," said a street kid, knocking on Donta's car window. "I got what you wanted." Donta handed the kid a five-dollar bill and directed him toward the back of his car. The boy threw a stack of newspapers into the open trunk and disappeared.

Donta got out of his car and walked around to see that the trunk was now half-full of newspapers and magazines. He had gone from town to town, paying kids and homeless guys to buy him a few papers here and a couple of magazines there. Even with one on top of the other, it was easy to see the common face that saturated all front-page headlines: the New York senator who had been attacked, Senator Hilary J. Tenenbaum.

Donta closed the trunk and drove as fast as he could toward Florida.

Same day.
London.

They assembled downstairs in the closed-curtain breakfast room, which otherwise would have had a beautiful view of the river Thames. Not a single person around that table gave a fuck about scenery. They were interested in their money. They were interested in how their chairman was going to make this situation in New York right.

Joe entered the perfectly ordered room feeling a little jet-lagged and stale from the flight. At the head of the table—in Joe's seat—was Tanner Blackwell, the owner of the Carolina territory *and* the promoter of one of the heavyweight champions of the world. Down at the other end were Jacque Kaouet and Jose Rios, who owned the Quebec and Mexico City territories, respectively. Sitting in the chair by the window was Niko Frann, the owner of the LA territory.

Joe started. "Thank you for being here, gentlemen. We're all a long way from home." He received a round of nods as he pulled out a chair for himself at the side of the table. "We need to discuss our loose ends," Joe said. "And we need to agree on a course of action to get us through this dangerous time for our business."

Tanner could sense that his opportunity was slipping away. Before their world changed, Tanner had made a deal that purposely created two heavyweight champions. Their unification match—match that would pit them against each other—was to be a record-breaker, a huge windfall. A windfall that would have benefited Tanner more than anyone else in wrestling, as he owned one of the champions, and Danno owned the other.

"Can't we *make* New York have the unification match? Before we change everything, we can still get this done," Tanner said.

Joe eased into his reply, but not before he made sure that his tie was centered. "I'm proposing to the executives here today that we go back to basics," he said.

"Hear, hear," came the response—from everyone except Tanner.

Joe continued, "We're going to honor our own rules, which state that all title changes and territory sales are to be sanctioned by us collectively, first."

Tanner jumped in again. "Listen, we can go back and get this match set up for the end of the month. We can't have two champions out there in the long term: that hurts the prestige of both belts."

Joe nodded in agreement. "But look around this room, Tanner. Look at the fucking empty chairs in here," he said. "One by one, we killed each other—for what? For New York, that's what. If we continue down this road, that place is going to be the end of us all."

"I know what this is doing to our business," Tanner replied. "Do I look like some kind of fucking idiot to you?"

"Well, then you know what the right thing to do here is," Joe replied. "If anyone is thinking of buying or selling territory, then it has to come here before anything else happens. We vote on what's best for business. This whole fucking mess was made by people making deals outside of this meeting, and as chairman of this council, I am useless if I don't know what the fuck is going on." Joe watched the room as he was given a quiet nod from everyone in the room—everyone except Tanner.

"No more side deals and secret handshakes," Jose Rios said. "We're supposed to be working the marks who buy the tickets, not each other."

"We work as a collective, like we used to before," Jacque added.

Joe looked to be doing what any reasonable and responsible chairman would do: he was putting everything back on the table, and was taking the decision-making away from the back-alley meetings and "wink-wink" deals that were killing their business. The other bosses weren't crazy about having a leash and a muzzle put on them, but no one had a counter-argument ready—not with the unprecedented mess that was left in New York.

"I am sick of lying low every couple of months because one of us gets greedy or stupid. Or both," Joe said.

"I second that," Niko said, nodding.

"That's fine for you guys," Tanner said as he picked some fluff from his trousers.

"Why is it okay for us, and not for you, Tanner?" Jacque asked.

Tanner wet his thumb and wiped the last nuisance from his suit. "Because to sanction this approach would mean that everyone else here would have to change *nothing*." Tanner turned his attention to Joe. "You know *I* want New York, and you know that *I* want that unification match. New York and I both have heavyweight champions out there. It was only a few weeks ago that we made the decision to create two titles, just so we could put them back together. Owning just one title is like having the dynamite but not the matches."

Joe leaned in so Tanner could see the whites of his eyes. "As of right now, this council is saying that New York is off limits. You hear me, Tanner? We're not bringing all their chaos into the council."

Tanner dismissively turned away from Joe. "What do the rest of you think?" he asked the other bosses. "You all think we should leave this much fucking money on the table to rot in Manhattan?"

"New York needs time," Niko said. "There are investigations and cops everywhere asking about who we do business with. We've never had this before, Tanner."

All the other bosses stayed quiet. Their silence told Tanner everything he needed to know. He slowly turned back to the table and gave the chairman a slight conceding nod.

"Do we have a plan to take the focus off New York right now, so we can go home and earn some fucking money?" Niko asked Joe.

"I already have something in motion," Joe replied.

With that short statement, Joe had won the room. The NWC would close ranks and play small, but safe. New York was out of reach. Kinda.

The next day.
Florida.

Donta walked across the old tough floorboards to the counter of the local store. Out of all the places he'd been in his life, he hated Florida the most. It might have been the travel, or it might have been the people. It also could have been the stationary ceiling fan above his sweaty head that made no fucking difference whatsoever to the stifling heat. In his experience, Floridians were by and large a friendly bunch who prided themselves on knowing their neighbors. This was a good thing for finding people—but it was also a bad thing if you were a stranger in their small town who didn't want to be remembered. For this reason, he had a fedora pulled down over his eyes—not that there was anyone in the tiny store who would notice. This was a tourist spot with no tourists. It was a swampy, off-road, brown-necked, sweat-stained store that sold milk, newspapers, postcards, and stamps.

Donta handed his purchases to the lady behind the counter so she could ring them up. She didn't care to talk, but smiled anyway. "Keep the change," he said as he took his postcards and stamps outside into the sweltering heat.

It was wet, warm, windy, and humid all at the same time. He'd only been back in Florida for a day and already he was looking forward to getting the fuck out of there. He pulled his hat down further and threw the postcards in the trash outside as he marched to his car. He sat inside and opened his glove box. He took out a pre-typed, pre-sealed envelope which was already addressed:

SENATOR HILARY TENENBAUM
UNITED STATES SENATE
WASHINGTON, DC 20510

Donta carefully took his newly purchased stamps, licked them, and stuck them at the top of the prepared envelope. He looked around a little and made sure no one was watching before he opened his car door and hurriedly walked to the rickety mailbox at the side of the store. Donta made sure that his face was covered before covertly sliding the envelope into the slot.

There was only one man who could tie the wrestling business to the attack on the senator, and that man lived about five minutes from where Donta posted his letter.

CHAPTER TWO

New York.

The Nightly View was a current affairs show that aired out of New York. It usually ran two or three investigative pieces with its studio anchor, Ant Stevens, directing traffic and linking one piece to the next before wrapping with an in-studio interview. This night Ant knew he had landed a big one. Both interviewer and interviewee were quiet, with their heads bowed and their faces freshly powdered, as they waited to be counted in.

"Three . . . two . . ."

Ant began on cue: "And now we turn back to New York, where in recent times the stories of murder, corruption, prostitution, and random acts of violence seem to grow by the day. We now live in a city where we have police dogs on the subways, whole neighborhoods are no-go areas, and not even New York's own politicians are immune to the city's slide. Tonight we have in studio Senator Hilary J. Tenenbaum, who was himself viciously attacked on the streets of New York only a few weeks ago."

Ant's golden voice directed traffic to Senator Tenenbaum, who was sitting opposite him. "And, because of the charges levied in today's papers about just *who* might be behind such an attack," Ant

said to Camera One, "we also have on the phone a wrestling promoter out of Tennessee, Mr. Joe Lapine."

"Thank you," the senator said as he managed a fleeting nod of thanks.

Ant was all business. "Senator, you say that this attack was because
of your investigation into professional wrestling in New York State.
You say that this sport isn't a sport, in fact, and that everyone
involved in it knows the same."

Senator Tenenbaum cleared his throat. "That's correct. On the
night I was viciously set upon, I was walking back to my home office
to finish up some papers that I needed for the pro-wrestling hearings the following day. I was trying to get a bill together to ban professional wrestling in the state of New York. I never made it home to
do so. I was warned—"

Ant interjected. "Warned, sir?"

"Yes, the man who did this to me didn't wear a mask, or a hood, or
anything to conceal his face. He was sent to intimidate me. He looked
me in the eye and told me to stay out of 'business that wasn't mine.'" The
senator took a drink of water to steady himself; he was clearly emotional.

"Mr. Tenenbaum, I hope you're doing better, sir," Joe Lapine said
over the connected phone line. Senator Tenenbaum shook his head
in disgust at Joe's phony concern.

"What do you think when you hear a story like this, Mr. Lapine?"
Ant asked, opening the conversation to Joe. "And, by the way, thank
you for calling in," Ant quickly added. "We find it hard to get people
from your line of work to come on the record."

The lights in the studio looked hot and a little oppressive. Joe,
however, was sitting back at his hotel desk in London. He was coming to the end of his forty-eight-hour visit, and this was one of the
last things he had to do before he left to return home. "Thank you
for taking my call," Joe said. "Just to say, I personally have no dog in
this fight. I know New York is having huge crime trouble in general,
but I just run a small circuit back home in Memphis."

"What do you mean by saying you have 'no dog in this fight'?" Senator Tenenbaum asked. "Aren't you the chairman over the whole cartel?"

Joe snapped back, "Cartel? Listen, Senator, with all due respect to you, I've had to listen to you go on every show on TV and radio, dragging our great sport through the mud. I've had enough. We're a business, just the same as boxing is. I don't know what exactly you think I'm the chairman of, sir. I hold my own promoter's license and I pay my share to the athletic commission—like I'm told to do—and that's about the size of it."

The senator jumped back in. "A few days ago, the wrestling promoter here in New York, Danno Garland, was shot dead."

"That case is ongoing," Joe replied. "And it was of a personal nature, nothing to do with the sport of wrestling."

"So you're saying this isn't all connected?" the senator asked.

Joe replied, "First, when I heard about Danno Garland's passing I was saddened, but not surprised. His dear wife was the victim of a robbery that caused her death. Mr. Garland seemed intent on dishing out his own form of retribution—and from what I know, his driver *allegedly*—"

The producer off-camera was nodding his head to the anchor. Ant interrupted. "Like you said, Mr. Lapine, the investigation is ongoing. I suggest that we stick to tonight's issue so as not to prejudice any case against Mr. Long."

The senator couldn't wait to get back in. For years, he had been trying to get something on these wrestling guys, and now he smelled the faintest whiff of blood. "This is all connected. All of a sudden, the wrestling business is responsible for a lot of criminality and bloodshed—"

Joe pretended not to hear and cut back in. "I'm sorry to hear that *anyone* got so brutally assaulted. It must be a confusing time for the senator."

"No, no, no," Senator Tenenbaum replied with frustration. "I'm not confused in the slightest."

"Did you guys have anything to do with the senator's assault and brutal stabbing on the streets of New York, Mr. Lapine? Yes or no?" Ant asked.

And that was the question Joe *needed* to be asked, the question he needed to set up the answer he had prepared. "Well, Mr. Stevens, some lunatic attacks Senator Tenenbaum on the streets of a city already racked with violence," Joe said in a considered tone. "Now, this attacker didn't even cover his face, according to the good senator. It sounds to me like Mr. Tenenbaum could identify this man easily if he was ever apprehended."

Ant Stevens held up a police sketch for his camera. To anyone who knew, it looked an awful lot like Mickey Jack Crisp. "This is him, folks," Ant said to the camera.

"Do you know this man?" the senator asked Joe, right on camera.

"No," Joe replied. "I do not."

That was true.

"You've never seen him before?" Ant asked.

"Only in the media—the same as everyone else," Joe answered.

That was a lie.

"Can you come on here, Mr. Lapine, and say that this man isn't one of yours?" Senator Tenenbaum asked.

Joe took his time in response. "No, I *can't* say that."

Joe's reply caught both Ant and the senator off guard. "Sorry, sir?" Ant asked. "You *can't* say that?"

Joe continued, "I know that man has nothing to do with *my* wrestling business here in Memphis, but I have no idea if he's connected to any other business out there. How could I?"

Both the anchor and the politician appeared momentarily stumped.

"The sport of professional wrestling is huge," Joe said. "There are thousands of wrestlers and promoters and ring crew, etcetera. I can't vouch for them all, sitting here tonight in London. No more than the senator can vouch for all the people who work in his area."

The senator thought that he was finally seeing one of the wrestling bosses mess up and drop their guard for once, and he was itching to get back into the conversation. "So you're saying that—"

Joe wasn't about to give the floor back now, though. "What I'm saying for sure is this, sir," he said. "If that man is found to be connected in *any way* to our sport, I will personally join the senator in making sure that the professional wrestling business as a whole is investigated from top to bottom, inside and out."

For the second time in a short segment, Joe had totally baffled the anchor and the senator.

"Even if he's found to not be from your neck of the woods?" Ant asked.

"I don't care," Joe said. "If my sport, which I love dearly, has caused this kind of hurt and distress to anyone—much less an elected representative of the people—then I'll shut myself down. Is that fair enough, Senator?"

Camera Two zoomed in good and tight to Senator Tenenbaum's face, waiting for his reply. The senator's political wiring was sparking enough to know how this was coming across to the ordinary American at home. "I welcome Mr. Lapine's offer and intentions," was all the senator could mumble. He knew that Joe had boxed him in with his faux kindness and concern. Anything other than thanks would have been ill advised.

"And to finish, sir," Joe said, "I sure would be grateful if you offered me the same courtesy. If this man *is* caught and if there's no hint that he is from our sport, would you consider informing the American people of that? All the accusations are needlessly hurting a proud hundred-year-old American staple. Professional wrestling doesn't deserve this. The families that work in this great tradition don't deserve to lose their livelihoods, their way of feeding their families."

Ant's producer was wrapping him up off screen.

"What do you say, Senator?" Ant asked. "Are you willing to telling the American people you're wrong if it comes to that?"

Senator Tenenbaum could only nod his head. "It won't come to that. These people have a habit of making sure nothing comes to the surface."

Ant Stevens once again held up the police drawing of a man that the senator knew as his attacker and the wrestling bosses knew as Mickey Jack Crisp. "Okay, I want to thank Senator Tenenbaum from New York, and Mr. Joe Lapine, who I understand is on vacation right now."

"That's right, Ant," Joe answered with a fake laugh. "But I'm looking forward to coming right on home."

Fucking right he was.

The next day.
Florida.

Florida was the noisiest quiet place on earth. Things moved in the bushes, grass, trees, and skies, and spending a coal-black night down there took some getting used to if you were just visiting. Mickey Jack Crisp thought that it was the greatest place on earth—especially since he had gotten his hands on some money. For the first time in his life he had a small place with air conditioning and a car that was reliable enough to get him from coast to coast. All thanks to the wrestling business.

Mickey wasn't an insider, or someone who had grown up in wrestling. He didn't even much like to watch it on TV. But he sure did like the money that the wrestling bosses gave him to do the things that they didn't want to do themselves. Most of the time they'd pay him and they'd end up doing the dirty deed themselves anyway.

But really, whether he liked the business or not didn't matter one tiny bit to him while he spent wrestling dollars at the bar, watching a blonde standing by the door. He smiled as the barman took her a drink that Mickey had paid for. She smiled at Mickey as the barman pointed him out. The bar was packed, but they seemed to home in on each other. Mickey had done much better with the ladies since he came back from New York. Money made him confident and generous, and the tourist ladies didn't seem to mind either trait. He left his stool at the bar and walked over to her.

A couple of hours later they both burst through the door into Mickey's place. She was wrapped around his waist, and Mickey was doing his best not to stumble over something, being both drunk and in the dark. Both of their breaths were strong with liquor. They stumbled their way to his couch and collapsed with her on top. Mickey broke away from her lips to see if she was like he pictured her in his head. She was—she was definitely as beautiful as he'd thought. He watched her arch her back and reach inside her purse for a condom.

"What's that for?" Mickey asked. She hushed him, and pushed him flat onto his back. "You see what's happening out there," she said.

Mickey tried to bluster and fumble his way through but she was insistent. No protection, no sex. And Mickey wasn't going to waste too much time arguing either way; his room was beginning to spin a little and he wanted to start while he knew he still could.

"What's your name?" he asked her. She wasn't a big talker. Mickey kicked off his shoes and shimmied his jeans to the floor. He tried to kiss her, but she wasn't interested in that anymore. No connection. No glances. No wandering hands. She just rolled on his condom, held his wrists, and fucked him until he came. No small talk. No finishing embrace.

She slid down and while Mickey thought a blow job might be on the cards, she was only interested in carefully removing the condom.

"Hey, while you're down there—" Mickey said as he lit a cigarette. His heart was pounding and the sticky Florida night made him feel even more like he was about to pass out.

"You want some water?" she asked as she stood and walked across his floor, naked. Mickey nodded. "Come get it," she said, leaning over suggestively to turn on the tap.

Mickey quickly stubbed out his smoke and tried to stand. He was disoriented. Dizzy. He immediately knew it was more than the effects of alcohol. His legs buckled; his breathing slowed down dramatically. The walls moved closer and his vision blurred. Mickey didn't even hear Donta enter his house and walk up behind him.

The blonde woman knew her part of the job was done when she saw Donta creep up behind Mickey and place the noose around his neck. Before Mickey could even attempt to fight back, Donta turned quickly and yanked on the rope, bringing himself and Mickey back to back. Donta arched forward, which lifted Mickey's feet off the ground, choking him. Mickey kicked a little and tried to breathe, but Donta tightened his grip and waited for a helpless Mickey to hang.

The last thing Mickey saw before he died was the blonde stranger picking up her clothes and leaving. She had spiked Mickey with such a large dose that by the time he realized he was being hanged, he could do nothing but accept it.

With Mickey Jack Crisp—the only physical link between wrestling and the senator's assault—dead, it was now time for Donta to lay out the bread crumbs for the authorities to follow. The letter he had mailed to Senator Tenenbaum earlier had a bullet and a letter inside it. That would be enough to lead the investigation in Mickey's direction. All that was left for Donta to arrange was all the pieces around him—to get the wrestling business off the hook completely.

Donta left Mickey hanging from his own bathroom door. He removed Mickey's few remaining articles of clothing and threw them into the hallway. Donta lined the floors, filled the bath, and covered the kitchen with magazine and paper clippings of Senator Tenenbaum's face. Every picture had Tenenbaum's mouth cut out and his eyes x'ed in red pen. Donta planted an untraceable gun—minus the single bullet that was on its way to Washington—under Mickey's mattress. He placed the typewriter that had been used on the envelope on the kitchen table.

Donta then took the contents of Mickey's condom and carefully emptied it on the clipping-covered floor, just under Mickey's body. Donta covered the walls with stab holes and angry gashes before he left.

Tenenbaum was everywhere and Mickey's cool little pad in the middle of nowhere looked like the lair of a madman.

A dead madman.

A dead madman who had had nothing to do with the wrestling business.

The next night.
New York.

After too long on his feet, Edgar Long sat in a daze on his couch. A hundred or more people had been through his house in the previous few days—but now all was quiet. His wife couldn't do it: she couldn't come back home after what had happened there. She never wanted to see that sitting room again. But Edgar wanted to clean it—and he did. He was a man of routine, and all of this change was playing with his nerves. His grandchildren made it out alive, but his son was in critical condition and despite all the scrubbing, Danno Garland's blood was still visible on his walls. Edgar washed and cleaned the room until his arms wouldn't wipe anymore. He got sick at the thought of his family in so much pain—so broken now.

He cried alone on his floor.

As he sat there, the light of day long gone, Edgar wanted his routine back. He wanted his grandkids back, and he wanted his son to live. He wanted to know what had happened. Nobody was saying anything, except that Lenny had shot Danno dead. This didn't sound at all right to Edgar; he knew his son, and he knew that he didn't have cold-blooded murder in him. Something else must have happened—something more.

Edgar sat in a daze on his couch and watched his TV. *The Nightly View* had been advertising all evening about how it was going to shed light on what was happening in New York. Edgar knew that his son was mixed up in the wrestling business. He just wanted to know what was going on.

Ant Stevens welcomed his viewers with his usual slickness and promised them an immediate update. It was the first time that Edgar was hearing the full story. A senator had been stabbed, and Danno's own wife had been murdered just days before Danno, himself, was shot to death. They showed a picture of Lenny on screen. Edgar couldn't help but fall apart again. What was his boy doing in the middle of all of this?

"We now know," said the anchor, "that the man who attacked Senator Tenenbaum was found dead in his own home today, of an apparent suicide. Just so our viewers know, the senator is down in Florida now, where he identified the man as the one who viciously attacked him. The man's motives aren't yet known, but we're getting word that the attacker's house was covered in disturbing images of Senator Tenenbaum, and that his fixation on the senator continued up to yesterday, when it's alleged that Mr. Tenenbaum received a bullet mailed—"

Edgar switched his TV off. His wife was right: this would be the last time that he'd ever set foot in his living room. No amount of scrubbing was going to get rid of what happened here.

1973.
Five months after Lenny was shot.
California.

Choosing Masquers Club in Hollywood had probably been a mistake.

"Y'all are going to have to move it to a bigger venue for next year," Minnie Blackwell told her husband as they waved and saluted their way through the crowd.

"Shut up," Tanner replied.

Even though the venue had the touch of prestige and history, it wasn't big enough to hold the owners, promoters, and athletes from both the wrestling and boxing worlds. On this night, the wrestling business itself needed to give its best performance. It was time to begin the process of moving on—of starting again.

Since the fifties, the Four Corners Social Club was a weekly coming together of boxing and wrestling personalities, which over time had turned into a fraternity. The club honored the greatest achievers and remembered the forgotten. It prided itself on not getting involved in the politics of the day.

The room was stuffed full of black ties, sparkly ball gowns, bald heads, and cigar smoke. Tanner pulled out his wife's seat and made sure that she was settled without incident. "Why are we sitting over here?" Minnie asked Tanner.

"Shut up," Tanner replied evenly and calmly. He walked around the other side of the table and sat opposite her. All the other tables seated six people, but Tanner's table was just for him and Minnie.

"Why did they put us up against the wall?" Minnie asked.

Tanner knew Minnie's patter well: she was asking just the right questions to get him annoyed. There was something about her that didn't like his mind to be too far away from her. "You said you didn't want to share a table with anyone," Tanner replied.

"A middle table would have been nice is all."

"If I had booked you a middle table, you'd want a fucking table on the ceiling." Tanner could feel his leg begin to bounce with anxiety, or anger—he never knew which when it came to spending time with his wife. "Would you like to move, then?" he asked.

"No thanks," she replied. There were a few seconds of silence, while Minnie and Tanner both scanned the room to see if anyone noticed them. "It's just—it's disrespectful, isn't it?" Minnie said. "You're put over here in the dark. I mean, what do they think is wrong with you?"

"I asked for this specific table in this specific spot because you *specifically* said you wanted a table in the corner on your own," Tanner replied.

"Even the bread is hard," Minnie said.

"What do you mean it's hard?" Tanner snatched the bread out of his wife's hand and squashed it in his hand until it crumbled. "Feels soft to me."

"Why? Did it feel like your dick?"

Tanner leaned in and whispered, "Did you really just say that, Minnie? Are you fucking nine years old?"

Minnie turned to the table next to her. "Excuse me, is your bread hard? In the middle, it's—firm, right?" The woman Minnie asked shook her head. Minnie turned back to her table with a look of disgust on her face. "What would she know? Looks like she hasn't eaten anything in years."

Tanner just switched off as his wife's mouth continued to move. It was a thing he could do to help survive being around her. He knew by her face that she wanted to say something more, but he pretended not to notice. She would never lean across a table, as it wouldn't be ladylike. When Minnie Blackwell was in public, she was an old southern belle. When no one could hear her, she cussed like a sailor and pronounced "dog" like "dawg."

"What a great crowd," Joe Lapine said, as he sat in one of Tanner's four empty seats. Tanner nodded and took a slug of water. "Anyone call you yet?" Joe asked quietly.

"No one in the Carolinas gives a fuck about what's happening in New York," Tanner replied.

"Why? What happened in New York?" Minnie wanted to know.

"Nothing," Tanner said to his wife. Joe smiled at Minnie, as a way of backing up her husband's story. Tanner turned away from his wife for some privacy.

Joe sidled up beside him. "New York is a fucking mess," Joe said.

"I heard Danno's driver didn't even fight his murder charge," Tanner said.

Joe shook his head. "That's what they're saying. There were some kids found in the garage too."

"Dead?" Tanner asked.

"I think they made it out alive," Joe replied. Tanner knew that Joe knew more—Joe always knew more. Tanner knew more, too. But he didn't want Joe to know that.

There might have been bloodshed there, but every wrestling boss in the US could see now that the mecca of wrestling, New York, was there for the taking with no one at the helm.

"What are we doing here?" Tanner asked. "Who gives a fuck about a Hall of Fame ceremony?"

Joe smiled and waved to someone passing, keeping up appearances. "We're showing the world that we've got nothing to hide. New York was a couple of bad apples, that's all." Joe leaned over to look past Tanner. "How are you, Missus Blackwell? You look lovely," he said.

"Thank you, Mister Lapine. Don't you look dapper, too," Minnie replied.

"I hope that your husband wins the award," Joe replied with a fakeness that only the wife of a conman could detect.

"I'm sure you do," she said. "Because there's not a single other person in here who deserves to be named promoter of the year like my Tanner. No one far—or near."

Joe smiled and nodded. He fucking hated Minnie Blackwell.

"Ladies and gentlemen," the master of ceremonies said into the microphone on stage, "What an honor it is to have the great and good from the worlds of boxing and professional wrestling here tonight." There was a warm round of applause from the gathered audience. He continued, "This room is more crooked than a retired boxer's nose."

That one died.

"Get the fuck off the stage," shouted someone from the back of the room.

"I hate these things," Tanner muttered to himself.

1974.
One year after Lenny was shot.
California.

Tanner and Minnie sat at the middle table and watched award after award get handed out. The bread was better this year.

Joe sat with the Blackwells. "It won't be long now," Joe said in Tanner's ear. "Danno's own lawyer couldn't make his way out of all of this unharmed. I heard that his doors closed yesterday. Lost everything."

"Does he still have the contract?" Tanner asked.

"No one knows," Joe replied, lying. Both he and Tanner knew that Danno's former lawyer was holding the contract to New York.

"When are we going back to New York?" Tanner asked. "I got a fucking unification match to cash in on."

"Soon," Joe replied. "I mean, it's a measure of how tight a situation is, when a lawyer as slimy as Troy Bartlett couldn't make it out of there with his own shirt."

It didn't go unnoticed by Tanner that Joe knew Danno's lawyer by name. Tanner bet that Joe knew his phone number, too.

1975.
Two years after Lenny was shot.
California.

"I've known Ricky for decades. Tell him I was asking for him when you see him," said Maw Maw Vosbury as he left Tanner's table. Little did the boxing promoter know that Ricky's name was poison around the wrestling tables.

"Don't worry, bunny," Minnie told her husband, as she wiped her lipstick off of his face. "This is bullshit."

Another year at the Four Corners Social Club Banquet without recognition. Tanner's heart was broken yet again. "I don't mind," he said. "It means fucking nothing, anyway."

No one believed him.

1976.
Three years after Lenny was shot.
California.

Tanner and Minnie ran for the door. "Hold it open!" Tanner shouted.

Minnie apologized to the doorman for being late. She and her husband handed in their coats and walked to the closed doors of the Four Corners Social Club Banquet.

"I love you, no matter what happens this year," Minnie said.

Tanner believed her.

1977.
Four years after Lenny was shot.
California.

"It's a rib," Tanner said, as he watched Jose Rios walk down from the stage with the promoter of the year award in his hand. "They're doing it to piss me off," he said to his wife.

"Don't let them see that it bothers you," Minnie replied, her poker face in play. "Next year."

1978.
Five years after Lenny was shot.
California.

The bar was quieter than the lounge. Tanner could hear the mumble of someone talking through a microphone in the next room. He couldn't even look his wife in the face. Both Tanner and Minnie were seated at the bar, ready to drink.

"You not going in, sir?" the barman asked.

Tanner shook his head. "Tell him why," Minnie said to her husband. Tanner, again, just shook his head. "This man," Minnie began, "is the most successful promoter in the country. He also promotes the world heavyweight wrestling champion, and every fucking year they—"

Tanner gently moved his wife away from the bar. She was only drinking soda, but it didn't take alcohol for Minnie Blackwell to cause a scene where her husband was concerned. "I love you," he said and kissed her shoulder gently.

"Tanner?"

"Yeah?"

"How is New York running small shows, still doing TV, and making their commitments if no one is boss up there?"

Tanner knew exactly how they were doing it.

1979.
Six years after Lenny was shot.
California.

Tanner stood with Joe in the parking lot. He could see Minnie waiting for him in the lobby, under the banner for the Four Corners Social Club Banquet.

"The other bosses want you to drop the belt, Tanner," Joe said.

"I did," Tanner replied.

"You dropped it to another one of your wrestlers in your territory," Joe said. "They want you to drop it to one of them."

Tanner didn't react much. "Open up New York. Then I'll—"

"I can't do that," Joe said, interrupting Tanner's request.

"I'll put my belt against the New York belt. We do this right."

Joe tried to keep his cool. "The other bosses aren't new anymore. They know exactly what you're doing."

"Yeah?" Tanner said. "I know exactly what you're fucking doing too, Joe."

Tanner stood on his cigarette and followed his wife.

1980.
Seven years after Lenny was shot.
California.

Tanner turned in his bed. He couldn't say that he was sorry to miss the banquet this year. Nothing much was changing and he didn't know how much longer he could look Joe Lapine in the face without calling him a cheating asshole. Tanner knew that something was going on in New York, but Joe was smart enough to fill the vacant bosses' positions with people who wouldn't question him.

Tanner was somewhat soothed by the fact that he still had the other heavyweight champion. The record books would show that New York had a heavyweight champion, and that Tanner Blackwell managed the affairs of the other wrestler who laid claim to the title. He rolled over in the dark and imagined what it would be like to put the titles back together again. He sipped the hot drink that Minnie had left beside the bed for him and imagined himself as the boss of New York.

The Carolinas were good, but Tanner Blackwell wanted the prestige.

"Joe called," Minnie shouted up the stairs.

"And?" Tanner shouted back.

"You didn't win again," she replied.

"Fucking bastards," Tanner muttered as he pulled the covers over his head.

1981.
Eight years after Lenny was shot.
California.

Tanner looked at his wife's empty seat beside him in the middle of the room. For decades he had wished that she'd shut up. How wrong he was. The room was bigger. The event was bigger. Everything had gotten bigger. As he got older, Tanner could feel himself getting lost in it all. Wrestlers were prettier and more asshole-like all of a sudden. Matches made no sense, and every fucking worker in the dressing room wanted to flip and jump around the ring. Winner after winner, Tanner didn't recognize any of the faces on the stage.

Joe sat where Minnie would have sat, had she still been alive.

"I want New York," Tanner said.

Joe put a consoling hand on Tanner's shoulder. Tanner picked Joe's fingers off of him.

1982.
Nine years after Lenny was shot.
California.

It had been ten years since the banquet first started, ten years since Lenny had gone inside, and ten years since Tanner had begun promoting his world heavyweight champion. Tanner wanted it, he wanted to win the prize; he wanted to be named promoter of the year. He wanted to be recognized for all the money he earned, all the records he broke, and all the bullshit he had to put up with.

He wanted to say his wife's name in public—he wanted to thank her out loud. He wanted her to be proud of him. He wanted. He wanted. He wanted.

But he didn't get. Again.

1983.
Ten years after Lenny was shot.
California.

Rust-colored piss was no good for any man, and certainly not for a man of Tanner Blackwell's age. Coupled with the way he had been feeling, he knew that things weren't getting better inside his body. But only queers and sissies went to the doctor.

Tanner had a banquet to sit through. Another year of being forgotten even though he knew he was out-earning everyone.

He zipped himself up and looked at his aging reflection in the mirror of the bathroom.

Tanner was too old—and now too sick—to have no legacy.

1984.
Eleven years after Lenny was shot.
California.

Outside, the dense Los Angeles air was adding to his frustration. Tanner pulled off his bow tie and ripped at his shirt buttons. His cane was still new and was more of an obstacle than a help. "Fucking—fuck," he raged under his breath. He was trying to compose himself as guests came and went. He tried to look up and smile, but he simply couldn't. The Four Corners Social Club Banquet had fucked him over again.

"Come back inside," Joe Lapine said, as he held the front door for Tanner. "It's only a stupid award."

"Terry Garland? That's who won! Terry-fucking-Garland is promoter of the decade?"

"Tanner—"

"I'm done with the politics of this," Tanner replied. "No one else is saying it, so I'm going to say it. I'm not asking you anymore. New York is back in play! It has been for years."

Joe could see that Tanner was far more upset than he had been in previous years. "Who cares about a fucking award, Tanner?" Joe said. "You're making more money than everyone in that room combined."

"You think this is about money, Joe?" Tanner replied.

"Absolutely," Joe said. "And that's all it's about, but a lot of people in our business have forgotten that."

Tanner downed the last mouthful of his peppermint drink and belched loudly while rubbing his stomach. "What do you want when you're old and rich, already?" Tanner said.

"I don't know. What else *do* you want?" Joe replied.

"I want my fucking due, Joe."

Joe stepped toward Tanner and tried a more diplomatic approach. "If you go marching into New York without the approval of the NWC, what do you think will happen?"

"One way or another, I'm doing this," Tanner answered.

"You can't undermine the NWC, Tanner," Joe said. "You, me, and everyone else who have been protecting this business are suddenly going to be fighting off every spick, nigger, and Paddy who wants to get into the match-fixing game. No one can see us fracture, 'cause if they smell weakness, we're all fucked." Joe could see that his words had sobered up Tanner's thoughts, somewhat. He continued, "If you want New York, then you do it the right way, the right way in front of the other territory owners, the right way in front of the athletic commission, and the right way in front of the law. 'Cause let me tell you this: if there's one place in the world that we have to look legit after all the shit we've been through, it's there."

Tanner rested his empty glass on the roof of a nice new car and walked toward the hotel door. "I'm going to get New York," Tanner said. "Don't fucking get in my way, Joe."

CHAPTER THREE

Kid Devine sat in the front row of an empty Madison Square Garden. He thought about his match that was coming up and how it would play out. He thought about his father, the wrestling business, the threats, and how all that would play out too.

He heard footsteps on the risers behind him.

"Let me smarten you up," said the voice in the darkness.

In wrestling, this phrase meant everything. A veteran saying those words to a rookie was a passing of the torch, a sign that you'd been truly accepted in the wrestling business. It involved a lot of trust—a lot of faith that the person learning would take on the old traditions, the proper way of doing things. That they would protect the secrets of the wrestling business.

On this night, the rookie knew the voice of the person that was about twenty rows back. The only lights were those above the ring, so Kid could only make out a silhouette in the stands.

"Can we let the people in?" a staff member shouted. "They're starting to go crazy out there."

"No," the man in the stands replied. "A few more minutes."

Kid stood up and leaned against the apron of the twenty-by-twenty red, white, and blue ring. He tried to look beyond the lights. "Why

*don't you come down here and show me something, old man?" he said.
"It's been a while."*

The man in the stands struck a match for his cigarette, and Kid caught a glimpse of his pained, pale face. "You okay?" Kid asked.

"I'm fine," the man answered. He took a pull from his cigarette. "Now, there's only four basic parts to a wrestling match: the Shine, the Heat, the Comeback, and the Finish. The Shine is where our hero starts off well, and wins a couple of small, early victories to get the crowd excited. They paid good money, so give them what they want." He took another pull and continued.

"To start with."

December 24, 1983.
New York.

Lenny just wanted to go home. When he had crashed the VW Kombi van, when Bree kicked him out, when he drove his family to Las Vegas, and when he killed his boss—all Lenny Long had ever wanted to do was go home. He had never wanted it more than on this night, though. As he lay on his dirty cell floor, blood dripping from his fingers and pooling in front of him, Lenny imagined his cozy log fire crackling at home. He tried to focus on the gifts he would wrap, and how he would lie on his belly with his sons to play with their presents. He could smell his kitchen and imagine the joy of home at Christmastime. With a flick of his tongue he checked the inside of his mouth. He could feel that his gums were torn by the fingernails of another man. That was the way the previous decade in prison had been for Lenny: beating after beating, because he was quiet and wanted to stay that way.

His cellmate—and attacker—began to whale away with lefts and rights and head-butts and scratches and bites. He screamed in Lenny's ear about something and nothing—it didn't matter. He grabbed Lenny by his hair and dragged him across the floor. The

sudden jerk reminded him of the other times this had happened—
times when he was petrified and would beg for his life. It was
Christmas Eve, and Lenny wanted to be with his family. But no one
in the wrestling business ever really got to go home—not as themselves, anyway. Only a scant few would turn up at their own door
finished with the business for good. After years on the road, in the
ring, and in the bars, living from a bag, a car, or a shitty motel room
every night, it was no wonder that children saw a stranger at home,
and that wives packed up and left. Lenny Long knew that more than
most.

In prison, he had no control over where he was going. There was
no left or right, no choice of paths, and no way home. He was moving in his head, though. He had always been small in size and quiet
in nature. He had grown up that way, and Lenny had always kept to
himself. He had never mixed much, and the only form of violence
he had been exposed to was in Madison Square Garden, where he
gladly paid a fair ticket price. That was before Attica Correctional
Facility became home.

After years of being terrified, Lenny now felt different. As his
attackers kicked and punched him, Lenny felt no pain. Each kick
was welcome, each stomp invited. No words or sounds had escaped
from Lenny's mouth since he had been put in that cell. Lenny just
thought that the beatings were what he deserved. It was what he had
coming. Over the years, his fingers were broken, and his teeth were
made jagged and loose. His eyes were smashed to yellow and black,
his arms were too sore to lift, his ribs too bruised to breathe. He was
in a hell that he felt was of his own making—until that freeing second where he knew he'd suffered enough.

In that instant, he launched from his stooped and subservient
position to crack the face of his assailant. *Bang. Bang. Bang, bang,
bang.* Lenny was releasing it all: every thought and every clogged
tear and word that he'd held in his head. *Bang. Bang.* His attacker's
lips opened to bleed, and his cheekbones became contorted and

swollen. *Bang, bang, bang.* Lenny's arms struck like pistons, freeing him from his daily stomach-churning fears, his years of being nothing. The face in front of him was beaten softer with every strike of his fist, until Lenny could do nothing but hit himself and his own chest as he roared and wailed over his unconscious cellmate. The power of beating someone else for a change, and the raw, unabashed option of murder—that permanent problem-solver—was there, in Lenny's hands. In turn, this brought calmness and understanding to him. He dragged the cell's bunkbed toward the door. He wanted all the other inmates to see him as he kicked his feet up and rested them between the bars, his vicious handiwork unconscious under him. Lenny didn't know whether this feeling was going to last, but there and then, in that moment, he knew that he was a bad motherfucker.

Such a notion made him smile for the first time since he had arrived there.

He threw a cigarette into his mouth and lit a match, old-school, along the coarse wall. He leaned back and he drew into him the most pleasure-filled intake of smoke that he had ever inhaled. Lenny Long hadn't suddenly become stronger, or more skilled, or deadly. He knew that he'd get beaten again, and he knew that his fighting wasn't nearly over. But he also knew that whoever was the next to grab his throat would be grabbing the throat of a man who knew he was done being pushed around.

And that man was the man nobody wanted to fuck with.

CHAPTER FOUR

1984.
Three months later.
New York.

Lenny Long was useful to wrestling again, so it was time to put him back into play. After years of silence toward Lenny from the National Wrestling Council, he now found himself walking to another meeting with an NWC representative. Lenny wished the setting were different, but all he could offer by way of a meeting place was the visitation area of the Attica Correctional Facility. The NWC chose a man who knew New York well; a man who had known Lenny's boss well. He was also someone whose life had changed forever when Lenny pulled the trigger on Danno.

Troy Bartlett looked around and knew that he was one dodgy deal away from being on the other side of the thick, dirty glass himself. As he waited for "the boss" of New York to be escorted to him, he couldn't help but think of how far he had fallen. Since Lenny had gone inside, Troy's business had been ripped open by the NYPD and the federal government; the investigation had bled Troy dry. As a lawyer of dubious moral boundaries, he couldn't withstand the forensic investigation that followed Danno's death. None of Troy's remaining clients liked new attention from the cops, so one by one they jumped ship until there was just one client left: the New York Booking Agency.

In the *real* world, the New York Booking Agency was the parent company that housed a professional wrestling company. In the *wrestling* world, the New York Booking Agency was the legally recognized company name of their New York territory. It was a legitimate front to make illegitimate cash.

Troy's part in all of this was his possession of the legal document that clearly stated Danno had signed his New York Booking Agency over to Lenny Long. The ownership of the company was even used as evidence in Lenny's trial, with the prosecutors submitting it as a possible motive behind Danno's murder.

Lenny was the boss on paper. And now that paper mattered.

Troy stood as Lenny sat down in front of him. "The offer is sixty thousand, this time," Troy said. "I can make the deal and we can all just move on." Lenny was unresponsive; he could hardly look up from the floor. Seeing again how much Troy had aged just made Lenny more aware that time was marching on without him. Troy continued, "The New York Booking Agency has other financial considerations, which the buyers are also willing to take on as part of the deal. I think you should kiss their feet, personally. This is money to you for absolutely nothing."

Lenny cleared his throat, as he hadn't spoken to anyone he didn't have to in days. "Why?"

"Why, what?" Troy asked.

"Why have they raised their offer?" Lenny asked.

Troy rubbed the prison phone receiver on his cheap suit jacket. "Why?" he asked in disbelief. "Because who gives a fuck why?" Troy waited for some appreciation; it didn't come. "You know," he said, "you can earn sixty-fucking-thousand to sign your name."

Lenny smiled. "You're telling me that it's as simple as that?"

Troy shuffled his chair closer. "Mr. Long, I get the distinct impression that this is the last time these people are going to ask. Do you understand? They will get this territory one way or another. Now, word is that your family isn't doing very well financially at the moment. Even if you don't want the money, I'm sure that your ex-wife could do a lot with it."

Lenny interrupted. "I'm done."

"Excuse me?"

"I've served enough time in here. I want out," Lenny said. He wanted to bring that money home; he wanted to be the one who handed it to Bree.

Troy smiled at the steepness of Lenny's request. "How do I do that?"

"I didn't fight the charges, or anything that anyone said in the trial," Lenny said. "I deserved everything I got. But I've paid enough, and I want to try to go home. I'll only consider any deal from here on out with that stipulation attached."

Troy wiped a bead of sweat from his brow. He didn't want to leave without an agreement. That would make him useless to proceedings. "Lenny, this isn't a bargaining position you've got here," Troy said. "You're not exactly sitting in a position of strength here."

"'Course I am."

"What?"

"If I wasn't, you wouldn't be here and they wouldn't be reaching into their dirty fucking pockets." Lenny drew a sharp breath and looked around. "They don't allow representation for appeals in here. You could do something about that," he said. "The night that it happened, Danno was an intruder in *my* parents' house—and it was *his* gun. I just disarmed him to defend myself." Troy tried to cut in. "You're all dirty pricks," Lenny continued. "Who know other dirty pricks. Now, get to someone on the parole board, and get me the fuck out of here. That, plus sixty grand, and we have a deal in the morning. You fucking tell them that."

Troy could only shake his head in disbelief as Lenny stood. "You did nothing to earn New York, you little fuck," Troy said. "Danno only put the business in your name because he knew you'd be the easiest one to get it back off when the time came."

"And how is that working out for you all?" Lenny asked. His sudden display of confidence knocked the crooked lawyer off his guard. "One more thing," Lenny said, "I want the original copy of that contract posted here for my attention. I will only leave here when I have it in my hands. You understand?"

Lenny hung up and walked back toward A block.

As he worked at the laundry, Lenny had all day to think about his meeting with Troy. If he was going to let himself even dream about getting out, he wanted to make sure that he was as ready as he could be. The wrestling business was different than any other; it ran on a different mind-set, and it was a way of thinking that Lenny hadn't used in a long time. Wrestling was all about what was happening where you couldn't see it. It was a business where you played checkers on top of the table, and chess underneath.

He needed to get out. It was too much knowing that his family was struggling. Every day Lenny planned the same scenario: he'd leave Attica, sign the piece of paper, and arrive at Bree's house with enough money for a brand-new start. Maybe she might include him too. Maybe not. But Lenny wanted to find out.

As he walked and daydreamed, he could still hear the thump of the metal press in his head as he left the laundry floor. He moved with the small huddle of men along the hallway toward the first of their guarded stops. They waited. Lenny looked up and saw the black sphere that was fixed on the wall, ready to dispense tear gas if the inmates started any trouble. The key was turned, and the heavy metal prison gate opened to let them through. They walked silently in line toward "Times Square," a small section of the prison where all the corridors met. Lenny continued along the sandy brick hallway, up two steps, and then four steps down. As he heard the voices and general chatter get louder, he stayed close to the wall, as always.

He ran his hands along the tall white radiators every ten or so paces and looked out the arched windows for the sun. As he got closer, the guard who smoked a pipe opened the last of their gates. The inmates filed into a single concentrated line at the door.

The mess hall gate was different than the other parts of the prison. It had decoratively twisted bars with little ornamental curls welded on top—it was about as pretty as metal and men and prison could get.

Inside, the room was huge, bright, and separated into three sections by giant white columns that shot from the floor to the high ceilings like clinical white oak trees. Lenny walked past the white tables and the mushroom-shaped stools that were bolted to the floor. He knew what was good and what to avoid; he knew who was good and who to avoid. Twelve years in and he was beginning to feel like a veteran, like the prison left him alone. New guys asked him questions and came to him about getting some work in the laundry. He ate his food, worked his job, wrote his letters, and read as much as he could. After the riots, the prison had gotten a little better at stocking the library and making programs available for inmates who wanted to learn.

The only thing Lenny Long had learned was a phone number. A number that he was thinking about dialing after he finished eating. If Lenny was worried about how to protect himself from the bosses, if he could get out, then this was how he figured he could buy some time. Underneath his mattress was a magazine, and on that magazine was a number that Lenny hoped was still in use.

"Hello?" Lenny said into the phone.

"Yes, hello," replied a man's voice, "*USA Wrestling Chronicles*."

Lenny looked around to make sure no one could hear his next words. "This is Lenny Long," he said. "The boss of the New York territory."

"You serious, man?" the voice asked.

A wrestling boss calling a wrestling magazine would be like a yeti calling the *National Enquirer*. "Yeah, it's me. I want to go on the record to talk about my hopes for the future. You got anyone there who'd be interested in that?"

1984.
Three weeks later.
Memphis.

Joe Lapine sat back on his jet and thought about nice things: a good wine that he'd had, a nice lady he'd met. He was feeling good, but he knew that the contents of the brown bag in front of him would ruin that. He put it out of his mind for five minutes. Five more minutes of nice thoughts before he knew he had to open that bag and read the magazine that was inside.

Joe reached in and opened the publication to the page that had been marked for him. The first thing he saw was an old picture of Lenny Long, and then a headline that read:

UNPRECEDENTED ACCESS: NEW YORK'S OWNER

He saw the highlighted quote from Lenny:

I know I'm new to the business, but I already love the intense competition from the likes of Joe Lapine from Memphis and Tanner Blackwell from the Carolinas. These guys have been around forever, and they are watching me closely. Everyone wants New York, but I know the old guys will guide me through all of this.

With that, Joe knew the game. Lenny couldn't be touched. It was easy to deal with someone who could disappear easily, someone no one would miss. Lenny just put himself front and center and told the world that Joe and Tanner were his rivals.

While wrestling liked to live mostly in the shadows, Lenny Long was positioning himself in the spotlight. The safest place he could be.

North Carolina.

Tanner shuffled around his pool with a giant cordless phone up to his ear and a copy of the same magazine in his hand. His swimming trunks were falling off his shrinking body. "What's he playing at?" Tanner shouted into the phone.

Troy was in a New York phone booth. "He wants to sell," Troy said. "I spoke to him this morning."

"He wants to sell?" Tanner asked. "Well, what the fuck is this shit I'm reading then?"

Troy cleared his throat. "He wants the sixty thousand," he said. "Plus his release. He has the contract now. You guys pick him up on the morning he gets out, and he'll do the deal."

Tanner could hardly speak with rage. "But he—"

"Well then, move on without New York," Troy said. "Forget about the place."

"Fucking no way," Tanner replied. "I'll be fucked if this business tries to forget me."

Troy dropped the level of his voice, as if Lenny might be able to hear. "He was smart, Tanner. Now you be smart too. Play along. You can't do shit *to him* or *with him* while he's in there."

Tanner could do nothing but throw the magazine in anger. Lenny *was* smart, and Tanner knew it. He had stumped the two master players, Joe and Tanner—for now. Tanner knew the only way to get New York quickly was to swallow his pride, open his checkbook, finesse his contacts, and do what Lenny wanted done.

And then make the little prick pay for it.

CHAPTER FIVE

1984.
One minute before Lenny got out of prison.
New York.

Lenny Long didn't know where home was, not anymore. He didn't know what state his family lived in. He figured they wanted to forget him, and he insisted that they did. He felt that it was the least he could do. But now that he was minutes from getting out he wanted to go home more than anything. He stood still, waiting for the prison door in front of him to slowly slide open. HANDS OFF read the sign on the bars. When the door was clear, Lenny stood inside the last small building that kept him from the outside world. It had a glass hatch to his left and a metal detector in front of him. Lenny wasn't allowed to move until the automatic door that had let him in closed behind him. He had spent twelve years of his life waiting for those doors to open and close, and now there was only one more to go. He walked forward to another prison guard, who sat at a desk beside the glass. Lenny could see the cold daylight forcing its way in through the front door past the metal detector. He was steps from freedom. Lenny could see cars parked outside: real cars, of different colors. He had missed colors.

The gray, intimidating prison walls that stood above him every day were now behind Lenny Long. They were just as bland and cold on the free side as they were on the yard side. As he looked outward with the prison to his back, there was almost too much space. The wrestling business had put him in there, and that same business had gotten him back out again. That was what he was wary of.

He felt the small comfort of the contract in his pocket. He knew that he was a prop that went inside when they didn't need him, and got taken back out when they did. There were no balloons, no trumpets, no waiting party. He wasn't even given a sly smile from any of the guards who might have wished him well. No one gave a fuck. The wheel kept turning, no matter if Lenny was in or out. He didn't tell anyone he was getting out, mostly because he hadn't believed it would actually happen.

The second he took his first step outside the walls was the second he knew just how valuable he must be. Lenny wanted to turn that fleeting value into lasting money. Everyone else in the wrestling business was making cash off playing the game. Lenny wanted his cut, too.

Once outside, some people ran from Attica's door; some strutted. Lenny meandered away from it, like someone who had just stumbled up out of a bunker. He knew that he didn't have any right to, but he looked for his family. Time and again, over the years, he imagined that they would be pacing as they waited for him to appear. They would come running and then their arms would be around him, and he would finally forgive himself for getting into the business— for putting them in harm's way. For not being there. Lenny knew that after more than a decade inside, he was a changed man. If only he could convince himself that those changes were for the better. The bruising on his face and the stitches above his eye were the last marks to remind him of the hell he'd been through. Another fight. Another situation that he ran toward, rather than away from.

Lenny didn't know where to go, but he began to walk. Attica was like the presence of a monster behind him and he didn't want to look back and acknowledge its existence, just in case it claimed him again. In front of him the skim of recent rain made the black tarmac shine as it led the way out to a changed world. He hoped for a normal life, but he knew that would be impossible until he made good on the deal he had made. Getting out hadn't happened by accident, and it certainly hadn't happened for free. Now, Lenny knew he had to pay up.

He was told to look out for a driver; someone would make himself known when Lenny got to the parking lot. There were a few scattered cars in the designated areas, but the place was mostly silent. Nothing was jumping out at him and it was miles to the city. He only had twenty-seven dollars in his pocket, saved from his fifty-six-cent-per-day wages. A taxi was probably out of the question, so Lenny put his head down and began to walk a little faster. Maybe they had just forgotten about him. Maybe they'd decided that he wouldn't have to sell his soul, after all. Lenny knew that was just wishful thinking as he crossed the wet grass that led to the road.

He needed them to come. He was out, and that was great, but it was the second part of his deal—the sixty grand—that was going to get him home. As he walked, he heard the chatter of an engine come from behind. He had a feeling it might be his ride. He was right, but not in the way he'd thought.

"Long time," said a familiar voice.

Lenny stopped and turned slowly to see a face as familiar as the voice. Lenny stared at Babu. Babu stared back. It had been years since they'd laid eyes on each other. To Babu, Lenny looked different: thicker around the shoulders, and way stockier in general, with shorter hair and an overgrown beard. Lenny saw Babu as roughly the same as he remembered him. Huge and menacing.

"What happened to your face?" Babu asked from his window.

"What are you doing here?" Lenny asked from a safe distance. As far as Lenny knew, Babu wasn't part of the deal that he had to complete. Lenny didn't want his former giant colleague making things more complicated than they had to be.

"Get in," Babu said.

The driver he was really waiting for was lying, unconscious, between two cars about a hundred feet away.

"Who told you I was getting out?" Lenny asked. Babu leaned across and opened his passenger door. "No thanks," Lenny said as he began to walk.

Babu touched the gas pedal just enough to stay in line with Lenny. "You have no idea what's been going on out here, do you?" Babu asked.

That simple question made Lenny want to run, made him feel as if he was in danger. Babu pulled the van across Lenny's path.

"I'm not asking you again. Get in the fucking van."

Lenny took one last look around for other options—other getaways—but there was nothing else. "What are you doing here?" Lenny asked.

"I'm here to change your mind on that deal," Babu said. "One way or another."

1984.
Two hours after Lenny got out.
New York.

Babu drove with Lenny, silent, beside him. Even though he had the driver's seat pushed back as far as it would go, Babu could still feel the steering wheel get lost in his growing gut. It was the result of a man who had all but given up.

As the miles ticked along, the sky got a little more overcast, and the scenery got more remote. Lenny couldn't figure out whether he was being driven by a friend or not; Babu was too quiet to give any indication. There was once a time when Lenny would have just known, but a lot of things had happened since Babu and Lenny had last seen each other. Some of those things they were both aware of—but others they chose to keep to themselves.

From the corner of his eye, Lenny could see that the giant looked older, and much heavier. Even the simple act of shifting in his seat made Babu wince in pain. His features were more pronounced: his jaw was larger, and his cheekbones seemed to be protruding a lot more. He had that tired look of someone who was always in agony, but even though the giant had changed, he was still the man who, years before, had come to like Lenny.

Lenny hoped that was still the case.

Babu turned from the highway and headed down a smaller, darker road. After passing a couple of wooden houses, the scenery soon became nothing but trees, hills, and neglected roads. Babu began to slow down as he looked out his window for a specific spot. After a minute or two of searching, he pushed on the brakes and the van jerked to a stop.

"I'm asking you to not sell to Tanner Blackwell," Babu said.

"I have no choice," Lenny replied.

"You're just going to have to trust me," Babu said.

Maybe years before there would have been enough trust—maybe before all that happened had happened—but not anymore.

Babu carefully exited the van, his huge feet dropping down onto a bed of wet leaves. There was no one around to witness anything, only hundreds of thousands of tall, skinny birch trees. Lenny had heard, years ago, that this was how they killed Proctor King. They brought him to a place that sounded a lot like where Lenny now found himself.

"Out," Babu said as he walked around to Lenny's side of the van. Lenny seriously weighed his situation before he joined Babu outside.

"What are we doing?" Lenny asked. He was terrified of the answer.

"You made a promise to him," Babu said.

"Who?" Lenny asked.

"Danno. And I want you to keep it."

"What are you talking about?" Lenny asked.

Babu took a step in and towered over Lenny. "We all have to protect the business. That's what we all signed up for when we were let in."

Lenny shook his head. "I just want to get my money," he said. "And head on my way. I don't give a fuck about the wrestling business."

"We can get you money, if that's all you want," Babu said.

For a split second, Lenny was curious as to who "we" was. He very briefly wondered what side Babu was on. "I've already made the deal," Lenny said.

"I can't let you sell us out," Babu replied. "New York can't get taken over by Tanner. Simple as that." Babu put his huge hand on Lenny's shoulder and pushed him toward the forest. Lenny took twenty or thirty slow, silent steps; the quiet was unnerving. In a place like this Lenny knew that there might not be anyone around for miles.

"I'm not going to let you kill me," Lenny said over his shoulder.

Babu could only laugh at Lenny's statement. "Keep walking, you piece of shit," he said as he pushed Lenny in the back.

Lenny staggered forward, but then stopped, firm. "I'm not taking another fucking step," Lenny said. He turned around and prayed that there wasn't a gun pointed in his direction. There wasn't.

"Where's your loyalty?" Babu asked.

"I already gave Tanner my word."

"What do you think is going to happen once you sign the papers?" Babu asked.

Lenny replied, "I know what happens if I *don't* sign them."

Babu moved closer. "New York isn't yours to sell."

"Whatever it's worth, I earned it," Lenny said.

Babu grabbed Lenny by the collar. His hamlike fist was half the size of Lenny's head. "And how did you earn it, exactly?" the giant asked.

Lenny knew that Babu thought he was inferring that he'd earned it by killing Danno. "I didn't mean—"

Before Lenny could finish his sentence, Babu slapped him across the face. The force of the blow lifted Lenny off his feet and dropped him onto his back. The left side of Lenny's head went instantly numb and his ear buzzed in a partial deafness, like a bomb had just gone off beside him.

"How did you fucking earn it?" Babu asked, as he stomped toward Lenny. Lenny struggled to get to his feet, but he managed to just before the giant got to him again. Lenny threw a punch that landed. Babu was stunned—not from the force, but by the fact that Lenny dared to hit him in the first place. Lenny backpedaled quickly with his fists still up. Anytime Babu got too close, Lenny would fire off another shot.

"All the history, and the blood spilled, and you're going to hand it to Tanner?" Babu asked. Lenny slipped momentarily and Babu closed in close enough to grab him by the throat. Lenny smashed two more shots to Babu's head before Babu pinned Lenny against a tree trunk. The grip strength of Babu's hands immediately immobilized his much smaller opponent.

Babu hoisted Lenny up into air as Lenny tried scratching at Babu's face and eyes. The giant head-butted Lenny in the sternum. It sounded like a cannonball hitting a bamboo shield. Any small reserve of breath that Lenny had was driven from his body.

"You're not going to take this from us. Do you hear me?" Babu shouted as he drove Lenny, time and again, into the tree.

Lenny began to fade under the sheer force of Babu's attack. The last thing Lenny saw before losing consciousness was the pain in Babu's face.

As much as Babu wanted to continue to rag-doll Lenny, his body wasn't able. He dropped Lenny and fell helplessly to one knee. Years of wrestling, and his body growing out of control, made for a lot of nerve damage and compression of the spinal column. When he broke into the wrestling business, the giant could lift several people per arm—but he was now regularly defeated by lifting anything more than a few pounds at a time.

Babu fell forward. "Lenny?" he asked. He couldn't turn over to see if Lenny was still alive. "Lenny?"

There was panicked silence, as Lenny tried to suck in any breath he could.

"Are you okay?" Babu asked.

Lenny didn't answer; he couldn't, even if he wanted to.

Babu was somewhat soothed by the fact that he could hear Lenny gasping for air behind him. It didn't sound smooth, but at least he was breathing.

As Babu cooled down and his adrenaline levels began to lower, he could feel a pain in the top of his head. He dabbed the area with his fingers to see that Lenny had drawn blood; there was a nice opening in the top of Babu's skull. Babu was half-proud and half-disgusted. The Lenny Long he had known would never be capable, or even want to be capable, of such a thing. But Babu was quickly coming to the realization that the man moving behind him wasn't the Lenny Long that he had known—not even close.

The giant found it hard to move. His back was in such excruciating pain that he had spent the better part of the last five years trying to drink it better. "Lenny?" he called from the ground. Babu could hear footsteps coming closer to him. He tried to roll over to see what was happening, because Lenny's silence was making him wary, to say the least.

As he began to roll over, Babu saw a flash of gray in his peripheral vision. Lenny had taken a thick branch from the ground and smashed it across Babu's shoulder and the side of his head. The giant threw up his hands in self-defense. He pushed himself through agony to make it to his stomach, where he could struggle to all fours. Lenny was scouring the ground for another, bigger weapon.

"Stop!" Babu shouted. He could see in Lenny's eyes that Lenny was afraid, enraged, tired, and tormented, all at the same time. Babu pushed himself onto his knees and managed to lunge his huge right fist at Lenny. It connected, and Lenny fell like a dropped curtain.

Babu could only moan loudly in agony himself. He just knelt there and watched Lenny's fingers curl as he drifted further into unconsciousness. The giant hauled himself toward Lenny to make sure that he hadn't bitten or swallowed his own tongue. "I'm sorry," the giant whispered in Lenny's ear.

Lenny snapped back to consciousness and tried immediately to get up. Babu held him firmly to the ground beside him. "It's okay, it's okay," Babu said in a calming voice. Lenny, panicked as to what had happened, and where he was, began to piece together his last five minutes.

"Take it easy," Babu said as he dragged Lenny closer to him.

From his back, Lenny could see the trees and the sky overhead. He knew that he was a long way from prison, and a long way from home.

1984.
Seven hours after Lenny got out.
New York.

Babu and Lenny were on the Washington Bridge, coming into the city. Both men were bruised and sore. They hadn't said a word to each other since they'd left the forest. Babu could feel that Lenny wanted to say something; Lenny could feel the same thing from Babu.

Someone needed to go first. After hours of silence, it was Lenny. "What option did I have?" he asked as he cleared his throat. "I loved Danno like a father. He told me that he was going to kill my wife if I didn't—"

"I know what happened," Babu said. "I don't want to talk about it." The giant turned to see a few tears make their way over Lenny's bruised face.

Lenny quickly wiped his cheeks; those tears had been twelve years coming, and only three seconds lasting. "I fought for my life in that prison," Lenny said. "I begged more than one person to let me live. I fucking hated myself for not being bigger or tougher." Lenny pretended to look out the window so he could cry in silence for another couple of seconds. He continued, "They would take weeks to break me. They'd threaten me, not let me sleep, and not let me eat. I was their fucking entertainment." Lenny turned to see if Babu cared, but his face wasn't easy to read. "And I cursed you into hell and back a hundred fucking times," Lenny said. "Where were you? Where was Ricky? I know what I did—and I wanted to pay for it. I *have* paid for it over and over and over again. But where the fuck were you guys?"

Babu didn't answer.

"So what choice did I have?" Lenny asked. "I served my time. I waited, and—nothing. My team wasn't fucking coming to rescue me. So I took Tanner's offer to get out and get paid—the only offer I had."

"We didn't just cut rope on you, Lenny," Babu said.

"Well, it sure as fuck felt like it."

The cracked roads shook Babu and Lenny in the van, and the loud honking of New York City outside kept them alert. Lenny hadn't seen his beautiful mess of a city in a long time. She seemed as dirty as ever, but a little happier, and maybe a bit richer, too. There were more nice cars and suits out and about. People looked shinier—brighter.

"I don't even know where I'm supposed to be," Lenny said.

"I do," Babu replied.

As they got closer to the deal, Babu wished that he'd had a better plan. The giant thought it wouldn't be too hard to change Lenny's mind—not the old Lenny, anyway.

Babu pulled into the building site. It was a metal skeleton of a huge building, half-covered, half-finished, standing tall in the gray sky over them. "Chrissy," Lenny said, calling the giant by his real name, "All I want to do is go home to my family."

Babu couldn't look at Lenny. He understood where Lenny was coming from, but the giant had a job to do.

Lenny got out of the van. There were only a couple of cars on the site and no immediate sound of banging or sawing or general work going on. There was, however, the hum of music: loud music that came from the back of the unfinished building.

Lenny walked to the mouth of the building without looking back. Exposed plastic sheeting flapped in the wind as Lenny kept his eyes on dark openings and any other place that might be hiding someone. The music grew louder. Babu drove off. Lenny wanted him to stay, but said nothing as the van left the parking lot. Across the road, Donta Veal watched the proceedings.

Inside the building shell, Lenny was met by a man who pushed Lenny toward the stairs.

"You Percy?" Lenny asked. "I was told to wait for Percy."

Percy nodded. "This way," he said.

As soon as Lenny took the first step up the bare concrete stairs, he heard the click of a hammer being cocked behind him. "Move," Percy said, holding a gun behind Lenny's head.

"You know that's not necessary," Lenny replied.

"Why's that?"

Lenny began to take the dusty exposed stairs. "Because you're bringing me somewhere I want to go," he said.

Percy was kind of put out. He wanted to use his gun. "How do you know you're going where you want to go?"

"Are you bringing me to see Tanner Blackwell?" Lenny asked.

There was a pause. "Yeah," Percy mumbled.

"Then I'm going where I want to go," Lenny said.

"Shut up, you faggot," Percy snapped.

Lenny and Percy went through a doorway into a room that was just a concrete box with exposed steel in the ceiling and square openings in the walls for the windows. The only piece of furniture in the whole place was a makeshift table in the middle of the room, with a bag underneath.

Lenny saw Tanner Blackwell first. He was sure that the man looking out the windowless square was, indeed, the boss from the Carolinas. He was older, skinnier, and more brittle-looking, but he was definitely Tanner. Also in attendance were Danno's former lawyer, Troy Bartlett, and two men whom Lenny recognized as the

Botchco brothers at the other side of the room. They had been handsome new wrestlers when Lenny last saw them—but now they were beetroot-red, balding, and three times the size they had once been.

Tanner smiled when he saw Lenny approaching. "We didn't think you were coming, seeing as how poor Percy here was knocked silly outside the prison this morning."

Lenny knew that had been Babu's work. He glanced at Percy, who dropped his head in shame. Lenny could see himself in Percy—his old self. Percy was a simple, young, scrawny kid trying to make his way into the wrestling business.

"I'm just here to collect my money and leave quietly," Lenny replied.

Tanner turned from the window opening and took his first good look at a free Lenny. "Well, you'll forgive us for thinking that you weren't coming," Tanner said. "Anyone associated with Danno Garland is an immediate traitor and liar, in my eyes."

Lenny took the contract from his pocket: it was creased, a little damp, and folded on the edges. "Do you want to do this or not?" Lenny asked.

Tanner smiled at Lenny's forthrightness. "Yes, sir."

Lenny couldn't help but notice the Botchco brothers pulling their best heel wrestler faces in the background. Troy took the contract and laid it on the table. The noise from the city was comforting to Lenny; he had missed it. He'd also missed the smell, which was one that only New York could cook up. It drifted its way into the building on a light breeze, which blew the edge of the contract up from the table.

"You know what I'm putting here?" Tanner asked. Lenny didn't really care. He just walked toward the papers to sign his name.

Tanner turned to the Botchcos to see if they noticed Lenny ignoring him, too; they had. Lenny's perceived ignorance was beginning to roil Tanner, and anything that roiled Tanner roiled his men, too. "Did you hear me asking you a question?" Tanner said.

"Yeah."

"Yeah, what?"

"Yeah, I heard you. Now have you got my money?" Lenny said.

Tanner pointed to the briefcase under the makeshift table. "Spoken like a true New Yorker. Danno must have been so proud of you, huh?" Tanner laughed, which meant that the Botchcos laughed. Percy followed, too, a little behind them. Lenny wasn't laughing.

"It's little fucks like you who poison our business," Tanner said. "No fucking respect." Tanner opened the contract to where Lenny needed to sign.

"Got a pen?" Lenny asked Troy. Tanner gave Troy the nod. Troy took a pen from his jacket and gave it to Lenny. "Open the briefcase and show me my money first," Lenny said.

"You don't trust me?" Tanner asked.

"No, I don't," Lenny replied.

"Give it to him," Tanner said.

One of the Botchcos—Lenny couldn't tell one from the other— kicked the briefcase along the floor toward him. Troy opened the contract, and Lenny approached it with pen in hand.

"Show me where," Lenny said to Troy.

Troy pointed to a few places, but before anything was inked, Lenny stooped and opened the waiting briefcase. It was full of freshly pressed cash. Lenny thought that, even if it wasn't all there, there certainly was enough to turn things around for his family. That was all that he wanted.

Tanner walked up to the table to witness the signature. Lenny cocked the pen and slowly brought it down toward the paperwork.

"It took a while to pay off," Tanner said. "But it was a good job for both of us that you shot that fat pig Danno in his fucking head."

Lenny instinctively turned and slapped the taste out of Tanner's mouth. The old man fell to the ground, holding his face. The whole room froze in shock—including Lenny.

"Have some fucking respect," Lenny said.

Percy tried to bull rush Lenny as the Botchcos hurried to help Tanner up. Lenny threw everything he had into his right hand and Percy hit the floor, but immediately wrapped himself around Lenny's leg as Lenny tried to bolt. The closest Botchco brother threw the briefcase at Lenny, who ducked. The briefcase hit the edge of the window opening and burst open, releasing an explosion of hundred-dollar bills outside.

"What did you fucking do that for?" Tanner shouted at his henchman's stupidity.

Lenny could see that the other Botchco brother now had a knife in his hand and was approaching rapidly. Lenny tried to untangle himself from Percy, but as the Botchco lunged, Lenny could only turn his body enough to take the knife in his shoulder area.

"I got him," shouted the knife-wielding brother to his boss.

Lenny kicked with his free leg and caught the Botchco brother as hard as he could in the balls. Both Lenny and Botchco hit the ground as Lenny struggled free from Percy, grabbed his contract, and scrambled for the doorway.

Lenny looked at the window opening and gave serious consideration to just fucking jumping, but it was too high. He scuttled down one flight of stairs and looked out again, but the drop was still enough to break his legs. He could hear the heavy footsteps of the Botchcos behind him.

Lenny's instinct was to try to lose them rather than outrun them, so he broke right and gently opened a door that took him out of the stairwell. He closed it quietly and ran toward the back of the building. His shoulder was throbbing and his blood dotted the gray concrete floor as he went from hallway to hallway.

The music he'd heard earlier grew louder as he approached the rear of the site. He took the steps down, two at a time, and slipped out of the building by pushing his way past a plywood sheet that covered an exit door.

Lenny stumbled straight into weirdness. He immediately hunched down behind a pile of bricks and watched a bunch of oiled, half-naked buff men scattered around the site. The fact that they were dancing and miming the lyrics of the song tipped it from the weird to the bizarre.

Lenny knew by the spandex, fanny packs, crop tops, and fingerless gloves that they were indeed his people. They were wrestlers, and probably southern, judging by the mullet haircuts, suede cowboy boots, and the chewing-tobacco teeth.

The more he looked, the more Lenny realized that these guys weren't wrestlers as he remembered them—they were a different breed. These guys were eighties wrestlers. The new school.

A camera crew filmed one wrestler in particular, as two others flexed their muscles into the camera lens from the side. They were "singing" along with everything they had:

When life is slammin' you down
And you ain't got no one around
You gotta be a man
You gotta clothesline what you can
Look great
grind your teeth
clench your fists
you can't be beat
You're a maaaaan
Grrrrr.

Huge men in tassels and bandanas were breaking planks of wood, swinging sledgehammers, and bending bars for the camera. The bad guys were full of menace and attitude, and the good guys smiled and posed any time they sensed the camera was near.

"What the fuck?" Lenny mumbled to himself as he backed away. This is what his business—the business of professional wrestling—had become since he went inside.

With so many of Tanner's guys between him and the exit, Lenny had no choice but to try the front gate after all. He carefully hurried around the side; it looked clear enough. He could see some of his sixty grand, his ticket home, literally blowing in the wind above him. He wanted to stop and collect every dollar.

"Hey," Babu shouted as he raced in through the entrance in his van.

Lenny stopped dead. He had Tanner's men behind him, Babu in front—and the money over his head. The giant slid to a sudden stop on the gravel driveway and waved at Lenny to come to him.

Lenny wasn't sure.

He'd already made a lot of stupid mistakes since he got out. He wondered if going with Babu was going to be another one.

"Hey," shouted one of the Botchco brothers as he charged out the exit.

Lenny quickly made up his mind. Babu it was.

As Lenny ran closer, the giant could see that blood was dripping from a stab wound in Lenny's shoulder. He turned off the engine and gingerly stepped out of the van.

"No, drive," Lenny shouted as he ran past Babu and into the van.

But Babu didn't run from nothing or no one—not even the two huge Botchco brothers who were rushing from the building site toward him. As Lenny watched from the safety of the van, Babu slapped the first brother into the nearest wall and cold-cocked the second with a head-butt. Two three-hundred-pound men, out cold in a couple of seconds.

Lenny slid into the driver's seat and started the van.

"You're not the driver anymore," Babu said through the driver's window. He opened the door and put one leg in the van. His weight made the vehicle bow down a little as he got fully inside. Lenny shimmied into the passenger seat.

"What did you do?" Babu asked as he started the ignition. Lenny didn't want to answer. "What did you do?" Babu asked again.

"Something stupid," Lenny replied.

Babu sped backward into the street and slammed the van into drive; he kept glancing at the blood stain on Lenny's shoulder as it grew bigger and bigger.

"What does that mean?" Babu asked.

"It means—I guess I'm a boss."

CHAPTER SIX

1984.
Seven hours after Lenny got out.
Memphis.

Joe Lapine took one hundred and thirteen steps through the packed boxes on his floor to get to his ringing phone. It was too many steps, he thought. As he got older, he had begun to see all the things in the world that could kill him. If he had a stroke or heart attack, he'd never reach the phone in time. He'd make sure to have a phone in each room in his new house.

"What happened?" Joe asked a little too loudly. "Is the paper signed over?"

"No," Donta said.

Joe clenched his fist and punched the air. "He didn't go through with it?" the chairman asked.

"No. I talked to Percy, like you said," Donta replied. "Lenny slapped Tanner across the face."

Joe sat down like a nosy housewife about to get all the street gossip. "He did?"

"Yeah. But it means trouble," Donta said. "They stabbed him, tried to kill him."

"That stupid fuck, Tanner," Joe said. "Get him the fuck away from that city."

Joe hung up and could feel all his hard work, negotiations, and personal plans slipping down the drain. Tanner was insistent that he would go after New York and Joe knew he should have acted then.

He wasn't going to make that mistake again. Tanner Blackwell looking for revenge wasn't going to be the thing that sank all Joe's plans.

It was time to deal with Tanner once and for all.

Joe dialed his office. "Martha, it's me," he said. "Call the other bosses immediately. Tell them that I want to honor Tanner Blackwell and make him the new chairman of the National Wrestling Council. Tell them it's an extraordinary agenda item and therefore I'd like to call the meeting for tomorrow night. We can do it in Vegas."

Down a dark alley, past three boarded doorways, and beyond a mountain of trash, they'd arrived at Babu's home. It wasn't what Lenny had expected. When he had gone inside, Babu was one of the most recognized faces in the country. He'd had national talk show exposure, women, money, and fame. Lenny didn't want to judge a book by its cover, but it looked like that was all gone now.

Through the flickering overhead lights outside, Lenny could see that his stab wound wasn't anything to panic over. He'd need stitches, but it didn't feel like anything was severed inside the shoulder.

Babu pulled the van up against the wall. "We're home," he said simply, as he delicately lowered himself out of the van. Lenny followed Babu's huge frame through his creaky front door.

Lenny immediately knew that Babu didn't live alone; he could smell home cooking, an aroma that hadn't visited Lenny in many, many years. "Up those stairs, there's a room and a place to wash," Babu said as he entered the kitchen.

His house was small for a giant, but it was well-kept and warm, and it had a woman's touch. Lenny looked up the dark stairs. "My shoulder is okay," he said as he followed Babu's direction.

"We can't leave it like it is," Babu replied.

Lenny peered around the door and could see a steaming pot of soup on the stove. "You wanna get something to eat first?" Babu asked. "Because we're going to look at that wound now, or later." Babu dished up a bowl for Lenny and a second one for himself.

Lenny sat at the table. He was getting a sense of Babu's home. It felt like what Lenny thought of as European: there was a small fire crackling in the corner, the beams over his head were exposed, and there was a rail of pots and pans hanging from hooks above the stove. Lenny took a second to digest the smell of the meal before it touched his lips. It was genuinely enough to make him emotional. He was out. All of that shit that happened to him, that had changed his life, was over. Or the last chapter of it was over. But he was out now, in New York, and with Babu again. They were different men, but they were still familiar to each other. Lenny slid his spoon around the inside edge of the bowl and blew on the thick spoonful as he lifted it to his lips. Babu sat next to him and looked intently at Lenny's new wound. Lenny didn't want to put the spoon down. The soup tasted too nice.

"Let me see," Babu said.

Lenny tried to play patient and eat at the same time. Babu tore a bigger hole in Lenny's already ripped T-shirt. The puncture was still wet and exposed, but it was nothing major, a clean cut. Babu rose from his seat and began to rummage through the drawers and little boxes on the shelves. Lenny took the opportunity to wolf down as much as he could.

"What's your plan?" Babu asked.

"To go home," Lenny replied with a full mouth.

"And how do you suppose you do that?" Babu asked.

Lenny hadn't worked out the details yet. "I don't know *how* I'm going home," he said. "Just that I am. And I'm going home worth something."

"Yeah?" Babu said as he put on a broken pair of glasses. "I told you I can help you with that."

"Next time I knock on Bree's door," Lenny said, "I'm going to be—something—more than this. More than who I was when I got put away—and certainly more than who I am now."

Babu sat back down. He had a tube of superglue between his huge sausage fingers that made him look clumsy and the tube tiny. His glasses were broken and Lenny wasn't even sure Babu could see through them properly. "I'll do that," Lenny said, as he took the tube for himself.

Babu wiped his hands along his shirt and proceeded to pinch Lenny's wound closed. Lenny then applied the glue along the cut line, careful not to get Babu stuck there, too. "You know Tanner has to come for you now," Babu said. "He can't have anyone putting their hands on a boss."

"I'm a boss," Lenny said. Babu peeked up from the wound to see that Lenny was smiling.

"We can stall them," Babu replied. "Bullshit them, and dodge them, but even then we only have a tiny window to get the territory moving."

Lenny finished applying the glue. "I'm not sure that's what I want."

"What do you want?" Babu asked.

"I don't know. Whatever is best for my family," Lenny replied.

Lenny walked up the dark stairs toward the small bathroom. He had no idea how Babu fit in there. Lenny needed a shower and rest. He had to try to get his head right, or at least right enough to catch up with what was happening. He had no idea where to go, or what to do—and he had no idea who he could trust.

He turned on the faucet and let the water slap down into the waiting bath. He locked the door and took off his clothes. He noticed his cuts and bruises in the mirror in front of him. His belly was fuller and rounder than it had been in a long time.

Below him, Babu waited until he knew Lenny was out of earshot before picking up his phone to make a call.

On the other end, Joe Lapine answered. "Joe?" Babu said. "It's me."

"What the fuck is going on out there?" Joe asked.

Babu spoke cautiously. "You need to pull Tanner, do you hear me?" he said, "Get him off the field any way you have to, or all this work will be for nothing."

"I'm dealing with it." Joe said. "Where's Lenny now?"

Babu thought carefully about his answer. He didn't want to say, but he had no choice. "I've got him—but I need more time to get him to bend," the giant said.

"Don't give him any other fucking option," Joe replied. Babu took a quick look up the stairs to make sure he and Joe were still speaking in private.

"You deal with Tanner and I'll deal with Lenny," Babu said. "Either way, New York is back in play."

Lenny sat naked in the darkness of the top step, listening to Babu's conversation. He felt the fear of being out of prison, and the anger of having been in there in first place. His bones were sore, and his wounds were throbbing. He missed his home—the same home he knew didn't exist anymore. Lenny grabbed his clothes and carefully opened the nearest window as quietly as he could.

Wrestling was looking for him, but Lenny was looking for family. He knew both things, yet again, were intertwined.

CHAPTER SEVEN

Kid Devine sat in the front row of an empty Madison Square Garden. He thought about his match that was coming up, and how it would play out. He thought about his father, the wrestling business, the threats, and how all that would play out too.

He heard footsteps on the risers behind him.

"Let me smarten you up," said the voice in the darkness.

In wrestling, this phrase meant everything. A veteran saying those words to a rookie was a passing of the torch; a sign that you'd been truly accepted in the wrestling business. It involved a lot of trust—a lot of faith that the person learning would take on the old traditions, the proper way of doing things. That they would protect the secrets of the wrestling business.

On this night, the rookie knew the voice of the person that was sitting about twenty rows back. Only the ring was lit, so Kid could only make out a silhouette in the stands.

"Can we let the people in?" a staff member shouted. "They're starting to go crazy out there."

"No," the man in the stands replied. "A few more minutes."

Kid stood up and leaned against the apron of the twenty-by-twenty red, white, and blue ring. He tried to look beyond the lights. "Why don't you come down here and show me something, old man?" he said. "It's been a while."

The man in the stands struck a match for his cigarette, and Kid caught a glimpse of his pained, pale face. "You okay?" Kid asked.

"I'm fine," the man answered. He took a pull from his cigarette. "Now, there's only four basic parts to a wrestling match: the Shine, the Heat, the Comeback, and the Finish. The Shine is where our hero starts off well, and wins a couple of small, early victories to get the crowd excited. They paid good money, so give them what they want." He took another pull and continued.

"To start with."

Kid moved to jump the barrier. "You can stay where you are," the man in the stands said. Kid reluctantly stayed where he was, but he had no idea why he couldn't go see his mentor.

"The second part of the match is the Heat," the man said.

"I know this stuff," Kid replied.

The man continued regardless. "And the Heat is where it begins to go wrong for our hero," the man said. "The heel sees an opportunity to win, and he takes it. It's the part of the match where the audience decides whether the babyface hero is worth supporting or not."

"Seriously, man. What are you doing up there? I can't see you," Kid said.

"This part of the match is when bad things happen to good people."

1984.
One day after Lenny got out.
New York.

Tad Stolliday fucking loved his job. While some people would say they enjoyed being employed, or that they didn't mind their work, Tad would have come in every morning to do his job for free. Being in charge of people actually made him feel better, as a human being.

He was too much of a pussy to be a cop, and too fond of himself to be a security guard, so he followed the road that best suited him: he was born to be a parole officer.

This day, however, was a bad day at the office. Word was coming down from the executive director of the State Division of Parole that a parolee had just shot a cop and wounded two others. The governor of New York, along with the mayor, had both called into question the effectiveness of the parole system in total.

"Tighten up on these cunts," was the director's supposed reaction.

Tad didn't need to be told twice. He was sitting in his home, waiting for 9:00 a.m. to come. He had given his shoes an extra shine that morning, and his tie was pressed perfectly and tied meticulously. The executive director wanted tightening and Tad wanted to impress. No coffee was needed and his push-ups were completed for the day. Well, that was what he'd tell the boys at the office. Truth be told, he loved the Raquel Welch fitness video. There was something about the breathless voiceover and synchronized breathing that pepped him up in the morning. His mustache was groomed and trimmed; his breakfast was squashed and scrambled.

This was going to be an awesome fucking day.

Tad Stolliday couldn't wait to talk to parolee number one: Mr. Lenard Long.

"Hey, hey! Stop that guy. Stop that guy!" roared the overweight taxi driver as Lenny jumped fences and cars and cut through lanes to get away. He felt like an asshole running out on a fare, but he had no choice.

After he bolted from Babu's house, Lenny stayed awake all night, moving from bus shelter to bus shelter. He waited for the morning before making his journey back to Queens. He didn't want to knock on his father's door in the middle of the night. Waiting till morning would make everything seem a little more normal, or as normal as it could be.

Lenny had written the address hundreds of times, but he'd never been there before. Long Island City didn't look like the safest of neighborhoods. Its riverbanks were strewn with twisted metal and forgotten debris. It looked to Lenny like an industrial area that had been hollowed out.

He turned the corner and walked through the morning smell of bakeries setting up for the day. Lenny walked up to the small, rectangular garden and knew right away that his father lived there. There were seashells pressed into the grass as a border, and in the middle was the faded gnome Bree had given Lenny as a joke present one Christmas. Seeing it made Lenny well up—it was the last piece left of his own home, and his father had kept it.

Lenny approached the door and knocked on the flimsy frame.

"Hello?" asked Edgar from inside.

"It's me, Pop," Lenny said.

There was a slight pause from inside. "Lenard?"

"Yeah, it's me."

Edgar took another couple of seconds to process Lenny's words.

"They let me out," Lenny said with his head pressed against the door.

Edgar hurriedly twisted some of the locks the wrong way, and some the right way. "I can't . . . wait, son," Edgar said. "I need to get . . ."

"It's okay," Lenny said, looking behind him to see if he was being followed.

Edgar opened the door, but not too wide. He had glasses on his face, and his hair was thinning. He was smaller, his shoulders narrower.

"Pop," Lenny said with a smile on his face and a tear in his eye.

Edgar was totally confused; he'd thought that his son had many more years to go. "Lenard?"

Edgar opened the door and he and Lenny hugged on his porch.

"Come in, come in," Edgar said as he moved his son indoors.

"I got out," Lenny said.

"What happened to you?" Edgar asked as he looked at his son good and proper.

Lenny had forgotten about his face, and the dry blood stains on his ripped clothes. He had never felt more self-conscious. "I . . . got . . . it's nothing. Honestly."

"The place is a mess," Edgar said as he closed a couple of the interior doors in his small hallway. He didn't want his son looking around too much.

Lenny could see into the kitchen where the table was set for breakfast. Three settings. "Are you expecting someone?" Lenny asked as he walked from the hallway into the kitchen.

"Yeah," Edgar answered. "I am."

Lenny could hear voices fast approaching his father's front door. "Who is it?" he asked. The look on Edgar's face made Lenny instinctively stoop down and look for a way out. "Is that my family?"

Edgar nodded.

"Fuck," Lenny said as he looked for a place to hide.

"Don't you want to see them?" Edgar asked.

Lenny wanted it more than anything in the whole world. "Look at me, Pop," he replied. "I don't want them to see me like this."

The front door opened and a voice called "Granddad" from the hallway. Lenny was boxed in. Edgar walked toward his front door and greeted his visitors like nothing was out of the ordinary.

"Thank you so much, again, Edgar," said another voice from the front door. It was her voice. Bree.

Lenny quietly slipped into the tight, dark pantry and closed the door. The new sounds of footsteps into the kitchen meant she was only a few feet away from him—but she would never even know that he was there. He couldn't see her, but her voice was soothing; it took everything Lenny had not to open the door to just see her one more time. But he knew what he looked like, and that he had nothing to offer her. He was a broken man, looking for his father to hide him, while he ran once again from the wrestling business.

He was Lenny Long. Still wrapped up in trouble. Still in danger. Still confused as to what to do.

"Can I put this down in my room?" Lenny heard a young voice ask. He knew it could only have been James Henry.

"Not right now, Jimmy," Edgar replied. "Wash your hands down the hall."

Lenny heard the boy's footsteps leave.

"You look really good, Bree," Edgar said.

"You too," she replied.

Lenny ran his squinted eye all around the door to see if there was a hole or crack he could see her through. He could hear Bree and Edgar pass plates, open bags, and pour drinks as they talked.

Edgar asked, "Was it a long way down? I miss you guys around the place."

"Just a couple of hours," Bree replied. "It's not that bad. We haven't got the TV or phone installed yet, so Jimmy's still a little restless. I understand him wanting to stay here. He feels like he's cut off from the world with me, for now. He'll settle down when he gets to know the new kids."

"I would have come up there and got you guys," Edgar said.

"Thank you, but I have some other things to do in the city before I head back, anyway," Bree replied.

"Coffee?" Edgar asked.

"You doing okay, Ed?" Bree asked. "You look a little distracted or something."

Lenny froze. So did Edgar for a second. "I think I'm coming down with a little cold or something."

"You want us to get out of here?" Bree asked. "Let you get some rest."

"No, please. I like having you guys here. And this breakfast isn't going to eat itself."

Lenny could hear a chair being scraped along the floor. He thought he could smell her perfume.

"As long as you're sure," Bree said.

"Of course. Have a seat."

Lenny stood silently in near darkness and listened to his family eat, laugh, and look after each other. It was still like a prison dream to him—being so close to his family again, but not being able to see them, see how they'd changed. But even their voices made him feel content. It made him want to be better, be accepted by them. He heard them pass each other juice and ask if anyone wanted more of anything. They talked about Bree's new place, and about another school for Jimmy. Their older son, Luke, was a man now and living in the city. It was a morning of catching up, and small talk, and it was all that Lenny needed to feel better.

Nevada.

Joe ordered the meeting, and the other bosses followed. The room was quiet, but full, except for one chair. It was dark and smoky, just how Joe liked it. It reminded him of the younger years of the National Wrestling Council, when he had been surrounded by some of the most ruthless promoters of all time, unlike this new batch. These promoters weren't nearly as plugged in to what was happening. The new NWC was made up of a few older, more tired bosses, and the rest were subpar relations of the bosses who were no longer around.

Joe couldn't have planned it any better for himself.

"Where is he?" Gilbert King, the Florida boss, asked. "This is very disrespectful, to you and the position of chair."

Joe shrugged. In a flash he remembered Gilbert's father, Proctor King, who had been dangerous and wily. Gilbert, his pampered son, was not the same animal at all.

"How much longer are we going to wait?" asked Hal Yellow from Texas. He reminded Joe of a train inspector, but he didn't particularly like him. "If Tanner is too good to show up, I think we should consider other options."

"I'll call his room now," Joe said as he left the table. He walked to the back of the room and picked up the pay phone. He pantomimed dialing a number and put the phone to his ear.

This was the kind of game that Joe Lapine had come up on. When he had been a young man at the NWC table, he'd watched boss after boss get eliminated from the game by stealth, technicality, or sheer politics.

To Joe, using force was a tool of the ignorant. He much preferred to ruin someone the good old-fashioned way: from the shadows.

Tanner awoke alone in his hotel room. Long flights used to knock him out, but now they nearly killed him. His phone had been ringing for about a minute before he came around and answered it.

"Yes?" Tanner said.

"Your wake-up call, Mister Blackwell," said the nearly undecipherable Irish accent on the line. "Your group is waiting for you downstairs."

Tanner hung up the phone. He dropped his legs over the side of his bed and rested his rough, wrinkly face in his hands. He felt around his cheekbone, where Lenny Long had slapped him the day before. It was still tender and sore.

He wasn't a big eater, anymore. He used to prefer a coffee in the morning, but now he didn't really feel like having anything to eat or drink. The cancer must have been in his stomach, too, he decided.

He shuffled around and farted as he bent over for his socks. There was a time in his life when he could pick up his socks with his toes and place them in his hand. Now he spent many more days just slipping his bare feet into his shoes—it was easier that way. His belt told him that he had lost even more weight. It was rapid now; a difference could be seen every day. Tanner was wasting away. Sometimes he pitied himself, but often he was too tired for even that. On other days, he bullied himself for being a fucking sissy who had gotten sick. Tanner had known that this day was going to come. It was something he had thought—he'd even talked about it with Minnie, when she was alive.

It was a day he knew that he deserved.

He put on his coat, even though he knew he wasn't going outside.

His back was hunched, his reflection was frail, and his body was dying. Tanner checked his fly one last time before he opened his door to see a tall, young, freckle-faced concierge waiting for him. It was then that he knew for sure.

"They're waiting for you downstairs, Mister Blackwell."

Tanner nodded and walked ahead. The concierge followed behind him silently. Tanner couldn't rush, even if he wanted to, so he and a man half his age moved slowly down the hallway.

"That's some accent you got there," Tanner said.

"It's a little hard for you people to understand sometimes, alright," replied the concierge.

Tanner's body was leaving him, but his mind was still very much his own.

"You been working here long?" Tanner asked.

"About a month only."

"Yeah?"

"Yeah."

They approached the elevator, and Tanner couldn't help but notice the squeak that was coming from the concierge's brand new shoes.

"That's out of order, I'm afraid, sir," the concierge said.

Tanner smiled to himself, before feeling a little insulted. "The stairs?" Tanner asked.

"Yes, sir."

Tanner turned toward the stairwell door, and began his slow steps. "Can I smoke?" Tanner asked, as he stopped and reached into his jacket for his cigarettes.

"You'll be late, sir."

"I'm not rushing to get there, and you know what I mean."

The concierge lit his lighter, and Tanner put his cigarette to it. The smoke bounced off Tanner's face as it rose toward the ceiling.

"You can tell Joe that I understand," Tanner said.

The concierge opened the door to the stairwell. "I don't know what you mean," he said as he looked anxiously over his own shoulder.

The young man's accent just served to remind Tanner that he was a long way from home. "You know, I always wanted to come to Ireland."

The concierge replied, "You'll have a great time here, sir."

"How much more of it do you think I'll get to see?" Tanner asked as he walked toward the open door that lead to the concrete stairs and raw brick walls.

"As much as you—"

"Tell Joe that I got the point," Tanner said. "And that I'm done."

The concierge moved Tanner closer to the stairwell. "They're waiting for you downstairs, sir."

Tanner shrugged off the concierge's attempt to move him along by the arm. "You tell Joe to leave me alone. Tell him that I'm out. I'm gone. Do you hear me?"

The concierge could see just how agitated Tanner was becoming.

"Do you fucking hear me?" Tanner shouted.

Before the concierge could do anything more to upset Tanner, Donta Veal appeared from around the corner and tapped the young man on the shoulder. The concierge quietly left.

Tanner tried to place Donta's face. He knew it, but he didn't know how he knew it. Then it hit him.

"Fuck," Tanner said, as he sat himself on the top step of the stairwell. Donta joined him.

"You just couldn't leave it alone, Tanner," Donta said as he lit his own cigarette.

Tanner could hear the squeak of the concierge's shoes moving away down the corridor. Knowing the way Donta worked, Tanner figured that the odds were high that the concierge wasn't a concierge at all. Donta would have no loose ends—no one to testify if it all went wrong.

"Every year you pushed the New York thing further and further," Donta said.

"That's because I knew that Joe was running it. He was telling the world one thing, and doing a deal with those snakes in New York to do the other."

Donta slid his hand into his jacket; Tanner waited anxiously to see what Donta was reaching for.

"I don't know why, because if it was up to me, I'd kill you. He just wants you out of the business," Donta said.

Tanner took another pull from his cigarette and thought about all the years he had been in the wrestling business, all the money he'd made, and all the birthdays he'd missed because he was on the road.

"Tell Joe I'm too weak to fight. I'm done."

Donta stood and moved behind Tanner in a deliberate attempt to frighten the frail old man some more. "Next time, you won't see me," Donta said.

Tanner understood completely. Donta's orders from Joe had very clear. The setup was perfect: no one was around. But Tanner was just an old man in a stairwell.

Donta was having a hard time walking away. "Hey?"

Tanner looked up from his seated position, and Donta hammer-fisted him across the face. Tanner moaned in pain as he covered himself up on the ground. Donta got a stomp or two in for his travel back to the States, and he felt better.

Nevada.

Joe knocked his knuckles on the table to call order. He acted annoyed that Tanner's chair was still empty, but he wanted to show the other bosses that the wrestling business waited for no man.

"We'll start without Tanner Blackwell, if there's a consensus in the room." Joe said.

"Where is he?" asked Gilbert King.

Joe took a second, like he was processing what he could and couldn't say. He wanted to look political—measured—like this wasn't personal.

"Fuck it," Joe said, as if he had just decided to be honest. "He didn't check in. As far as I can tell, he never even came to Vegas."

"What?" asked Gilbert. "You try to give him the chair, and he has one of the world heavyweight champions, and he doesn't even show up?"

Joe sighed and played along like he'd never asked his secretary to book a meeting room in Vegas for them, and a separate room out of the country for Tanner. Joe's plan was if Tanner became stubborn and refused to leave the business, then something would have been done to him—but outside of America, outside of New York, and it would be made to look like an accident.

Joe's other option was that Tanner would leave quietly, and Joe would "suspend" him from the NWC for not showing up. One way or another, Tanner was either dead and out or suspended and out. But he was fucking out. And that gave Joe a clear line to New York, and a room of bosses who just moved firmly behind him.

No war. No drama. No more dissension.

"To be honest with you all, this is the last straw for me. This disrespect toward you, the council, and the position of chair can't continue. It makes us all look weak," Joe said, as the trained seals in front of him clapped. "Add that to the fact that Tanner tried to secretly buy New York, again, yesterday . . ."

Joe waited for the outrage and mumbling, which came just on cue. "Yes, that's why I called you here today," Joe continued. "I just learned myself this morning. So Tanner was never going to get the chairmanship of this great council here today. I was going to fucking suspend him indefinitely for breaking our rules, for going behind our backs, and for putting all of our territories at risk. Again!"

As Joe looked at the other bosses, he could feel the grip that Merv used to have before him as chairman. Joe talked about how the sky was falling, and how he was the only one who could protect the business from it. He had them all wide eyed and scared.

Tanner was to be suspended, and New York was to be marked.

"Marked?" asked Hal, trying not to sound like the rookie owner that he was.

Joe explained, "We put it out there that any wrestler who works the New York territory from today on is to be blackballed by the rest of the business."

Joe's plan received a slow clap as everyone eventually figured out what he was doing.

"Let's see how long they can hold their TV without any wrestlers to feature. How long will they hold their venues without any matches to put on? How long will New York survive without any workers?" Joe asked.

This was the grand power of the NWC: with all the other territories backing him, not a single wrestler in the country would attempt to cross the line into New York.

"We all know the rules. Most of us live by those rules. If you don't, then we will kill you on the vine," Joe said.

CHAPTER EIGHT

New York.

Lenny sat on the avocado-colored toilet in his father's house. It was peaceful, a place to catch his thoughts. He leaned over and ran the faucet on the avocado sink. The water was cold to the touch. Lenny dipped the corner of a towel under the stream of water and dabbed around the edges of his glued-up shoulder.

"Lenard?" called Edgar from the sitting room.

"Yeah?" Lenny replied.

"C'mere."

Lenny entered the sitting room and saw Tad, his parole officer, waiting for him.

"This man is here to see you. Says you gave this address," Edgar said.

Lenny nodded. He'd never seen Tad before but instinctively knew what he wanted.

"I'll leave you to your business," Edgar said as he tried to leave.

"No, I'd like your father to hear this, too," Tad said, as he sat down in Edgar's sitting room with his coat on.

Lenny and Edgar took his cue and sat down as well.

"What happened to your face?" Tad asked.

"Just a goodbye present from Attica," Lenny lied.

Tad wasn't sure; he didn't trust anyone who wasn't wearing a badge or a uniform. Despite this, he began the speech he'd prepared hours before. "We have fifteen state parole commissioners, but two of those positions haven't been filled. It's these people who take on the cases of fifteen thousand inmates who are looking for an early release from prison. People like your son, Mr. Long. Do you understand?"

Edgar wasn't expecting to be called upon. "I do."

"Lenard?" Tad asked, "Do you understand?"

Lenny nodded.

"I need a verbal statement," Tad said.

"I do," Lenny replied. "I understand."

"Okay. When people such as yourself get brought before the courts, judges do the sentencing," Tad said, "But the real sentencing seems to be done by the parole board nowadays." Tad looked suspiciously at Lenny. "By what criteria, I don't know. I have no idea how these people arrive at their decisions, and who am I to second-guess them?"

Neither Lenny nor Edgar replied. They didn't know they had to.

"That wasn't rhetorical," Tad said. "I have no idea how the parole board came to their decision, and who I am to second-guess it?" Tad wasn't being subtle in letting Lenny know that his release from prison was raising some questions.

"I understand," Lenny said.

"Me too." Edgar followed his son's lead.

Tad crossed one leg over the other. "When a decision is reached, however, it is then up to people like me to make sure that people like you, Lenard, don't go back into society and cause further suffering to civilians. Last year, there were one hundred and thirty-eight thousand felony arrests in New York State. I'm happy to say that only six hundred and seventy-five of those were parolees. Do you understand me?"

"I do," Lenny said.

"Me too," Edgar said.

"Last year, I was responsible for forty-two cases. You're my seventieth this year, so far. I just want you to know that, because you're special to me in that way. I've never had such a case load in my life, and you, Lenard Long, sit on top of that pile." Tad stood up. He presumed by the engaged, respectful reaction he'd gotten that his point had been made. But fuck it: he wanted to make it again. "They let a guy out, and he just killed a cop and injured two more. When they looked at his record it was discovered that his parole had not been revoked, even though he had been arrested twice and convicted once before the shooting. That makes people like me look incompetent. If you so much as get picked up for littering, I'm going to put you back inside. Do you understand that, Lenard?"

Lenny nodded again.

"I need to hear you say it."

"I understand," Lenny said.

"Me too," said Edgar.

"Mr. Stolliday," Tad said to Lenny.

"Mr. Stolliday," Lenny replied.

"Good," Tad said with a smile.

Edgar stood and walked Tad to his front door. He was polite but surgical in removing the parole officer from his house. Lenny followed behind.

Tad reached for, and produced, a perfectly cut business card from his pocket. "Monday morning, come see me. We'll be working on making you a better citizen."

"Can't wait," said Lenny.

"Or I might visit you again," Tad said, smiling.

"That would be lovely, too," Lenny replied.

Tad walked away from the house and got into his car. "Be good out there."

Lenny nodded and smiled as Tad drove off.

"What are you bringing to this house?" Edgar asked.

New York.

Ricky Plick sat outside the administrator's office in a sharp suit and tie. His forehead was glued and bandaged, his hips were throbbing, and his knees were blue underneath the nice material of his trousers. He noticed the secretary watching him.

"Is this going to take long?" Ricky asked.

"I don't know, sir," the secretary replied. "He's usually very punctual."

"Just . . . I've got a flight."

On Ricky's last word, the door with ADMINISTRATOR on it opened.

"Mr. Plick?" asked a man who looked like a middle-aged doctor.

"Yes?"

The administrator stood in his office doorway and waited for Ricky to walk through.

Inside the office, the men sat on opposite sides of a wide desk. The office was compact, but functional. The wall behind the administrator had a black mark on it from him leaning back in his chair with a head full of lacquer.

"How is he?" Ricky asked.

This most basic question seemed to catch the administrator off guard.

"He's, eh . . . he's to be expected. I suppose. But we need to talk about other matters, first."

Ricky felt like belting the guy across the face. Instead, he slid his hand into his inside pocket and took out a stack of cash. "This?" Ricky asked, showing him the money.

The administrator nodded. "It's just that we can't keep doing this. You're late every month, and short sometimes."

"But it balances out," Ricky said.

"There are other options here, Mr. Plick. If you can't afford your . . . *friend's* stay here, then there's state options that you should . . ."

The administrator knew from Ricky's thunderous face that he had better stop talking. "State options?" Ricky asked. He wasn't waiting for a reply. "Over the last six years, I have given you people every penny that I have. I paid the fees and the extras and the tests and the medicines. I have done all of that. You're right in that, nowadays, the money is a little late sometimes, but I don't work around the fucking corner from here. I can't just skip on by and hand you your fucking money." Ricky threw the cash he had on the table. It was a thick little stack, but it was not enough to keep Ginny there for a month.

"Sir—"

Ricky continued. "Now, here's what's going to happen. You're going to make sure that *my friend* doesn't miss one meal, or one single activity in this place. He stays in his ground floor room, because that's what he likes. You're to make sure that his life here is like your brochures say; people are happy on your brochures. He deserves to be the same. And I'll make sure that you get your fucking money on time, and in full. Deal?"

The administrator tried to talk, but Ricky was looking for a one-word reply. "Deal?" Ricky asked again.

"We need the rest of the money by the end of the month, or we can no longer have Ginny stay at this facility."

"His name is Mr. Ortiz," Ricky said as he stood slowly and turned for the door.

"Mr. Plick?"

Ricky stopped. "I will have your money."

"Mr. Plick, we also don't accept foodstuffs from the outside, and we can't have unsupervised persons in the rooms of our patients."

"I don't know what you're talking about."

"The ice cream, sir. You can't keep sending in deliveries of ice cream."

"Like I said, I have no idea what you're talking about," Ricky said before leaving the office.

He called the same number at the same time on the same day of every week, and on every Wednesday, at six o'clock sharp, Pagladoni's

Ice Cream Parlor would make their delivery: twelve scoops, four bananas, three candy toppings, whipped cream, and a long spoon. Only this time, they were advised by Ricky to do it in a different way. Pagladoni's youngest son, Carlo, tiptoed in the evening darkness and approached Ginny's ground-floor window. Through the net curtain, Carlo could see Ginny waiting, with his chair facing the door.

Carlo gently approached and tapped lightly on the window, leaving the tray of ice cream behind him. As he walked off, he could hear the window open, and the sound of the tray being slid into the room. Week by week, Ginny forgot most faces, names, places, and old times, but he never forgot Wednesday at six. It was his favorite time of the week, and he even made an effort to dress up nicely and brush his hair for it.

Ginny looked forward to his delivery more than anything in the world, but for Ricky, it was his weekly apology. Like a man who sends his wife flowers, Ricky sent ice cream to soothe his conscience. Even though, somewhere in his head, he knew that he was doing all he could, Ricky still felt bad that he spent so much time away from Ginny. His heart was broken that he couldn't hug the man he loved, so ice cream was a tiny comfort both to Ricky for sending it, and to Ginny for getting it.

As Ginny got worse, Ricky had days where he worried about what would happen to him when he could no longer remember anything. Ricky had been assured by the doctors who were taking large chunks of his money that Ginny would be in no pain, and that some people were "happily unaware" that they even had anything wrong with them. Ricky prayed that would be the case for Ginny. To a large degree, it was. Ginny had his routine, his own room that he loved, and his meals ready-made. They informed Ricky that Ginny loved music hour, and that he would regularly dance with the other patients, if they let him. This made Ricky smile. Ginny was the kind of man who loved to dance when no one was watching. Not once in their long relationship had they ever danced together.

As Ricky stood outside of Ginny's room, he weighed time and again the cost of entering. The previous few visits had upset Ginny hugely. Ricky thought that Ginny knew him, but didn't know how to process who they were together. The doctors said that it was simply that Ginny didn't like strangers, and Ricky was now a stranger.

So Ricky did all that he could do: he walked away with his heart broken.

It got colder as he stood there, but Babu was willing to wait another ten hours if he had to. He was around the back of an old truck stop, about four miles away from the airport. This was the meeting place. With all that had been stirred up, Babu figured that somewhere different was probably safest. The second he saw the frame of the man approaching him, he knew it was his old friend.

"Chilly enough for you?" Ricky asked as he approached.

"Good to see you," Babu said, as he shook the man's hand and pulled him in for a bear hug. "How's Ginny doing?"

"Good. Seems to be totally at home there," Ricky said.

"Good. Thanks for taking the time to see me," Babu said, as he ushered Ricky to a little picnic table at the side of his van.

"Lunch?" Ricky asked.

"I got hot tea, and some sandwiches," Babu said. "There's a chicken dish in there, too, if you want it. Or you can take it with you."

Ricky patted his old colleague on the shoulder and sat down. Babu took his seat with a little more caution. "I never fucking know if I'm going to fit—or, if I do, whether the bench is going to just disappear up my ass or not."

Ricky laughed a good, much-needed laugh.

"You could stay here if you wanted," Babu said to Ricky. "There's no one looking for you here anymore."

"I would stay here in a heartbeat, you know that. But I can't earn here."

Babu set out the cups and handed Ricky a wrapped sandwich. "What if I said you could?" Babu asked.

Ricky knew what was on Babu's mind.

"New York is about to be swallowed whole by the greediest, filthiest scumbags in the country," the giant said. "And while they're fighting each other, we have a chance to stand the territory up, ourselves. We just need the money."

Ricky stopped and thought about the situation for a second. It was something he wouldn't have ever allowed himself to do before, but having to leave home again was becoming unbearable for him. "Do you know they blackballed New York at their meeting this morning?"

Babu shook his head.

Ricky said, "Yeah, because Lenny slapped Tanner—and everything else that's going on—they've put the word out that if any wrestler works this territory then they're blackballed forever."

"Fuck."

"So, I'm just wondering—if we could miracle up the money somewhere, how do we work around the fact that no one will work for us?" Ricky asked.

"I don't know," Babu said.

"You don't know?" Ricky laughed. He knew he shouldn't have even entertained the idea.

"That's what I need you for," Babu said.

Ricky looked around. They were at the back of a shitty truck stop, drinking tea from a thermos like some low-level scumbags on the run. This wasn't what he wanted from life at his age. "Look at us," Ricky said. "Even if we could get wrestlers, what would we do with them today? It's all baby oil and jacked-up bodies. It's a bodybuilding competition now. They're all fucking coked out of their minds."

"You mean to tell me that if Lenny Long asked you to run New York, you'd say 'no thanks' and move on?" Babu asked.

Ricky bit into his sandwich as he thought. "It's weird that he is holding the paper."

"He wants you in, Ricky. I know he does. He doesn't know what he's doing. You could come home, and make New York for yourself."

"It's almost impossible to turn this around," Ricky replied.

"I'm sick of bowing and scraping. These other prick bosses didn't do nothing for the business here," Babu said.

Ricky caught himself dreaming again and stopped immediately. He looked at his watch and stood. "I've got to go."

"How many more bumps have you got in that body, you old fool? How much longer can you make it in Japan?" Babu asked.

Ricky didn't know how to answer.

Babu said, "We have the pieces. They might not be the shiniest, newest, most perfect pieces, but we have them."

Ricky walked back to the giant and gently said, "I know you've got some kind of deal with Joe Lapine in all of this."

Babu stood up. "That's correct."

"And how do you think I'm supposed to take that?"

"Take what?"

Ricky thought about saying more but turned to walk instead. Babu wasn't done. "Danno was gone. You disappeared. And I was in a deal where I held one of the world titles," he said. "New York was a fucking fire pit. Joe kept the lights on."

"That was nice of him," Ricky said.

"You think I don't know *why* he kept this territory on life support? You think I don't see him coming to collect now? But what choice did I have? I could have walked away like you did."

"Walked away?" Ricky shouted. "You think I got out of here because I wanted to?"

"It's a very simple thing, Ricky. I know why *you* did what you did. I know why *Joe* did what he did. And I certainly fucking know why *I* did what I did."

"How much did he pay you?" Ricky asked.

"What did you say?"

"You heard me. What deal have you two got?" Ricky asked.

Babu came close to punching Ricky in the face. "He needed me on the card to keep New York alive, and I needed him paying the bills under the table for the same fucking reason. For that, he promised me that there would be no more killing, that people would get paid on time, and you'd get safe passage back into New York to see Ginny. That's what I got."

There was a pause as both men calmed down a little.

"I appreciate that," Ricky said.

"No problem," Babu replied.

"Have you told Lenny what you did yet?" Ricky asked.

Babu hung his head a little. "One thing at a time."

1984.
One month *before* Lenny got out.
New Jersey.

There were body builders, beauty queens, face paint, mirrored sunglasses, white suits with the sleeves rolled up, pretty boys, wild island men, hair spray, fanny packs, and a new guy standing around the ring.

Everybody's eyes were on the gruff Texas veteran who stood in the middle of the ring.

"If you're a babyface and some ladies in the audience think you're their hero, you better keep them happy out there. Entertain 'em, fuck 'em, or do whatever they want you to do with them. Remember: the fat gals have the biggest mouths, so if you're going to nail her, nail her good. We have to come back here every month, and you will not embarrass this company with your small or drunk dick. Do you hear me? On the other hand, if you're a heel, you can drink and fight as much as you like. Hell, I had a boss who used to pay me some extra coin just to go to the local bar and start some trouble. Just remember: if you lose a fight, you're fired," Wild Ted Berry said from the ring.

He was once a journeyman wrestler, paid to lose in every territory he went to, but when he retired, Ted had found that he was more suited to the booking end of wrestling. A booker had to be creative, be tough, and know every wrestling scenario in order to make the matches seem varied and unique. It was his job to put on matches that the audience wanted to see, and to pick the winners that they wanted to cheer for. Ted had put forty years into the business, and not even he had seen anything like what was planned for this night. That was why he felt the need to give the back-to-basics speech. He wanted to remind the roster of what it was to be a pro wrestler, and to focus their minds so they wouldn't revolt or riot when they heard the main event.

"It's my job to put you in this ring," Ted continued. "It's your job to give them what they want."

The new guy, Kid Devine, watched the gruff Texan lay down the law from the ring. It was his first night, and he could tell by the human shit already left in his travel bag that he wasn't very well liked.

It was the way that wrestlers communicated—especially to new guys.

"Call your wives and girlfriends, and tell them you're going to Tunkhannock, Pennsylvania; Rochester, New York; Lancaster, Pennsylvania; Long Island, New York; St. Louis, Missouri, for TV; then Altoona, Pennsylvania; Salisbury, Maryland; Landover, Maryland; Johnstown, Pennsylvania; Garfield, Pennsylvania; Kingston, Howell, Lyndhurst, and Somerville, New Jersey. Don't forget to tell them that you'll see them next week when we do all this again."

Kid chuckled, because he thought the insane travel was, well, insane. That action cost him entry to the dressing room, though. He had to take his shitty bag and get dressed outside in the hallway on his own. He couldn't figure out who had it in for him—maybe it was everyone. Laughing at the schedule hadn't helped, nor did the fact that he was about to wrestle the legendary Babu in his first match.

"Go home."

Kid was lying in the corner with his head on the second turnbuckle; he was coming to the end of his first match. His chest was chopped raw, and he was pretty sure that more than one tooth was loose. He also had a broken toe. It wasn't over yet, though. The referee slid down and pretended to check on the well-being of the rookie challenger. "Do you hear me? Go home," the ref covertly whispered in Kid's ear.

The Holy Cross High School gym in Queens was full, and it was the referee's job to relay messages between the wrestlers without the audience spotting it. The ref could tell by Kid Devine's face that he had no clue what "go home" meant. Kid wasn't smartened up to the business; no one had told him that the outcome was what it was.

"Hit him with your finish, and pin him," the ref whispered, as he lifted himself from the mat.

Babu walked gingerly across the ring toward his downed challenger. The giant's condition, injuries, and level of fitness were all causing him pain and severe mobility issues. He had to hold the top rope just to move on his feet. His body was shot, and had been for a long time, but he needed to protect the belt, like he was programmed to do. At that stage of his life, with all the political uncertainty out there, Babu thought that the best way to protect it was to give it to someone he could trust: someone without any history. So, one more match it was.

"Is the kid still with us?" Babu asked the ref.

"Kinda," the ref answered.

Babu hid his smile and advanced. He was giving Kid the ultimate honor—but he was going to make the rookie work for it. That's what all of the old-timers did to the new guys, beat the living fuck out of them. It was a rite of passage, a way to determine which of the new guys were cut out for the wrestling business. It would damage the business to let them all in on the inner workings if only one or two were ultimately going to make it.

Even with Kid's head ringing, he started to piece together what was happening: Babu was handing him the world heavyweight title. The young, handsome, masked wrestler had been in training for only a couple of months. He'd run ten miles a day and done five hundred Hindu squats. He'd gotten stretched by some old veteran until the veins in his eyeballs broke and his tongue swelled up. The young man kept coming back, though, because he was the man of the house. He had no more options but to come back to try and make some money for his family.

The next day, the training would be even worse.

"Get up," Babu shouted, as the referee pantomimed trying to stop the giant from doing more damage.

Kid Devine then remembered seeing a younger Babu in his prime. He remembered the giant before he limped and grimaced in pain. Kid remembered the champ before he started dying.

"Get up, I said," Babu roared at the rookie on the canvas. His visceral tone sparked a rush of adrenaline that lifted Kid Devine from the mat. The young challenger looked out at the small crowd and imagined himself as a champion outside of the gym. Both men locked up again as the tepid response from the crowd swelled.

"What's your finish?" Babu asked in the clinch.

Kid was taken aback that the giant was talking to him. "What?"

"Pick me up and slam me," Babu ordered.

Kid reached down and hooked Babu's huge frame. He could immediately feel Babu lift his own weight up for him. Kid planted his feet and put everything he had left into getting the iconic champion in the air. He could see the two enormous feet leave the canvas as he heaved Babu up for a slam. He imagined the giant going up ten feet into the air, only to be slammed down with such force that the ring would give in, too. In reality, he got Babu up to about his hip, then fell backward with the giant on top of him.

"Get out of there," the ref shouted to Kid, as he slow-counted the pin.

"Get him out of there," Babu shouted too.

Kid tried every which way to move the immense body on top of him.

"One," counted the ref.

Kid, with Babu's help, and maybe even a little shove from the ref, managed to turn his situation around. He found himself where he should have been: pinning the champion.

It used to be that when a new heavyweight champion got crowned, the world heard about it. Babu hoped that would be the way this time, too. But for now, his job was to make sure that the lineage of the title stayed true. In a business of smoke and mirrors, it was the wrestling guys themselves who cherished nothing more than lineage. Winning the title—any title—only meant something because of who had held it before you. The ten pounds of gold in and of itself wasn't worth that much, but all of the classic matches and former champions that came attached to that gold meant everything.

Kid walked backstage, where Babu was waiting for him. Backstage was a school locker room with toilets so small that Babu had never even bothered trying them.

"Put out your hand and thank me," Babu whispered.

Kid wasn't sure what was going on, but he trusted Babu with his life.

"Thank you," Kid said, as he shook Babu's gigantic hand and bowed before him. With the rest of the locker room watching, it was a little gesture that moved the needle of hatred a half millimeter in Kid's favor.

Kid was happy with himself. He removed his boot and carefully inspected his toe. He should have been changing in the hallway, as he was told to do.

"You were going a little rough on me out there," Kid said innocently to Babu from across the room.

Kid's half millimeter of good grace evaporated, and the needle moved to nuclear.

"Get out!" shouted Babu.

Half of the people in the locker room jumped with fright, as they had never heard the giant raise his voice before. He'd never had to. Babu got up, walked over to Kid, grabbed him by his hair, and dragged the new champion to the door.

"Get the fuck out," Babu said again, this time throwing him out himself.

From the floor of the hallway, Kid could see regret in Babu's eyes. Babu didn't want to do what he was doing, but he knew that the others in the dressing room would do a whole lot worse.

"Don't ever fucking question me again," Babu said as he slammed the door.

Kid had a lot to learn about the wrestling business. He just had no time to learn it.

New York.

Lenny sat on the back step of his father's house, looking at the small garden. It was perfect. Not a blade of grass out of place, not a weed in sight. Edgar was a man who lived on routine and order, and just having Lenny back was upsetting his father's small universe.

"I'm going into the city to see your boys. You wanna come?" Edgar asked from the back door.

Lenny shook his head. "Not now, you know."

"What is all of this?" Edgar asked, cutting through the bullshit. "I mean, what is everyone supposed to do now, exactly?"

Lenny stood and turned to his father.

"I mean, do I talk about you? Do I even say that you're out? What do I do here?" Edgar asked.

"No. Don't say anything. Not yet."

"Not yet?" Edgar said. "Why? Have you a fucking plan or something that I should know about?"

"I'm working on something," Lenny replied.

"Well whatever that plan is, can you hurry it the fuck up? I'm not comfortable with you in my house," Edgar said. "I'm sorry. I'm not."

"I should have told you I was coming. But I have no other choice. I have to be here—or they'll send me back," Lenny said.

"I saw you watching my front window earlier. Who were you looking for?" Edgar asked.

"No one," Lenny replied.

"You think I'm a fool, son? I don't know how you got out, or why. But I know it's not for nothing."

"I've got this," Lenny said.

Edgar walked to Lenny and let the storm door slap closed behind him. "You've got this?"

Lenny nodded. "Yeah."

"You know how much Bree had to move around when you were inside? You know how many jobs she's worked? The younger boy didn't handle it so well. He got himself into a lot of trouble without his father around. Even getting to see you inside would have been something. But no, you didn't want that either."

"I'm sorry," Lenny said. "I had my reasons."

"Your boys were raised by other men. Some of them did good, some of them didn't. But they have a consistent house here with me. No drama. Nothing out of the ordinary. And I adore those boys. You're not coming back in here and fucking that up for them. You hear me? You sort out whatever shit it is you've found yourself in this time. And you do it without hurting this family again."

Lenny understood. There was nothing he could say that would put his father at ease. He just had to act. He knew it wouldn't be long before all the players presented themselves and all the snakes came out of the bushes. They smelled weakness and isolation coming from Lenny—an irresistible combination for the other bosses.

Lenny knew his position was fragile, but it was in that fragility he saw opportunity. It was an opportunity to do what his mentor, Danno Garland did: outfox them all.

Even though he hadn't yet left, Ricky imagined coming home. He was on the verge of another twelve-hour flight, another six-week tour. His body hadn't even begun to heal up from the last one. If there was even a small chance that he could come back home for good, he owed it to himself and to Ginny to at least find out. It would certainly do no harm just to see if he could find some backers for the New York territory.

So now he was standing at a pay phone at JFK Airport, on hold. He hadn't spoken to her in years, but he knew she had money. At one time, Ricky had handed her five hundred grand himself. It was Danno's money, but she had earned it. Word was that she used that money in a smart way, and soon it doubled and doubled again, and maybe even again. Ricky knew that she was fucking around with him: twenty-seven minutes and she still hadn't come to the phone. Ricky knew why. But still he kept feeding the coin slot.

When she lost her husband, Danno had sent Ricky to inform her of her shitty terms. When Danno tried to buy her business, he had left Ricky to explain just how badly they were fucking her over. Now it was his turn to eat some shit. Ade Schiller didn't forget. Anything.

As he waited, Ricky noticed a small party at one of the check-in desks: it looked like a check-in lady was retiring. He was a little jealous. They'd brought her cake and a lot of people seemed to like her. Maybe she had saved a few dollars and would enjoy herself after she went home for good. She certainly didn't have to ask for money over the telephone, or fly to Japan to survive.

"Hello?" said Ade's voice on the line.

"Ade?"

"I haven't been called that in a while. Ricky, is it?"

Ricky knew she knew, but felt he had to play along. "Yes, it's Ricky here. Thanks for taking my call."

"What have you got for me, Ricky?" Ade asked.

"Well, how about New York?" Ricky replied. He could almost hear Ade smiling over the phone. She hadn't expected Ricky to get to the point so quickly, and she hadn't expected the point to be so out in the open. Ricky knew that someone like Ade had been following the whole story from the sidelines: it was just in her blood. He also knew that she felt she had unfinished business in wrestling.

He continued, "I hear you've been doing some things in the boxing world, and I was wondering if you wanted to bring some of that money—"

"Who told you that?" she asked.

"We all know the same people, Ade," Ricky said. "The last time we met, I handed you some money that I hope changed your life. I was hoping you might like to put it to work, invest it back where it came from."

Ade thought that she might want something more from the wrestling business this time. It had burned her badly in the past, but that was half the appeal of getting back in. She wanted to put a lot of things right. Exorcise a lot of past demons.

Ade wanted to get back on the field and settle some old scores.

"New York?" she asked, "What's that going to cost me?"

CHAPTER NINE

1968.
Nevada.

Before Danno was killed, before Babu was champion, before Lenny was even in the wrestling business, and before Merv died, there had been Proctor King and Ade Schiller.

Proctor was the boss of Florida, and Ade was the wife of the chairman at the time, Merv Schiller.

As they sat at a large round table in a Las Vegas conference room, Ade tried her best to not rip her husband's eyes out, and Proctor was doing his best not to blow Ade's husband's brains out. It was a typical National Wrestling Council party.

At the beginning of the night, Proctor and Ade were separated by many others, but as it went on and the band played faster and louder, they found themselves the only ones left at the table. He was ten glasses deep into a bottle of whiskey, and she was sipping on soda water and lime. He was trying to act more sober than he was, and she was trying not to watch her husband buy drinks for every pretty girl in the room—girls he had already paid to be there.

Proctor noticed that the tables around the room were still occupied by the other bosses. It seemed to him that the only one having fun was Merv. Ade made the same observation. She would have had to be blind not to see that he was fucking around with other women.

In the meeting before the party, Merv had just sewn up yet another year for himself with the champion. All the other bosses looked like they were doing their best to look happy for him, but secretly a lot of them wondered what a wrestling business without Merv in it would look like.

"He's a brave man," Proctor shouted across the table.

Ade heard him, but she pretended not to. "Sorry?" she said, as she moved to sit next to him.

Proctor took a split second from studying his glass to look up. "If it's any consolation, it's this business," he said. "It makes us all do stupid things."

Ade shook her head in disgust. "There's no business in the world that makes a man such a prick . . . such a gluttonous pig."

Both Ade and Proctor watched silently as Merv ran his old hand up and down a young thigh.

Proctor stopped swirling his drink and sat his glass down on the cheap paper tablecloth. "I've seen guys who weren't even booked to wrestle leave their house with their bag on their shoulder. For two days, they would pretend to be working different towns just so they could fuck, fight, drive, and drink what they wanted. The wives didn't know any different."

"They knew," Ade simply replied.

Proctor had never thought of it from the wife's point of view. He felt stupid now for even bringing it up.

"So, I'm supposed to be grateful that at least my husband is up front about it?" Ade asked.

"Of course not. I didn't . . ."

Ade turned straight to Proctor and asked, "Just what are you saying?"

Proctor tried to jumble together a sentence that was soothing or political or soft to hear, but nothing came quickly enough. He raised his glass and finished its contents.

"You're all the same," Ade said as she turned away from Proctor and back toward the dance floor. Her anger was for her husband, but it was leaking out everywhere else.

Proctor shook his head. "We're not all the same."

"You've never cheated?" Ade asked.

Proctor looked her squarely in her eye. "I've never cheated on my wife. I've cheated on just about everything, or everyone, else in this business, but not my lady."

Ade smiled at the honesty. She believed him, too—or at least she wanted to. She didn't even know why she cared.

"Never?" she asked.

"Nope."

"Isn't that what you all do?"

"Men? Or wrestling promoters?"

"Both."

"I don't know the answer to either of those. What I do know is that people will only treat you the way you let them."

Ade knew that what he was saying was absolutely true. She just needed to hear it for some reason. "Really?"

"Yes, ma'am."

Ade took a cigarette from her purse. Proctor lit a match for her.

"Everything is just too perfect in your home, I bet?" she asked.

"I never said that, either," Proctor replied, as he blew gently on the used match. "Things can be sour without being disrespectful."

Ade sipped her drink. She didn't even know why she was still sitting beside Proctor; there was just something in the way that he talked to her. Most of the other bosses were too scared to even look at her with Merv around.

"So, I'm letting him treat me this way?" Ade asked.

Proctor took his jacket from the back of his seat, and stood. "I don't know you well enough to answer that, Mrs. Schiller. For all I know, I open my mouth, and then your problems become my problems."

Proctor waved good-bye to some of the other tables. "Nice to meet you again," he said as he left Ade's table.

She watched him leave before something inside her made her follow him.

In the parking lot, she could see the beam of two headlights being switched on, followed by the roar of an engine. She moved faster and her heart beat in rhythm with her march. When she got closer, she could see Proctor alone in his car. "Wait," she said, too soft for anyone to hear. "Wait!" This time, she was louder and more confident.

Proctor pressed his brakes and reached for his gun as he tried to make out who was approaching him. The fact that it was Ade Schiller didn't make him comfortable enough to put his revolver away.

Ade tapped the window, and Proctor leaned over to roll it down a little. "Why are you going home so soon?" she asked.

"You really want to know?" he said.

"Yes," she replied.

The whiskey made Proctor a little less political than he might have otherwise been. "Because my job here is done. I congratulated your husband in public. Now I have to go home and try to look at myself in the mirror."

"Me too," she said.

Proctor smiled. "Well, Mrs. Schiller, I dare say that you're going to have to climb a lot more stairs, and walk on nicer rugs before you get to your mirror."

"Let's talk," she said. "We might both have the same problem."

Proctor pulled his car away from Ade slowly, until he knew that she was out of harm's way. He then floored it.

1969.
Portland, Oregon.

"I saw the giant son of a bitch, myself," Proctor said, as he wolfed down the house special. The Old Spaghetti Factory had only opened that day, but the food was perfect, and the hospitality was great, too. "Danno flew us all in to watch him wrestle. He's greener than goose shit, but that giant has money written all over him."

Ade Schiller sat opposite him in the booth and pushed her unwanted food around her plate. "And are you going to meet Danno here?"

"Yeah. It's out of the way, and somewhere that none of the other bosses would come in a million years."

Proctor looked intently at Ade. "You were right that Danno's the missing piece of our puzzle. I'm one hundred percent sure of that, now," he said.

Ade smiled and thanked him.

"Just remind me to never fuck with you," Proctor said.

"Why's that?"

Proctor wiped his mouth and leaned back in his seat. "'Cause you saw the angle long before I did. You picked Danno; you picked me."

Ade knew what he wanted to say, so she said it for him. "And I picked that my husband should die?"

Proctor nodded and began eating again. "There's no other way to do this, and that's another thing you were right on. We can't move in on all of Merv's things right away. Danno gets the belt first; everyone forgets and moves on with their lives. Then we come back and get everything we want without any heat on us."

Proctor rubbed his last piece of bread around his plate. He was energized from having met Ade, and from listening to her plan, as well as from the trust that went with it and the risks of seeing it through. Proctor King hadn't felt so alive in years. He knew that his mouth was kind of full, but he couldn't resist the urge to smile, regardless. "I struck a deal with Merv to vote against Danno today. My ballot pushes the numbers back to Merv. Danno's proposal is toast in there, and he doesn't even know it yet. What do you think Danno is going to say when I offer him the belt after he gets humiliated?"

Ade smiled at Proctor's underhandedness. She could have stayed there talking for hours, but Proctor always made sure that they were careful. Any conversations between them were under thirty minutes, and they were always face to face. That meant that getting to talk to him was a rare thing. He never wrote anything down, either: he had memorized phone numbers, addresses, and people's names.

"What about the guy?" she asked. "You know, the guy from Florida?" Ade wanted to know the answer, but she really just wanted Proctor to stay longer.

"Just like we discussed. He'll go to San Francisco and take care of Merv after I get Danno signed up." Proctor dabbed both sides of his mouth. "You better go back to the hotel. The NWC meeting is in a couple of hours." Proctor put out his hand and smiled. Ade wished it was more, but a handshake would have to do for now. She rose from her seat and walked away from the table, as if she and Proctor had never met.

He took a matchbook with the restaurant's name printed on it and slid from his seat. He noticed that one of the waitresses who was taking a break had sat right up against his booth. She politely nodded, and he returned her gesture. He was sure that she hadn't heard anything, but not sure enough.

The NWC meeting went just as Proctor had told Ade it would. Danno's proposal to make Babu the heavyweight champion was ruled out. Proctor was the "no" vote in the secret ballot that had killed Danno's chances. Voting against Danno did two things for Proctor: it made him more of an ally in Merv's eyes, and it made Danno seem vulnerable, and therefore more open to a plan B.

After the meeting, when no one could see, Proctor arranged a time to meet Danno in The Old Spaghetti Factory. That was where Ade and Proctor's plan would come into being; that was where she would get what she wanted, and Proctor would get what he wanted. All he needed to do was get the unsuspecting Danno Garland to hold the hot potato—the world title—until Proctor was ready to take it from him.

1969.
San Francisco.

There were midgets, beauty queens, tattooed faces, gold sunglasses, new white suits, hugely obese twins, a bald old woman, toothless mountain men, islanders, a one-legged man, and a widow. San Francisco welcomed difference admirably. But even it raised an eyebrow at this funeral.

The outer fence was lined with people who wanted to know what the spectacle was. Some younger voices chanted their favorite wrestler's name. When the time came, they all tried, with varying degrees of success, to bless themselves.

"John Merv O'Reilly, may you rest in peace."

Ade watched not the grave, and not the priest, but the other promoters. As her husband's body was being covered, the reins of the San Francisco territory were transferred to her. She'd had no choice: her husband was wealthy, but she was not. Such was his cloak-and-dagger mentality that she had no idea where he'd put his money.

Merv Schiller, like all the other wrestling bosses, wasn't the kind of man to use bank accounts; they would only let it be known just how much he was worth. The only paper trail that any of them left on the surface for scrutiny by the law was their ownership of their wrestling companies. Everything else was cash, secret handshakes, illegal, or buried somewhere safe.

In Ade's case, it was too safe.

So fucking smart, but so fucking stupid, she kept thinking over and over.

The crowd turned and walked away from the grave. A few people touched her arm as they passed, or offered their help if she ever needed anything. Ade nodded, like she thought a grieving wife should do. In reality, she wanted to tell them all to shove their fake condolences.

A few hours later, her backyard was filled with black clothes and somber people. Everyone spoke in hushed tones, and trays flew around like silver frisbees. Ade sat on her back step, smoking and running her years with Merv through her head. She had no idea why she'd stayed with him. She had consoled herself by saying that it was easier to get into that bed, turn on her side, and convince herself that tomorrow would be better. With Merv, though, tomorrow was never better.

Danno Garland walked down the steps past her and made his way to the quiet huddle. Ade liked Danno. Or at least she certainly didn't dislike him, and she was happy to think that his life had changed for the better. She watched Danno's lips as he spoke to his slight, out-of-place driver.

"Where did you put the car?" Danno mouthed.

Lenny answered, but Ade stayed focused on Danno.

"Good. I want to get out of here soon. Have you seen Proctor anywhere?"

Ade wondered the same thing: where was Proctor?

As if on cue, he emerged from the crowd on the other side of the garden and made his way over to Danno. Lenny was dismissed as he and Proctor discussed something that wasn't for everyone's ears. To Ade, Proctor seemed fine about what had just happened to Merv. She knew that she'd wished for Proctor to get rid of him, but maybe she would have liked to have seen a little bit of remorse. The more Proctor and Danno spoke, the more uneasy Ade felt about being left out of the loop. She finished her drink, rose uneasily from the steps, and navigated through all the fake heartbreak to get to where Danno and Proctor were talking.

Proctor nodded over Danno's shoulder, and let him know with one simple carny word that someone from outside the business was approaching: "Kayfabe."

As if she hadn't heard that word before; as if she hadn't been around the wrestling business long enough to know what it meant. She instantly knew that Proctor saw her as an outsider, and it cut her. That word had immediately let Ade know that she was always going to be excluded from the boys' club, but she did what she always did: she smiled.

Danno immediately changed the subject. "You can't say that Nixon doesn't have that something that Johnson didn't. He's clean, and on the—"

Ade locked onto Proctor, ignoring Danno. "You staying?"

Proctor warned Ade with his eyes. "No. Why would I do that?"

She waited for him to say something else, but he didn't. She shook her head with disgust. Maybe it was the drink, or maybe it was the day, but Ade Schiller couldn't smile any longer. "Fuck you," she said as she walked away.

"Is everything alright here?" Danno asked to break the tension.

"It must be the shock, or something," Proctor said as he watched her leave.

"Yeah, shock," Danno half-heartedly agreed.

Inside the house, Ade threw back another drink. Proctor entered and stood behind her. "Leave me alone." Ade poured another.

"I need to know if you're going to hold this together," Proctor said.

He gently closed the door. Ade didn't respond, so he turned her around. She tried to kiss him, and he backed off.

"What are you doing?" he asked.

She picked up an empty glass from her sink and fired it at him. Proctor lunged at Ade, wrapped her hands up, and held her tight, with her back against his chest. He looked out the window to make sure that everyone was still oblivious to what was happening.

"We didn't do this, do you hear me?" he said.

Ade tried to bite his face as it came over her shoulder. Proctor squeezed her tighter, until she was wrapped up completely. She stopped struggling and began to cry. "I don't know what I'm going to do," she said.

"I thought this was what you wanted," he said.

"Well, you certainly got what you wanted."

Proctor put his lips to her ear and hushed her. "I sent a guy to get to Merv, but Merv had already been dealt with by someone else. That's the truth. You got free from him, without having to—"

Ade didn't know what to believe. "I wanted us to be together."

"I'm sorry," he whispered.

"What did I get?" she shouted. "You're getting the belt next, that brings the money, and the power. All of these fucking men will be kissing your feet in due time. What did I get from all of this?"

Proctor covered her mouth with his hand. "You got exactly what you asked for," he said. "You got this house, the money, and more importantly, you got yourself a clean slate. You are a beautiful, single, filthy rich woman who can do whatever she likes."

Ade shook herself free, took a huge breath, and wiped her face. She could only smile with embarrassment as she fixed herself up. "Of all the bosses, I had to grow fond of the one who doesn't cheat."

Ade wanted Proctor to forget himself and be with her. She didn't care about sex; he could be with her all of his life without being unfaithful to his wife. That would suit her, too, because a woman like Ade wasn't looking for sex, or certainly not just sex.

He said, "You should take whatever you can and get out of this business, Ade. You're too soft for it." Proctor put out his hand for her to shake. She felt odd taking it, but shake Proctor's hand she did.

"We didn't do anything wrong here, and we still got what we wanted," he said as he turned and left.

Ade stood in her kitchen with mascara on her cheeks and a head full of regrets.

CHAPTER TEN

1984.
Three days after Lenny got out.
New York.

Lenny stood across the road from his father's house. He was wearing fresh new clothes, and the cut around his eye was starting to heal a little, too. He wasn't sure if Edgar was home, so he didn't want to go in. Lenny just wanted some room to himself. For the last few days his father had been following him around, talking nonstop. When Lenny was growing up his father hardly even looked at him. Now Lenny couldn't get his old man to shut up. He didn't know if it was because his father was getting older, or because he was nervous about having Lenny in the house.

The new neighborhood was nice, but it wasn't home. Home was somewhere else—somewhere Lenny hadn't really asked about yet. He imagined walking up to Bree's house and knocking on the door. He'd have a way out. Be done with the wrestling business. Maybe even have a little money. He remembered the house he and his wife started out in, with the stubborn back door and the front door that was slightly too small for their couch to fit through. They would talk at night about what kind of people they wanted to be, and about what kind of people they wanted to raise. Back then, Lenny dreamed of making it in the wrestling business, and Bree talked about going back to singing when their sons were a little older. Even though it was all said in earnest, Lenny couldn't shake the feeling that they were both lying to themselves.

He had so much to say he was sorry for—so much to try to make better. He just didn't feel like he deserved his wife's forgiveness, or that of his ex-wife, as she had come to be.

Out of the corner of his eye, Lenny saw his father appear from the side of the house. Lenny covertly walked away before Edgar could see him. He knew that his father liked his space, too. Both men were just sitting on top of each other while Lenny waited for something to happen with the business.

"Hey!" called a voice from behind him.

Lenny kept walking.

"Hey!" the voice called again.

Lenny turned slowly.

"Got a light?" a boy standing behind him asked.

Lenny shook his head and began to walk. The boy kept pace with him. "Why are you so interested in that house?"

Lenny didn't want to make a scene, so he cut down a side street between two buildings. When the boy turned the corner to follow him, he found Lenny waiting for him. The boy stopped, but didn't back off.

"What's your name?" Lenny tentatively asked.

"What's your name?" the boy replied.

He was about thirteen or fourteen, with a mullet, a sleeveless denim jacket, and a pack of cigarettes hanging out of his pocket. Lenny immediately knew the boy's eyes, his mouth. They were the same as his mother's.

"I'm Mike," Lenny replied.

"No, you're not," the boy replied.

It was a standoff; Lenny took a second to figure out how to proceed.

"How do you know?" Lenny asked.

"'Cause I've seen picture of you. You're Lenny."

"And you're James Henry."

"Jimmy."

"Jimmy?"

"Do you know what happens to kids with two first names around here?"

Lenny laughed; Jimmy didn't.

"Okay, Jimmy," Lenny said. "Nice to meet—"

Before Lenny could finish his sentence the boy walked over and hugged him, like it was the most natural thing to do in the world. It was a soft, innocent hug—one with no anger or resentment. Lenny was a little uncomfortable at first, but he soon settled into the embrace. The last time Lenny had seen his youngest son, he couldn't even talk yet.

"How have you been?" Lenny asked. He couldn't think of anything else. What do you say to your son after twelve years?

Jimmy let go of his father and looked him right in the eye. "I need you to help me." The sincerity in his request knocked Lenny off guard a little.

"Okay," Lenny said. "What can I do?"

"Can we get out of here?" Jimmy asked.

"Where's your mother?"

"Working. She's picking me up at Granddad's later."

Jimmy could see that Lenny wasn't totally sold on following him. "There's a place on the corner, down here."

"It's not a bar, is it, Jimmy?" Lenny asked, smiling.

"I don't drink," Jimmy replied very matter-of-factly.

"Okay," Lenny said. "This way?"

Lenny took a second to look around for Bree.

"This way," Jimmy said, as he gestured for Lenny to walk ahead.

Jimmy watched his father walk, and a small smile broke out onto his face. A couple of steps in, and Jimmy began to mimic Lenny's stride until their walk was identical.

"I'm big for my age, don't you think?" Jimmy asked. "Big shoulders."

"Ah—yeah. You're—yeah."

Jimmy could hardly hide the excitement on his face. "I could run this neighborhood in a few years."

"Yeah?" Lenny said.

"Yeah. Easy. What happened to your face?" Jimmy asked.

"I fell," Lenny said.

"You fell into someone's fist."

Lenny laughed. "Yeah, something like that."

Japan.

The Pacific Hotel was where all foreign wrestlers—or *gaijins* as they were known locally—were put up when they wrestled in the Tokyo Dome. Even though Ricky wasn't wrestling buildings that size anymore, Mr. Asai, the Japanese promoter, made sure Ricky still had a room there. Ricky and his Japanese boss had battled each other time and again when both men were younger and making names for themselves across Japan. There was a deep respect between them, which only grew as they got older. Even though Ricky was well past his prime, he knew that Mr. Asai always had a job for him, always had a room for him. Always had a paycheck for him.

Jet-lagged and thousands of miles away, all Ricky could wonder about was whether Ginny got his ice cream.

As he looked out his window, he couldn't help but reflect on his years in Japan since Danno died. When he first got there, his huge advantage was that he was white, American, and part of a tag team he formed with the huge Texan, Wild Ted Berry. Neither man liked each other much, but they had both been around long enough to know that coming to Japan and splitting the work in a tag team made sense. At least, it did until they got sick of splitting the money, too.

They started out as a big attraction to the Japanese audience. Every night, in every venue, Ricky and Ted would find themselves well paid and at the top of the card. After a couple of years, the money and the crowds shrank. Ted did some final tours in the late seventies, but headed back to America to wrestle off and on in New York again. Ricky couldn't return home safely, so he stayed—or maybe overstayed. That was when Ginny got real sick. Ricky had no choice but to go find the best care for him. Both men snuck back to New York. Ginny stayed; Ricky left again to make some money to pay for Ginny's care. He found himself traveling Japan for small to mid-sized companies, wrestling for one hundred and eighty dollars a day. To supplement his money, he sold pictures and autographs from his gimmick table at the back of the halls for any fan that wanted them. He dreamed every day about going back home for good, but all he knew how to do was wrestle and book wrestling matches. After what had happened in New York, Ricky didn't even know if he could keep getting back into the US alive, much less get employed there.

He stayed in Japan because every penny he made was saved for Ginny. The only treat he allowed himself was a trip at the end of every tour to a small, nondescript steakhouse in Gotanda, Tokyo. Even then, he left the phone number of the restaurant with the receptionist in his hotel, in case something happened with Ginny.

Ricky knew that he couldn't do all that much anymore, with his body as broken down as it was, so he had turned to other means to attract an audience and keep himself employed and on the booking sheet. If he couldn't entice the crowds with speed or skill, there was a growing market for blood in Japan; they loved their technical classics and bloody brawls equally. Technical exhibitions were many years removed from Ricky's capabilities, so he leaned on the bloody brawls to keep the crowds interested in him. His matches weren't about headlocks, body slams, or suplexes, but about barbed wire, blood, and sharp objects. His old body couldn't go sixty minutes anymore, but it could bleed with the best of them, and that's what it did to pay the bills: bleed.

New York.

Ginny spent however long it took for hot water to go cold looking at his plastic razor. He had no idea what it was for, so he kept looking at it until it came to him. He knew it was close to 6:00 p.m., and 6:00 p.m. was ice cream time. There was shaving cream on his face for a reason, but he couldn't piece it together, so he used the now-cold water to wash it off and he threw the razor in the bin. Somewhere in the middle of the night, he'd remember what it was for, and he would hide it again.

They didn't like him having razors in his room.

He laid his shirt on his bed and his shoes on the floor. His neck and ears still had a little shaving cream on them. He decided to go with a tie. He dragged his favorite soft chair into the middle of the room and had the TV ready to go on his channel. Sometimes he'd forget to turn on the TV, and sometimes he'd forget to get fully dressed, but he never forgot that 6:00 p.m. was ice cream time.

He just didn't know that it was coming from Ricky.

Shirt on, tie on, pants on—his shoes were forgotten this time. Ginny waited, facing the door. He watched the seconds tick by on the clock. It wasn't a minute past, or a minute before; the ice cream always came at six. The second hand made its way around and excitement made Ginny want to pee, but he dared not move. The mixture was the same every Wednesday, but it still seemed like Christmas to him. It reminded Ginny of being a boy or something, and it made him happy. It made the stressful day of remembering and forgetting a little less terrible.

Tick, tick. Tap, tap. It was six o'clock, and there was a tap on the window. Ginny was facing the wrong way due to months of getting his delivery through his door.

Tap, tap. Ginny tried to identify where the sound was coming from, and then it hit him.

Ginny stood and walked to where the man was standing outside his window. He put his two fingers underneath the slim frame and pulled up. There it was: Pagladoni's twelve scoops, four bananas, three candy toppings, whipped cream, and a long spoon. He could hardly control himself as he took it. He never looked around to see who had left it, and he never bothered closing his window. It was ice cream time, and nothing else mattered.

"See you next week, Ginny," the ice cream guy said as he walked away.

Ginny's mouth was too full to reply, but he tried.

Japan.

Ricky usually rode the bullet train. He did so at his own risk. He was a heel bad guy in Japan, and the Japanese took their wrestling very seriously. Even though he covered up and wore a hat, he stood out pretty easily among the Japanese commuters. The promotion hired a bus for the heels and a separate bus for the babyfaces to get them to the buildings—but Ricky preferred to keep to himself. He was usually one of the only *gaijins* onboard those buses, so he always felt a little like an outsider. He knew that it was his own fault for not learning the language, but when Ricky arrived in Japan, he had never imagined that he'd still be there ten years later.

At first Mr. Asai knew that Ricky might be a little isolated, so they insisted that Ricky take their English-speaking referee, Masa Kido, as his travel partner. Masa was a veteran who had been designated to look after the foreigners, to make sure that they made their bookings on time. Now, Masa was one of Ricky's most trusted friends on the road. The foreign wrestler and the local referee had spent hundreds of hours around each other. Ricky had met Masa's family and slept at their house anytime Ricky was working a match close by. In Japan, at this point in his career, Ricky turned nothing down—no matter how violent or dangerous the match. He knew that Mr. Asai was running out of ways to hide his broken-down body, so he appreciated every single booking he got.

In the locker room, Ricky watched as a "young boy" took the boots off a Japanese veteran who had just finished his match. Sometimes these young boys were indeed just that, but more universally, they were rookies looking to get into the business. They slept on floors, carried bags, and washed the ring gear of the established wrestlers.

In the showers, a forty-year-old young boy sumo wrestler—who wanted into the business—washed the feet of the Japanese champion. It made Ricky uncomfortable to see, but to everyone else in the locker room, it was a sign of respect and tradition.

"You ready?" Masa asked Ricky from the door of the locker room. Ricky nodded. It was show time.

The hall was full with a good main event on top. Ricky walked through the curtain, and his presence garnered an audible "ahh" from the crowd. He was a New Yorker, but his gimmick in Japan was that of a cowboy. He made his way to the ring with black ropes and white turnbuckles as the crowd patted him on the back and showered him in paper confetti. Ricky tried to heel it up a little by threatening to punch the fans who leaned out to touch him. They still applauded him; they liked Ricky, and they knew that he was a "one hundred percent" kind of wrestler. They wanted blood, they wanted effort, and they wanted the right man to win. Ricky had mastered all three of those categories in Japan.

The building was industrial looking, with different levels separated by exposed concrete. The ring sat on a perfectly shiny wooden floor, and the audience around the ring was cordoned off to give the wrestlers a pathway around it to work. Inside the ropes stood Masa, the ref, in his lime green trousers and his lemon yellow shirt. Beside him stood some pretty local girls, waiting to hand their bouquet of flowers over to the combatants. Of course, Ricky, in character, wouldn't take his, and this made the crowd finally boo him.

Ricky's opponent, Genji Shin, made his entrance, and the crowd became noticeably more excited. Genji had once been the face of the company, but a betting scandal had rocked him out of the top spot. He was still a good worker, but he was the sleaziest man in the company—not an easy feat. Genji was always on the end of his nerves, with his nails bitten down to nubs and his greasy hair barely clinging to his head. He took delight in ripping the fans off at the bar, his merchandise stand, or wherever he could. He was also not shy about taking advantage of the female fans in every town he worked in. He was a classic example of a holier-than-thou persona in public, but a scumbag in private.

Ricky wasn't the only man in the match who was past his prime and needed money. The two men needed it for diametrically different purposes, but in wrestling, that didn't matter. The ring announcer began to introduce both Ricky and Genji Shin, but Genji smashed Ricky in the back of the head before his name could be read out. Ricky could tell by the snugness of Genji's punch that there was going to be very little acting involved in their match. Genji was supposed to be the babyface good guy in the match, so his attack from behind made no sense to Ricky. He stomped down on Ricky's head, and all he could hear was the piercing high-pitched squeal of an eardrum blowing. Ricky quickly got out of there and took a knee while he tried to figure out what was going on.

"Are we working, here?" Ricky asked Masa.

"Be careful of this guy," Masa whispered.

Ricky knew that his opponent was going to use Ricky in the territory to make himself look like a killer. Genji wanted people and the promoter talking about him. And he was going to take liberties with the broken-down foreigner to do it. Especially now that there was a rumor that Ricky was going back to New York for good. If you wanted to make yourself look good at Ricky Plick's expense, now was the time.

Ricky rose as fast as he could, but the blow to the ear made it harder for him to stand straight. Genji rushed Ricky backward into the turnbuckle and began to "potato" the shit out of him with punches. Every strike, usually measured and careful, bounced directly off of Ricky's skull for real. Ricky fish-hooked his overzealous opponent and spun him into the corner. He gave his receipt in strong right hands: one, two, three hard shots just above Genji's eyebrow. Ricky could see the scar tissue there, and he went to work on it. Genji raked Ricky's eyes, giving Ricky a hard time both hearing and seeing what was coming for him. After a stiff elbow to the jaw, Ricky was down in the corner.

Genji slid into the corner with Ricky. He wormed his way in and brought his face close to Ricky's. Ricky could see that the Japanese wrestler was trying to bite him in the clinch. There wasn't much room to move, as Ricky was trapped between the turnbuckles in the corner and a crazed-looking wrestler in front of him. Ricky grabbed Genji's head and slowed everything down. He felt a measure of control come back to the match—that was until Ricky felt the sting of a blade above his eye, and then the resulting warmth of his own fresh blood running down his face and neck. Fuck that. Genji had cut Ricky, without Ricky's permission. This was a practice that old-timers used to practice with greenhorns who didn't know how to blade properly. But Ricky Plick was no greenhorn.

Ricky bullied his way back to his feet and stood away from Genji. It was totally disrespectful to "get color"—to blade a veteran—and it was a killable offense to draw blood from them if they didn't know it was coming.

"What the fuck are you doing?" Ricky shouted to his smiling opponent.

"That's a bad cut," Masa said as he flew by.

"You fucking think?" Ricky replied as he dabbed the blood running down his face. Ricky advanced to Genji and stiffed him with a forearm across the face. He then head-butted Genji for real across the bridge of the nose, and the local wrestler stumbled back into the ropes. Ricky could see blood. And not just his own. He then grabbed Genji by the throat and fired him as hard as could between the ropes, out to the shiny wood floor. Ricky followed. He wiped away his own flowing blood so he could see where to grab a chair. Genji watched as Ricky approached with his new weapon, so Genji "fed" Ricky his back to hit. He bent over, and made his back as long and straight as possible for Ricky to aim for. Ricky wasn't having any of Genji's sudden wish to work together; he swung as hard as he could toward the back of Genji's head. The chair bounced off the back of his skull, and blood immediately squirted out into the audience from the resulting gash. Genji went down hard. Ricky kicked his opponent's head and stomped on his face as Genji lay unconscious on the ground.

Masa slipped in between the two men and tried to push Ricky off. "Enough," Masa shouted. "He's out. He's out!"

Ricky spat on Genji as he lay on the floor with a pool of blood growing beside his skull. The audience booed and heckled Ricky. He was in no mood for working. He was pissed off and there was no way he could act any other way.

As he stood there and looked around, Ricky couldn't come up with a solid reason to stay in Japan anymore. He was tired and beat up, and he missed Ginny more than anything else in the world. With New York showing seeds of growth back home, Ricky didn't feel the choking pressure to stay here.

"I'm going home," Ricky said to himself. He walked, in peace, in the middle of a chaotic building.

New York.

Jimmy was on a mission to impress his old man. He was known around the neighborhood, and he wanted Lenny to know he was known. Jimmy saluted, greeted, and nodded coolly to anyone in sight as he and his father walked by.

"I'm well known around here," Jimmy said.

"Yeah?"

"Yeah."

"That's good," Lenny said.

"Yeah," Jimmy replied.

"Yeah."

Jimmy continued to lead the way.

"So, where are we going?" Lenny asked.

"Just another block." Jimmy crossed the road between traffic. Waiting for cars to stop was for little babies, and Jimmy Long was no baby.

Lenny could finally see where his boy was bringing him. "I . . . uh . . . we should go somewhere else."

"What, you don't like pie?" Jimmy asked, with a look of utter confusion on his face. "Who doesn't like pie?"

Then Jimmy realized that Lenny had no money.

"It's my treat," the boy said, as he continued walking.

Lenny followed. "Your treat?"

"Yeah, I got my pocket money."

Lenny noticed that the guy behind the counter in Pizza Pizza didn't smile at Jimmy, even though Jimmy was polite and smiled back. The guy didn't look like he wanted to hand over the slices of pizza, but Jimmy pointed to Lenny, and the guy behind the counter reluctantly slid the slices to the boy.

"Here you go, Pop," Jimmy said, as he slid the cheese supreme over to Lenny.

"He saying something to you?" Lenny asked.

"He just wanted to make sure I wasn't in here on my own."

Jimmy didn't seem to notice, or care, about the guy who served him, so Lenny left it alone.

"Thank you," Lenny said.

Even though it felt all-around weird to meet his son for the first time in twelve years, and not have the money to treat him, Lenny couldn't help but feel a joy in actually getting a chance to study his boy's face.

"You shouldn't eat it all at once—it'll burn your mouth," Jimmy said.

Lenny wasn't sure if Jimmy was advising Lenny, or if he was reminding himself that it would burn him.

"Can we keep this to ourselves?" Lenny asked.

"Yes," Jimmy replied, very matter-of-factly. "I won't say anything to Mom."

Lenny felt the need to explain. "It's just that I haven't seen your mother in—"

"Twelve years." Jimmy looked up from his slice for the first time. His eyes were identical to Bree's. "You haven't been home in twelve years."

Lenny nodded. "What I'm trying to say," he continued, "is that I want to be different when I see her."

"You want your face to be better?" Jimmy asked.

Lenny took a bite. So did Jimmy.

"Yeah, I want to look a little better. But I want to show your mom that I'm . . . not the same. It's hard to explain. Like I have prospects, you know. Like I can look after you guys. Like I'm a fucking man."

Jimmy took a second to let Lenny's words settle in. "I understand," he said as he took another bite.

"How—how is she?" Lenny asked.

"Good."

"Good?"

"Yeah."

"How good?"

"What?"

Lenny paused. "Is she happy?"

"She cries sometimes. I don't know whether that's because she misses you or not."

"She cries?" Lenny asked.

"Not as much now."

Lenny's heart was broken. "She cries?"

Jimmy nodded. "How's your pie?"

"It's weird," Lenny said.

Jimmy laughed a little. "Weird?"

"It's been a long time since I had pizza like this. It doesn't taste real anymore."

Jimmy leaned in, like he was about to discuss serious business. "How would you break into this joint?"

Lenny wasn't sure if Jimmy was serious or not. "What?"

Jimmy kept eating, and his eyes stayed on the table. "Just say that we're casing the joint. How would you get in?"

"Why would you ask that?" Lenny said.

"'Cause you're a con," the boy said simply.

Lenny wanted to answer. He wanted Jimmy to think he was cool, even if it did mean talking, in theory, about breaking the law. "It can't be done," Lenny said. "There are windows all along the front of the building, and foot traffic outside. I'd say it would be impossible to get in and out without being seen. Why?"

Jimmy said, "Just trying to learn the business."

Lenny laughed. "Learn what business?"

"For when I grow up." Jimmy took another gigantic bite. He had a little snot beginning to form in his left nostril.

Lenny noticed the guy behind the counter staring at them again.

"What is this guy's problem?" Lenny asked.

Jimmy saw where his father was looking. "Can I tell you something?" he said with a full mouth.

"Yeah," Lenny said.

Jimmy took a couple of chews and wiped his mouth. "I have no money."

Lenny spat his half-chewed mouthful onto his plate. "What?"

Jimmy smiled. "I don't have a single cent. I don't even get my pocket money until tomorrow."

"You got no money?"

"Nope. I lied," Jimmy said. "I told the guy you were going to pay."

"What? Why did you lie?"

"I don't know why I do it. But I lie all the time," Jimmy said. He calmly picked up his slice to have another bite but Lenny slapped it out of his hand.

"What?" Jimmy asked.

Lenny leaned in and whispered, "You can't eat it if we can't pay for it."

"The guy that owns this place is an asshole." Jimmy took what was left of his slice and slipped it into his pocket. Lenny couldn't believe his eyes.

"We can't do that," Lenny said.

"Well, I don't know about you, but I have to run," Jimmy said.

"Hang on, this is crazy," Lenny said.

Jimmy looked his father dead in the eye. "I can't get in any more trouble with the cops, or they said I'd end up in a home."

Each sentence was making Lenny more exasperated. "What?" Lenny saw the guy behind the counter look out at them again from the kitchen. He had a phone to his ear.

"Go," Jimmy said. He nodded his head toward the door as the guy behind the counter walked into the back.

Lenny didn't have much of a choice—he didn't have any money of his own and he knew if the cops came he was straight back inside. He slowly moved to the edge of his seat.

"You doing it?" Jimmy excitedly asked.

Lenny nodded. "Go."

Father and son bolted out the door and scrambled up the road as fast as they could.

"Hey, hey!" shouted the guy behind the counter.

Lenny never ran so fast in his life. In the middle of the panic, he could see the look of pure exhilaration on his son's face.

The railroad tracks looked like a rusty steel mess. The surrounding banks were overgrown, and the eyes of a few homeless people watched Jimmy and his father walking home. The boy was eating the last bites of his pizza and Lenny feeling the sun on his face and the stones under his feet. Both of them felt content.

"Mom used to work at that pizza place. Did you see the guy working there?" Jimmy said. "He doesn't like me."

"Why not?" Lenny asked.

"Because he stiffed Mom on her paychecks. He always said that she didn't work enough hours, or that he'd pay her the next time. That's why we moved. She got a job somewhere else." Jimmy stopped walking. "That's why it's not stealing. That asshole owes Mom a ton of cash. It's our money. She worked for it."

Lenny could see how passionate his son was about protecting his mother. "I understand."

Lenny's words made Jimmy chill a little. "You looking to make some money?" Jimmy said.

Lenny smiled. "Why?"

"'Cause I've got a thing going here."

"And what would that be?"

"It's a little grift," Jimmy answered matter-of-factly.

"A grift, eh?"

"Me and a friend of mine do it together. I jump in the river and pretend I'm drowning. Nine times out of ten, whoever tries to help me takes their keys and their wallets out of their pockets. So my friend's job is to rob the hero. Simple."

Lenny had no idea what to say. He wanted to scold the boy, teach him something. But the reality was, Lenny was still a stranger to his son.

Jimmy continued. "So, a couple of days ago, my partner tried to take an unfair split. I took what was mine. Then his brother found me, pushed me around, and kicked me in the ribcage."

Lenny stopped and turned Jimmy toward him. "Does your mother know about any of this?"

Jimmy shook his head. "I wasn't joking around about the cops putting me in a home."

"What home?" Lenny asked.

"Juvie." Jimmy smiled at his father. "Like you, Pop. I'm like you."

Lenny stooped to Jimmy's eye level. "Don't ever be like that."

Jimmy had a huge grin on his face. "You're not the only one who deals with the law."

"Jimmy, I—I didn't deal with anything. I was—"

Jimmy put out his hand for his father to shake. "We're buddies, aren't we?"

Lenny wondered just how wild Jimmy was. He remembered him as a little pudgy baby who wouldn't do much for himself. "Yeah, we're buddies," Lenny said as he shook his son's hand.

"Did you see Luke yet?" Jimmy asked.

"Not yet," Lenny replied.

"He took up the family business, too. The other family business," Jimmy said.

Before Lenny could inquire further, Jimmy was straight back in. "Will you take me home? Mom would love to see you."

"Not yet."

Jimmy and Lenny walked the railway home.

"Tomorrow?" Jimmy asked.

"No."

"The next day?"

"Is that money I hear rattling in your pocket?" Lenny asked.

"No," Jimmy lied.

Japan.

In all of Ricky's time in Japan, he could never get used to one thing: the food. After a big match, he liked to make his way down to the little steakhouse close to his hotel. It was a treat to himself because steak wasn't as cheap or plentiful as it was back home. Ricky liked to bring the owner a few gifts every time he went down there. He had never gotten to know the owner's name, but Ricky was always treated right. In return, the owner had given Ricky a satin red jacket with the steakhouse's name on the front and the silhouette of a bull's head above it. Ricky wore the jacket at shows, and the steakhouse would look after him when he came in.

It was a small place with raw wooden stools facing a long, simple counter. There were a few tables with the same simple wood. Ricky was sore and slow. He didn't know what had happened in his match, but he knew that he couldn't wait to get the fuck home. While he devoured his steak, Ricky figured out a few different ways to bring New York back to the top. He needed to convince Ade to buy the contract from Lenny. She would have the resources and contacts to light the territory up again. Maybe even take the black mark off the place. In the meantime, he'd build stars, make his way back into the NWC's good books, and start to trade wrestlers again. The more he thought about it, the more excited he became. He could honestly, finally go home, and be closer to Ginny. He could work behind the scenes and stop bleeding for money.

"You got room for one more?"

Ricky turned to see his old tag-team partner, Wild Ted Berry, standing behind him with a huge grin on his face. He too was wearing a satin steakhouse jacket.

"What the fuck?" Ricky said.

"They paid me main event money to come over for another tour," Ted said, as he sat down. His beard and teeth were stained with chewing tobacco, and his eyes were puffy from the long haul over.

"I thought you were taking care of New York?" Ricky said.

Ted leaned in. "Where do I even start with that fucking place? You know what's happening there, right?"

Ricky shook his head, refusing to admit he knew anything about the territory. "Been a long time since I was in the loop."

"Lucky you," Ted said, looking at Ricky's steak. "Hey, can I get one of these?" he asked a passing woman. He wasn't even sure she worked there, or understood him.

Ricky was happy to see his old tag-team partner. It had been a long time since both men were together—much less in Japan.

"New York misses you," Ted said. "Ever since Danno—you know. And then you left. Joe Lapine comes sweeping in through the back door. They think I don't know what's happening. But I knew. Joe putting just enough money into it to keep the place alive. Making sure we kept TV."

"Really?" Ricky simply took a drink, leaving room for Ted to continue.

"Looks like Joe wasn't happy to hear that you were coming back," Ted said.

"Coming back?" Ricky replied. "Who said—"

Ted smiled. His teeth were freshly painted in tobacco juice. "You don't have to try to work me, Ricky. I've been around a long time. I know how all this plays out."

Ricky slowly cut another piece of his steak. "I don't have nothing in concrete."

Ted opened his little carry bottle and spat into it. "Joe blackballed me. Said I should have known what was going on. So I had to come back here."

Ted was too old to start again; he knew it, and Ricky knew it. "Is there any way that I can convince you not to go back to New York?" Ted asked.

Ricky didn't take any pleasure whatsoever in shaking his head. "I have to go home."

"I thought as much." Ted signaled to the counter for a drink. "Will you have one too?" Ted asked. "A welcome drink for me, and one for the road for you."

"Of course," Ricky said.

In the space of a day in the wrestling business, Ricky was heading home, and Ted was banished back to Japan.

"I will bring you home if I can," Ricky said. "I've got something going over there. Maybe it comes off and we get to go back home."

"I appreciate that," Ted said, as he held his drink up.

Ricky picked up his drink and did the same. He could see that Ted didn't really believe it. Ricky didn't really believe it either. Doing business with Ade was a long, long shot.

"Are you sure there's no way I can talk you out of going home?" Ted asked again, this time with the clear sound of desperation in his voice.

"I'm sorry," Ricky said.

He was tapped on the shoulder, and through a series of hand signals, nods, and smiles, Ricky figured out that there was a call for him. In all his years of leaving the steakhouse's number at his hotel, it had never been used.

His blood ran cold.

"Everything alright?" Ted asked.

Ricky slowly stood and walked to the waiting receiver. It must have been Ginny. Something had happened. His hand began to tremble a little as he put the phone to his ear.

"Hello?" Ricky said.

"Leave now, Ricky," said a familiar-sounding voice. "Just walk out of there."

Ricky looked around the steakhouse. Everything seemed normal. Everyone was minding their own business. Could it be a rib by some of the other wrestlers?

"Who is this?" Ricky asked, trying to recognize the voice.

The caller on the other side hung up. Ricky put his phone down too. It sounded like Masa, who was great for letting Ricky know what was really going on, but Ricky wasn't one hundred percent sure that it was him.

"Everything okay?" Ted asked, as he signaled for another round of drinks.

Ricky didn't know what to make of what had just happened, but Japan felt off this time. He probably never should have come back, but what choice did he have? "Back in a sec," Ricky said, as he walked toward the restroom.

The steakhouse had a tiny, pale green toilet at the end of a small corridor. Ricky headed straight to the side exit off that corridor. Ricky was now pretty sure that it was Masa who had called him, and Masa was a friend who didn't fuck around.

Ricky walked to the exit and tried to figure out how to open it without making too much noise. He heard someone approach him quickly from behind. Before he could turn, he felt the sharp, cold blade of a knife stab his lower back repeatedly. Ricky lashed back with everything he had and cracked his attacker in the face with his elbow. He could feel the cold sensation of shock run up his spine; he tried instinctively to reach back to get a sense of how bad it was. Blood was spilling on the floor. He turned to his attacker, but the face was unknown to Ricky. He was Asian—nobody Ricky knew in wrestling. It was never the person you could see that you needed to worry about.

As his attacker began to get up, Ricky kicked him in the face as hard as he could. Ricky stumbled over the man and slipped on his blood as he cracked the exit door open. He fell outside to the ground. Across the narrow road was a gas station. Ricky knew he didn't have much time, so he tried to drag himself to where passersby might see him. Where someone could help. He threw his right arm out in front and hauled his faltering body a few inches at a time. He didn't know if anyone was behind him, waiting to strike again. He didn't know who was in the restaurant and if they were there for him too. He didn't know if Ted was involved. He just knew he needed to get as much space between him and the steakhouse as he could.

He also knew he wasn't going to make it to the gas station.

Ricky rolled over; he wanted to see the sky above him rather than the dirty street under him. He felt his eyes getting heavier, and the sounds around him getting softer. His own blood began to choke him. He had never experienced a stranger feeling than knowing it was his time; knowing that there was no one around to tell he was leaving. No one to put him at ease. He was so far from the wall he'd held onto when he tried out his first bike; so far from his first match; his first love.

He felt a calmness come over him.

Ricky stopped trying to move, and he stopped panicking. He just waited until his eyes closed and he could open them no more.

CHAPTER ELEVEN

1970.
San Francisco.
It started as a little thing: a few floorboards here, a few floorboards there. Merv was old school, which meant no banks, no checkbook, and no accountant. He'd made millions between the wrestling business and other deals. But Ade couldn't find a single fucking cent—not yet.

She was sure that he'd put it all underneath the floorboards in the attic, so she started removing one board at a time. She struggled to lift the first one, and every single one after that, until she had the whole space taken up. She found nothing but signs of mice. After a couple of months of living in the big mansion on her own, Ade sat doing absolutely nothing. She looked at her house, big and cold, and wondered why she was still there. Merv was gone, but she felt that he was watching her, and judging her. He was still everywhere: in every picture, every seat, and every lamp. Merv's awful taste in design, decor, and art caused Ade to panic.

Fuck it.

She entered her dusty gardening shed and emerged with a wheelbarrow. Her garden was full of tiny test sites; mini graves where she had been digging for Merv's money. She just had another nine acres to go before she covered the whole garden. In the kitchen, her cupboards had been totally emptied, and her hallways had floorboards missing. She was randomly testing parts of her house, too. One night long ago she had tried to coax the money's whereabouts from a drunken Merv, but all he said was he'd "tell her some night in April." Whatever the fuck that meant. She wasn't even sure if that's what he'd said. So with Merv dead, and nothing to go on, she had no other choice but to look for it herself. April was the fourth month, so she tried every fourth room, every fourth step, every fourth floorboard, and every fourth foot outside. There were millions of dollars hiding somewhere. Ade knew it.

Merv used to come home from events with his bag heavy with cash. Ade would go to bed and by the next morning the bag was always empty and waiting by his car keys, ready to be filled again.

She tried to follow Merv once, but she had only gotten halfway down the stairs when he caught her. "You ever snoop around on me again, and I'll break your jaw," he told her.

She believed him, too.

Floor after floor, she tossed Merv's every belonging down the stairs. Clothes, old title belts, model boats, watches, bedsheets, and records all went tumbling down to the waiting wheelbarrow. Ade didn't know what she was going to do with all Merv's crap, but she did know that she had to get rid of every trace of him. Wheelbarrow after wheelbarrow, she dumped his stuff onto her nighttime lawn. She was angry, guilty, sweaty, and without a plan. She knew that just dumping it outside meant she would only have to deal with it the next morning, so she filled the garage with it. She lived in the house, and what was left of Merv lived in the garage.

Eventually the car company came and took the car back. Then they came again, and took the second car. All of the bills stayed in their envelopes by the door. Ade hid from anyone who knocked. She didn't know who any of the people at her door were, and she didn't care to check. At first she'd hear her doorbell and hide under her bed, but the more she got used to it, the more she hid in plain sight. She didn't panic, because she knew that there was money. She had seen it for decades. Their house was big, with a lot of under-floor options and crawl spaces in the walls. She thought it might take her a while, but Ade had time. At least, she felt like she had time, until the wrestling company Merv left behind began to lose the crowds. Ade was the de facto new boss, but she wasn't a wrestling person, and she didn't understand how to draw people into her territory over a sustained period of time.

With money drying up, her hunt for Merv's hidden treasures took on a new importance.

Her failing wrestling business made the other male bosses very happy; nothing brought them more glee than watching a woman slowly drown in their industry. None of them wanted her at their closed-door meetings, except maybe for Proctor King. It was hard to tell, though; he didn't let out much, and she didn't care to ask. All Ade could see was that Proctor and Danno were playing the game beautifully, and when the time came for Proctor to have the title belt, he would be one rich man—just like he and Ade had planned.

Ade was supposed to be rich right alongside him. Instead, she was taking the house apart.

"Ma'am," said the foreman, as he walked toward Ade.

"Yes?" Ade replied.

The foreman looked unsure. "This is what you want?" he asked.

"Yes."

The foreman unfurled the plans on her table. "Can you please have another look to—?"

Ade leaned into his view. "If I have to say 'yes' once more, I will find myself another contractor."

The foreman nodded and left the room. "Start her up, boys," he shouted up the stairs to his crew.

On his word, the thump of sledgehammers and the deafening squeal of electric saws began.

1971.
San Francisco.

Ade Schiller—Adrienne Hulse before she married Merv—had grown up on the road. Her father was a pro wrestler, her mother was a pro wrestler, and she was their only child. Although the road took them everywhere, New York was a place that animated her child's mind, and it did so even more when she was a teenager. It was the lights and the glamour: the big city.

It was also the place where her father died in the ring.

Only a couple of times in history had a wrestler actually died within the ropes. Ade's old man had died of a heart attack, which had left him cold about sixteen minutes into a match in New York. Ade wished it had been in Madison Square Garden. She wanted her father to have at least gone out in a full house with people chanting his name. Unfortunately, he died in the back room of a bar. He never saw the big time, never made the big money, and never worked for any of the big companies.

Ade always dreamed of putting their family name right, for him and for herself. She imagined her father taking his last breath alone, with no one caring, no one noticing, because he wasn't top of the card. He wasn't rich, powerful, or a star.

Lance Root—now there was a star. Back when Ade was a younger woman, he was the guy that everyone used to pay to see get beat. She remembered his thick lips, and the palms of his hands, which were always so much whiter than the rest of his body. He grunted, mostly, and looked annoyed to be alive. Ade had figured that he might have been just the man to revive her ailing territory. Back in the day, no one drew more money as a bad guy than Lance. Mr. Root, smelling desperation, called the terms of his deal: the ludicrous, non-sustainable terms, which Ade agreed to.

She'd figured that Merv's money hidden in the house was about to pay out, and with Lance Root on her roster, she was sure to be covered in the wrestling business too. What she didn't know was that Lance didn't really feel like working all that hard. He had come to San Francisco to retire, more or less. He just never told Ade that before they both signed a multi-year deal. He was slow, old, fat, and nothing like the heat magnet that he'd been back in the day. No one, least of all Lance, cared if he wrestled or not.

Ade had just paid out more on a guaranteed contract than she would have for the world heavyweight champion, and all she'd gotten was a useless sack of meat.

1972.
San Francisco.

The house was a skeleton, with only tightly woven industrial plastic sheeting holding it together. The grounds were completely overturned, and all of the bricks that had been removed lay perfectly stacked beside the house. It was a neat destruction, but it was destruction, nonetheless.

Ade never found a single cent.

It became like a sickness to her. When she could afford a crew, they picked through the house. When she couldn't afford them any longer, she gently deconstructed the house herself, piece by piece. She was so infatuated with finding the money, she neglected the wrestling company she was now in charge of. It was dying without her attention, and costing her money to run shows, because her audience was shrinking week by week. Ade was quickly nearing financial ruin.

When the roof came off her house, she had slept in the garage for fear that someone would come along in the middle of the night and simply stumble onto the jackpot that was right under her nose, somewhere. Sleeping there just made her sick. Even when her doctor strongly advised her against it, she came back to the house and worked through the night, again and again. She was desperate for the money, but more than that, she couldn't let Merv win. She was sure by now that the wrestling business as a whole entity was an albatross to her life, but she couldn't get out now even if she wanted to. So she kept going, even when she didn't want to, when she was too sick to, and when she knew better. She was already this far in; what other option did she have?

Ade sat in the attic of her house. With the tiles gone and only the bare roof timbers left above her head, she could look down on the bay at the end of the hill. It was a beautiful night, but there was rain in the air. She needed to move soon to get back to ground level before it got too dark. She knew her way around the missing boards, but not so much that she wanted to navigate them without light. She planted her hand and pushed herself up to a standing position, but she'd moved too quickly. She hit her head on a beam, which knocked her sideways and sent her face-first to the floor.

Ade just managed to stop herself from going through a missing section, an open gap down to the next floor. As she lay there, she could feel the pain in her head as it swelled and throbbed. She could only hang on where she was and lie there, crying.

She managed to make it down to the ground floor and was walking to her car when it began to rain. She had a warm coat and a flashlight. When she reached into her pocket she realized that her car keys had fallen out of her pocket in the house. She wasn't going back up there in the dark and the rain.

She beat the lock off of her garage with a rock, but by now, she was bleeding from her head, dizzy, sore, wet to the bone, and physically weak. She was glad to get in out of the rain. She tried the overhead light in the garage, but knew that she hadn't paid the bill. The space was packed to the gills with Merv's old things, but in the corner was the mattress that Ade slept on. She lay down gently and pulled her wet sweater over her head. She had very little left in her. She was just about done until she heard a noise outside.

One eye shot open as she felt around the mattress to see if there was anything that she could use as a weapon if she needed one. She quietly sat up and tiptoed to the door to see what was outside. She saw a heavy candlestick that Merv had loved. It would certainly do to crack a head if she needed to. She slowly peeked out the door only to see the neighbor's dog taking a shit right beside her car.

Ade stomped her foot and shouted at the dog, which made it run away into the night. In anger, she threw Merv's candlestick holder into his pile of possessions, which started a noisy mini-avalanche. Ade didn't care. She fell back onto her mattress, where the contents of Merv's overturned desk were now waiting for her. There were pens, unopened bills, a Rolodex, and some cufflinks. Ade just swiped it all into a box and fired it back into Merv's pile of crap. But not before checking it for cash.

Ade lay down again. She didn't want to think—thinking kept her awake more nights than she cared to remember. But she knew that Danno was making a fortune, and that Proctor would soon get his turn. What did she have? She would just wait for sleep, and start again tomorrow.

Ade looked around and was yet again surrounded by Merv and his mountain of useless things. Only this time, she was in a small musty garage instead of a mansion.

Among all the crap, something kept drawing her to an envelope that was stuck against the wall, which read:

Sausalito Yacht Harbor

She had no idea what that was, but it was chipping away at her. Something familiar about that name. She lay, cold and wet, looking at it. Something wouldn't let her thoughts move on. She reached to grab it and opened the envelope. It held nothing of interest. She dropped it on the floor, rolled over, and tried to sleep.

She got a minute or two of rest, until it hit her.

CHAPTER TWELVE

1972.
San Francisco.

Morning couldn't come soon enough. Ade waited for the pier to open. She had been this excited before, but it had always led to nothing. Merv's hide-and-go-seek game always won out. She timed her journey from her house; Merv could have easily done the same.

At the pier, she waited patiently for a middle-aged woman to open her small wooden office. Shortly after her came what was obviously her twin sister, who also walked into the hutch. It was showtime. Ade darted from her car. "Hello?" she called.

The twin ladies turned to see a disheveled, bleary-eyed woman in bloodstained, slept-in clothes approach them. Ade saw that their name tags read Emma and Sarah.

"Emma, Sarah, how do you do?" Ade said.

"Good, thank you," they both replied together in perfect synchronicity.

Sarah pushed Emma forward to talk to Ade alone, while she tiptoed off in the background. "Can I help you, ma'am?" Emma asked.

"I'm sorry," Ade said, suddenly becoming self-conscious about her appearance. "But, I think my husband had a boat down here."

"You *think*, ma'am?" Emma asked.

"He was . . . a secretive man. He didn't say much about things. But I got this—" Ade reached into her pocket and pulled out the letter from the garage. "Sausalito Yacht Harbor. That's you guys, isn't it?" Ade asked, as she pointed to the sign above them.

"That's us, ma'am, yes."

Ade began to let herself get a little excited. "And I'm presuming that there would be no point in paying club fees here, unless there was a boat somewhere?"

"Some people just join for the clubhouse and tennis courts," Emma replied. "But charges of this nature would be mooring fees."

Ade could feel it. "Can you check? His name was Merv Schiller."

As Ade said his name, she could tell that the woman had heard of him. Her face noticeably shifted.

"Do you know my husband?" Ade asked.

Emma nodded. "Mr. Schiller was a regular here, up until a while ago. He worked long hours and needed to get to his boat pretty late at night, if I remember."

Ade could have cried with joy. This was it, she knew it. "Can you show me that boat?"

Emma could see the relief on Ade's face. It was hard for her to realize that the woman in front of her was Merv Schiller's wife. "Do you know the name of the boat, at least?" Emma asked.

Ade shook her head. "He never even told me that he had a fucking boat."

"I don't know, ma'am. I'm not really supposed to—"

"April something," Ade said emphatically.

"Let me go check," Emma said reluctantly. She entered the hutch.

Ade's whole body was flooding with adrenaline. Even if she wasn't allowed to see the boat right now, she knew that it could be overcome with some ID. Ade ran to her car and got her driver's license. It still said Schiller on it.

"Ma'am?"

Ade could see the woman waiting outside the hutch for her. She looked the same, but her nametag said Sarah.

"Where's the other—where's your sister gone?" Ade asked.

"She's on the phone, ma'am."

"Okay, I'll wait."

"There's a problem," Sarah said.

"I have ID," Ade replied, as she flashed her license. "I'm his wife."

Sarah drew a large breath. "It's not that. The *April Showers* isn't here anymore, ma'am."

Ade heard, but didn't understand. "Excuse me?"

"It was taken away."

"To where?"

"We wrote to you several times. We called. I even personally went to your house," Sarah said.

"For what?"

Sarah pointed to the white sign that was posted on the outside wall of the hutch. It read:

ALL FEES MUST BE PAID ON TIME

"What?" Ade asked. "Are you serious?"

Sarah could hardly look up from the ground. "We tried everything to get you, ma'am. I personally put you—" Sarah stopped and looked around to see if anyone was listening. She continued with a hushed tone, "I personally put you down as paid for over a year, because Mr. Schiller was such a longtime member."

Ade grabbed Sarah by the shirt. "Where's his boat?"

"It's gone. They get taken away, if—"

Ade screamed, "Where is it?"

"Waldon's. They take the boats from here and impound them."

Ade collected herself somewhat. The boat wasn't there, but at least she could find out where it was. "Where are they? Where's Waldon's place?"

Sarah didn't want to answer. "I—I—"

Ade could feel her stomach turning. She knew something was wrong. "Answer me, please," she said calmly.

Sarah could hardly get the words out. "They closed down suddenly."

"They did what?" Ade asked.

"They're gone."

Ade tried to laugh, but no sound came out. Her shoulders shook and her eyes filled with tears. "You know what happened?"

Sarah was scared of the look in Ade's eye. "No ma'am. They were in business for twenty years and then they disappeared. Didn't tell anyone. Just left."

Ade laughed as she hunched over and slapped her own thigh. "They got my fucking money," Ade said to no one in particular. "They got to it before I did."

Emma emerged from the hutch. "Ma'am, the boat was impounded due to lack of—" Sarah stopped her sister from talking. Both women watched Ade gently lower herself into a sitting position on the dock, laughing and crying and curling herself up into a ball.

1972.
New York.

Ade traveled to New York as quickly as she could. She'd heard about what had happened to Proctor's son and she wanted to see if he was doing okay. She also wanted to see a friendly face.

Ade wanted to get away from San Francisco.

She wanted to see Proctor.

After pooling everything she had and selling anything she had left, she bought herself a ticket. At this stage, she was hardly going to wrestling shows at all. Venues were looking for her, and wrestlers were looking to get paid. She needed a break; she needed someone to put their arm around her.

When she arrived at the hospital in New York, she immediately saw Proctor at the pay phone in the lobby. "Put me through to Danno," she heard him tell whoever was on the other end of the call.

Ade looked around until she found her reflection in the glass doorway. She looked good: confident, not desperate.

"You fucking cunt. I swear to God, I'm going to kill them, Danno. Then you," Proctor said into the phone. "This is how you keep your fat, greasy hands on the belt? You take out my boy? Is that where we've gone in all of this?"

Ade waited before advancing any further. Proctor was ready to blow, and she didn't want that to be the backdrop when he finally saw her again.

He removed the phone from his ear and screamed into the mouthpiece. "Where's his fucking foot, Danno?" Proctor slapped the phone back on the hook and fired a potted plant through the candy dispenser glass in front of him.

"Move him," Proctor shouted to no one in particular. "I want to bring my boy home to Florida with me."

Ade watched as Proctor stormed down the hallway. She followed him. She watched as Proctor turned left and right and walked past door after door until eventually he came to his son's room. She walked up and listened for quiet in the room. The whole building was quiet. No visitors and no staff to be seen. She also heard no voices inside the room, so she was sure Proctor was alone. Ade peered around the doorway and saw Proctor sitting alone at the side of his son's bed. Gilbert King was bandaged and unconscious.

"Hi," she whispered.

Proctor turned and looked at Ade. She could see he was confused. He didn't look too thrilled to see her, either.

"Sorry to—" In that second, she knew that it was all a big mistake. She turned to leave.

"What are you doing here?" Proctor asked as he stood up.

Ade couldn't think of anything that didn't sound crazy. She had built their story up in her head while she was tearing her house down. Maybe after a couple of years, she would reintroduce herself to Proctor and he would be delighted to see her. Maybe he would even want to be with her. It was fucking crazy, all of it. Ade knew it and felt it, but she couldn't do anything to change it now that she was in front of him.

Proctor marched her roughly into the hallway. "My wife is here," he said looking around to see if anyone could see her.

She shrugged him off. "You're hurting me."

Proctor leaned aggressively into her ear. "I don't want you around her; she doesn't have anything to do with this fucking business."

"But there's nothing going—"

Proctor shoved Ade headfirst toward the door. She landed badly, but all he did was kick her shoes after her. "Get the fuck out of here."

Ade's head was bleeding, her shoe heel was broken, and her eyes were blurring with tears. She tried to scream, but he put his hand over her mouth, grabbed her by the hair, and dragged her away from his son's door like she was less than human.

Ade lay there after he left. She was stunned, hurt, and shamed. She lifted herself from the floor and made her way to the exit.

1972.
New York.

A couple of months later, Ade found herself back in New York. This time she didn't have to pay for anything, which was good, because Ade didn't have two coins to rub together.

Lenny inched Ade Schiller through the traffic leaving JFK International. "How was your flight, Mrs. Schiller?"

Ade was freshening up her face in the back of the car and reading the giant billboard to her right. "The Great White Way to New York. Is that what they say now?"

"Mr. Garland is really looking forward to your company tomorrow after you get settled," Lenny said.

"How is Mr. Moneybags? I hear he's having to deal with a lot of shit from that asshole, Proctor."

Lenny concentrated on finding the smallest opportunity between the Buick and the Mack truck in front of him. "I wouldn't know about those things, I'm afraid. The word is, though, that Proctor hasn't even been heard from since the boss gave him what-for about the match at Shea."

"Really?" Ade seemed intrigued.

"No one has heard a single word," Lenny said.

This update seemed to make Ade very happy. "Really," she said again.

Lenny popped the cigarette lighter and handed it back to Ade, who duly lit up.

"How did Danno know I was coming out here?" she asked.

Lenny shrugged at his boss's mystical ways. In truth, it was more than likely that a wrestler from her territory said something in passing about them not working this week because their boss was coming to New York. This, of course, would have been overheard by his tag-team partner, who was a brother of the ring announcer in LA, who met with Ricky last week to see about working some towns with them while his brother finished up a messy divorce in Jersey.

Telephone. Telegram. Tell-a-wrestler.

The phone rang.

"Ade?"

"Yes?"

"It's Danno. How are you?"

"I'm doing great. I'm coming right down."

"Do you mind if I come up?"

"Um . . . I guess not."

"Good."

Ade was overdressed for her room and now she felt foolish. She had torn her garage to pieces to look for something to wear. She just wanted out of the wrestling business, and something told her that Danno Garland hadn't flown her to New York to talk about the weather. She had heard that things were getting heavy between Danno and Proctor. Their big match, during which Danno would have to release the belt, just like Ade had planned, was just around the corner. She had been all over the plan at the start, and now that it was coming to an end, she couldn't have been further away from it.

All she wanted to do was distance herself even more.

She opened the door. Ricky Plick walked in first; Danno quickly followed him.

"Sorry about this, Ade," Danno said, as he put his hat on her glass table. "I've got to be careful."

"I understand," Ade said.

Ricky nodded at Ade, and she nodded back.

"I'd like to buy you out," Danno said before he'd even taken his coat off.

Ade could hardly hide her joy. "Can I get you a drink?" she asked.

Danno smiled and shook his head. Both he and Ricky were clearly in a hurry. "I've got to do my favor for Proctor soon," Danno said, "And I think it would be a shame to have all of this power right now, only to go back to where I was when the belt is gone. Don't you?"

Ade nodded. "I don't want to sell, though," she said, lying.

"You're losing everything, Ade," Ricky said. "Your territory is hurting, you've built no new stars, your gates are down hugely, and your contract with old Lance Root still has years to go."

"I'm going to step out," Danno said, rising from his seat.

"Why?" Ade asked.

"Ricky here is going to look after things," Danno said. "I'm in a tight spot at the moment, Ade. I've got a lot of people breathing down my neck. I hope you understand."

Danno kissed Ade on the cheek, picked up his hat, and left the room.

"So you're his mouthpiece again?" Ade said to Ricky. She remembered that when Merv was killed, and Danno was next in line to take the title belt, it had been Ricky who came to her house and negotiated on Danno's behalf.

"I'm doing a job," Ricky said.

"How much?" Ade asked.

"Three hundred grand."

Ade scoffed.

"That's more than it's worth," Ricky said. "We both know that."

Ade could hardly take the fucking business anymore. It had ruined her life and made a show of her, pulling her first one way and then the other. She couldn't take these men anymore. Even the good ones like Danno seemed to be assholes.

"And you pay off Root's deal," Ricky said.

"Ricky—"

Ricky continued, "Danno can't be seen buying up such a bad contract, Ade. Do you think Babu would be happy being the *second* highest paid wrestler on the roster? You made a bad call. You have to fix it."

She thought about it for a second, but she didn't have any wiggle room. "Deal," she said simply. "Deal."

The biggest match in the history of professional wrestling didn't even happen. Danno was supposed to drop the heavyweight championship of the world to Proctor. He was to do it by ordering Babu to let Proctor's son, Gilbert, beat him and become champion in front of a record crowd.

Instead, neither Babu or Gilbert made it to the match. They were driven by Lenny Long, fresh in the business, when Gilbert caused their van to crash.

Gilbert then lied to his father and said that Danno's side was to blame.

Proctor, hearing that and seeing the huge injuries to his son, started a war. A war that Danno eventually won. At least, it looked that way.

As Danno was celebrating overturning Proctor, his wife lay dead on the floor of a motel room in Texas. Proctor heard what happened, and knew he would be suspect number one, so he immediately went into hiding.

1972.
San Francisco.

"You're going to have to stop," he'd said when he saw her carrying the bricks back toward the house.

Ade looked up and saw Proctor King standing submissively in her driveway. She had heard about Danno's wife, too, and knew exactly why Proctor was standing in front of her. She was out of the business: no one would come looking. Even if they did, it would be after everyone else had been searched first.

"What are you doing?" he asked. His question sobered her up a little. She wasn't really sure herself what she was doing.

"I'm not giving up, I guess," she replied.

He approached her like a dog looking to get out of the rain. "I need your help," he said. His head was bowed; his voice was broken. "I didn't kill her."

Ade knew he hadn't. She threw her last brick down for the day and wiped her hands. Something in her head told her that she'd never come back to that house again. She felt neither happy nor sad, but was sure that was it for that house. It was time to move on and do what she wanted to do with her life.

"Fancy a motel room?" she asked.

Proctor was asleep in his single bed, tired from the flight. Tired from running. Ade sat on the edge of her bed, looking at him. He had been true to the end; he hadn't fucked around. Even with only a couple of feet between them, she couldn't even make him look—not that she wanted anything to do with him anymore.

Outside, she delicately dialed a number on the pay phone. She knew that she'd never get Danno, but Ricky was always available to do business on his boss's behalf. The phone rang and rang, until eventually Ricky answered.

"Hello?" he said, sounding sleepy.

"I heard about Danno's wife," Ade said.

"Who is this?" Ricky was clearly trying to wake up.

"It's Ade."

Ricky didn't know what to say. He was caught in the middle of chaos and didn't really have time for sympathy, especially from someone unimportant, like Ade was now. "I'll tell Danno you called—"

"I have him here," she said.

"What are you talking about?" Ricky asked.

"Proctor King. He's here with me, now. Tell Danno that I'll give him over for five hundred thousand dollars."

"What?"

Ade replied, "Proctor told me that he had her killed, Ricky. I don't want anything to do with that. Five hundred grand, and he's yours."

There was no pause to think; no permission sought. "Deal," he said.

CHAPTER THIRTEEN

1984.
Three days after Lenny got out.
New York.

Lenny was woken up by Jimmy banging on his window from the outside. "Incoming," Jimmy shouted through the glass.

"What?" Lenny asked, unsure both of what was said and who was saying it.

"Uncle Babu," Jimmy replied.

"What?"

"He's here."

The boy disappeared from Lenny's window. It took a little while for his words to melt through Lenny's layer of sleep, but when they did Lenny sat up immediately. "Uncle" Babu was coming to see him, and Lenny still didn't know which way the giant was leaning.

He got up quickly and dressed even more quickly. He peeked out from his bedroom door and down the hallway. He saw nothing out of the ordinary, so he tiptoed into the kitchen—where Babu stood drinking coffee. Lenny froze.

"What are you doing here?" Lenny asked, trying to look surprised.

"I owe you an apology," Babu said.

Lenny wasn't expecting those to be Babu's first words to him. "Oh yeah?" Lenny said. "Why's that?" Lenny wanted the giant out of his father's house before his father showed up.

"I've been keeping something from you," Babu said.

In scenes like this, Lenny was hit all over again by just how massive Babu was. He didn't fit well in a normal house. He was in the way of everything and unable to sit in the limited space around the kitchen table.

"What have you been keeping from me?" Lenny asked, not really wanting to know the answer.

Babu took a worn picture from his pocket. It was of Babu and Kid Devine—with Kid holding the world title. It wasn't old; it had just been carried around too long in Babu's pocket.

"Who's that?" Lenny asked, keeping his eye on the door to see if his father was around.

"That's your son," Babu replied. "That's Luke."

Lenny wasn't sure if Babu was fucking with him or not. He looked closer. He could see himself in there a little, maybe. "He likes wrestling?" Lenny asked, totally confused. Luke had always hated wrestling when he was a boy.

Babu said, "Look at him. He's handsome. Big too."

The more Lenny looked at the photo, the more the smile on his face grew. "He's—all grown up."

"I gave him the title," Babu said.

Lenny, lost in the picture, wasn't paying enough attention. "Oh yeah? Did he love it?"

Babu put his hand over the picture to get Lenny to focus. "He's our new champion," Babu said.

Lenny looked up expecting to see Babu grinning, but he wasn't. "He's . . . what?" Lenny asked.

"I should have given up wrestling years ago, but I couldn't find anyone I could trust to hand the belt to."

"What?" Lenny asked again.

"He's the world champion."

Lenny laughed a little; Babu didn't. "You serious?" Lenny could tell, without Babu having to answer, that Babu was serious. "You brought my fucking child into the business?" Lenny asked.

Babu nodded. "Well, kinda. It was more Ricky than me."

"Ricky is in on this, too?" Lenny began pacing. "You're fucking kidding me."

Babu caught Lenny's eye. "He was a star in college—football and wrestling. His knee gave out on him, though. Ricky would roll with him when he was a boy, and he felt Luke had something. But he never encouraged anything, never put pressure on him to be anything."

Lenny slammed his hand on the kitchen table. "What the fuck were you thinking? What was *Luke* thinking? He should have told the two of you to go fuck yourselves."

Babu snatched the photo back out of Lenny's hand. "He was thinking about putting food on the table, Lenny. I'm sorry to say it but things got real tough when you went inside. When your boy knew for sure that football was out for him, he immediately came down here looking for a break."

"And you made him the fucking champion?" Lenny shouted.

"I did that for *you*. Who else was I supposed to hand it to?" Babu replied. "He was the one guy in the business who I knew wouldn't go running to Tanner the second he had the title as leverage. Your boy is new and green as gooseshit—but he's cut out for this business."

Lenny just couldn't imagine his boy as aggressive or athletic. Not the boy he knew. Not the boy he left.

Babu continued, "The locker room has given him hell. He can walk away anytime he likes, but he doesn't. He's driven. He wants the big money. And he's young and cocky enough to think that he can get it."

"And what do you think?" Lenny asked.

"I think he's right," Babu said. "I think he'll make money."

Edgar pushed open his front door and walked in with his arms full of grocery bags. Babu immediately stood taller. Lenny could clearly sense tension between Babu and his father.

"I left the door open," Edgar said to Babu. "You should use it."

"Yes, sir," Babu said as he left the kitchen.

Jimmy passed Babu in the hallway and immediately hugged his massive leg.

"Hey," Babu said, as he slipped the boy a ten-dollar bill. "How are you doing, little man?"

"Good. You're not staying for breakfast?" Jimmy asked.

Babu looked back into the kitchen. The reception hadn't been exactly warm. "No, I've got some things that need seeing to. I'll catch you down the road." Babu's hand covered Jimmy's head as he tousled his hair before leaving.

"I don't want anyone from wrestling in my house again," Edgar whispered to Lenny. "I fucking mean it."

"I didn't know he was coming," Lenny said.

Jimmy stood in the hallway and listened to his father and grandfather talk in the kitchen.

"Things have been good around here. Calm," Edgar said as he put away the groceries.

Lenny took some juice from the fridge. "I heard you," he replied.

Edgar stopped what he was doing. Lenny could see that Edgar was nervous about the wrestling business creeping back into their lives.

"I know what I'm doing, Pop," Lenny said. "I know how this game this works."

"Me too," Edgar replied. "I know how this works too. They keep you around and then when they're done with you they get rid of you."

"I won't let them," Lenny said.

"You think you have a choice in that, Lenny?" Edgar asked as he left the kitchen.

The apartment building had small, grimy corridors, plenty of doors, lots of noise, and kids running wild. This was where the world heavyweight wrestling champion lived. Lenny took a breath and knocked on the door of Apartment 26.

"Hello?" asked the voice from behind the door.

"Hello? Who's that?" Lenny asked.

"You came to my door—who are you?"

Lenny paused. "It's me. Lenny. Your—ah, father."

Lenny heard the click of the lock opening and the removal of the safety chain inside. After a couple of seconds, Kid stood back and left his door slightly open. "Come in," he said.

Lenny walked in slowly. The apartment was tiny and clean, but it needed a lot of work. He could see that the bed was made and the dishes were washed and drying on the rack. It reminded Lenny a little of where he'd just come from. He kept looking around the room for something to fix on because Lenny couldn't look his boy in the face.

"How are you?" Lenny asked.

"You want a drink?" Kid replied.

"Please," Lenny said. He waited until Kid turned around before he stole a look at his boy. From behind his son was muscular and athletic, but not too thick. His ears were bent up and swollen, and he had an ice pack taped around his knee.

"Luke?" Lenny said.

"Can you call me Kid?" he asked.

"Kid?"

"That's my gimmick. Everyone in wrestling calls me Kid."

Lenny saw that his son's face was handsome, and his hair was washed; he looked after himself.

"But you want me to call you that, too?" Lenny asked.

Kid took a soda from his tiny refrigerator and left it in front of his father. "I'm already getting the worst time just for being your son. Please don't walk into the locker room and call me by my first name, too. They would never let me live it down."

Kid made a whole lot of sense. Lenny took a seat by the window; the next building was close enough that he could nearly touch it. "I want you to try something else," Lenny said. "Wrestling is a—"

Kid smiled. "Try something else? I'm the world heavyweight champion."

Lenny looked around at Kid's tiny apartment. "World champion can mean a lot of things."

Kid sat down and put his feet up on his rickety coffee table. "I'm not leaving wrestling. I can make good money there."

"And you can also get killed," Lenny said. They paused. Lenny's last sentence was a little too sharp for them both—but for different reasons. Lenny thought that he'd try to take a little heat out of the room. "How long have you been here?"

"Are we just straight into the small talk?" Kid asked. "Like we only seen each other yesterday, 'cause I got to get to the gym soon."

Lenny wanted to hug him. He remembered him as a little boy. "You used to want to do anything *except* wrestle," Lenny said.

"I remember a whole lot of things about you, too." Kid stood. The sheer weight of his sentence hit his father hard.

"I'm sorry," Lenny said.

"Do you want to catch up? Is that it?" Kid said. "Here are the relevant points in my life: you killed someone and went to prison. Then you told your *own fucking family* that you wouldn't see them anymore if they tried to visit you."

"I was ashamed," Lenny said. "I was getting beat pretty badly and I didn't want you all to see me like that. I honestly thought I was going to die in there. I wanted you to move on."

"Well, you got your wish. 'Cause we did," Kid said. "Except for the times we nearly went under. We're still trying to clear bills. Ricky and Babu had to give us money. They bailed us out. They kept us going even though their own families had no money. And where were you?"

Lenny was stunned. "I didn't know they helped you guys out like that."

"Helped us? They raised us. Still do," Kid said.

Lenny was totally taken aback by what he was hearing.

"Are you my boss right now?" Kid asked.

"No," Lenny replied.

"Then go."

"Luke."

"I'm serious," Kid said as he opened his door. The wild noises from the hallway outside came parading in. "I want you to go. When the time comes, we'll do business 'cause they tell me you're my boss. But for now—"

Lenny turned slowly and walked to the doorway.

On the way home from the city, Lenny wanted to make a stop.

He had gotten good directions, but his legs wouldn't carry him to her grave. He wanted to say good-bye, but he might have already done that; maybe that was why he wouldn't take another step. His mother was gone and he didn't want to see where she had ended up. Some other day he might, but on this day, Lenny was happy just to stand at the gate of the cemetery. He said what he had to say to her from afar.

He was done.

As he walked through the parking a lot, he could hear the wheel of another car pulling up slowly behind him. "You ready to do some business?" asked a female voice from the car.

Lenny turned and saw a face that was immediately familiar; he just didn't know from where.

"Get in," she said.

Then it hit him: Ade Schiller.

She pulled in a little ahead of Lenny, opened the passenger door to her gray Mercedes-Benz two-seater, and said as he walked by, "You remember me, don't you?"

"I do. Nice to see you again, Ade." Lenny didn't know if this was a setup, if something or someone was about to blindside him, or if Ade was there to talk business. But he knew he was about to find out.

She pulled the car up beside him again. "Ricky called me," she said. "He said that you guys were interested in doing a deal, but maybe he was wrong?"

"You're not working with Tanner Blackwell, are you?" Lenny asked as he passed his father's empty, waiting car. He didn't want Ade or anyone else knowing what he was driving.

Ade laughed at the notion. "I heard about what you did. You slapping that old bastard Tanner created as many friends as it did enemies," she said. She patted the leather passenger seat for Lenny to get in.

She was obviously older, but still beautiful. Lenny's last memory of her was from when he had picked her up at JFK at Danno's request.

She parked and got out of her car. Lenny stopped too. It was a public enough place—he could see the entrance and exit clearly. Nothing seemed off enough to cause him too much anxiety.

"I don't know about you," she said, "but I don't have to wait for Ricky to get back from Japan to figure out what I want to do here."

"Ricky doesn't talk for me," Lenny said.

"Yeah? Well, he wants *my* money to buy *your* territory," she said, taking off her sunglasses. "How about I just give you the money, and you just walk away from all of this right now?"

Lenny smiled. It hadn't taken long for Ade to get to it. In a way, he admired that.

"Well?" she asked.

Lenny shook his head. "No, thanks."

"No? New York is nothing right now, you know that, right?" Ade asked.

Lenny replied, "It's still something, otherwise you wouldn't be here, Tanner wouldn't be chasing it, and Ricky wouldn't be calling you."

"And Joe Lapine wouldn't be funding it. You forgot that part," she added.

Lenny had no idea about Joe, but he knew enough to not let her see that.

Ade continued, "You think I don't know what's going on?"

"I'm sure you do," Lenny said.

Ade took out a cigarette pack, opened it, and offered Lenny a smoke across the roof of her car. He declined. She took one for herself, tapped the end of it on the pack, and lit it. "So, you've been to Babu's place, slept in a bus shelter, and visited your father. Now you're here. And you're still not dead. What does that tell you?"

"That you've been following me?" Lenny said.

Ade laughed. "Well, not me personally. But yeah."

"Apart from that, I don't know. What does it tell me?" Lenny asked.

"That you're safe. For now. If I can find you, then the bad guys can find you too. And you don't want that to happen. Let me take all the heat from you."

"That's very kind of you," Lenny said sarcastically.

She took a big drag from her cigarette. "Most people in your situation would have gotten drunk and fucked a couple of whores or something after getting out. I admire that about you."

Lenny began to walk away.

"You're not thinking of staying in this business, are you?" she asked.

Lenny shrugged as he made his way away from her.

"It's going to take years," she said. Lenny stopped. She said, "To get this territory healthy again, and to get it making real money. It's going to take years." He turned around. "I'm just saying it, because I get the impression that you're aiming for something quick." She stood on her cigarette butt and walked toward him. "Even when you have the pick of the litter, it takes time to build stars, it takes time to build towns to see those stars, and it takes time for your TV to reflect that. And that's with all the other bosses on your side." Ade picked a pretend hair from Lenny's shoulder. "Joe marked New York. There isn't a wrestler in the world who is going to work with you guys. Do you think your TV is going to hold your time slot if you don't have the wrestlers to fill it? How about the venue owners? What about the granddaddy of them all, the Garden? How long do you think they're going to remain exclusive to you guys if you don't have matches to go in there every month?"

"I'll figure all this out," Lenny said simply. "I appreciate your time."

"You're just a driver. You don't know anything about this business. You need to act, Lenny. While it's still safe."

Lenny was acting. Just like he hoped, all the players were revealing themselves.

Lenny circled back after Ade was gone and got his father's car. The city outside was different. The music inside on the radio was different too. It was more direct, it started with a bang that never stopped. Lenny was rocking the fuck out to "Dancing in the Dark," cruising along 47th Avenue. He didn't know all of the words, but that chorus—he could roar that chorus with the best of them. He beat the steering wheel in time with the drums and tried to not look like an absolute mental patient when another car was driving close by. Other than that, Lenny was on stage, and the world was singing along with him. Music was a great release, and a happy tool to help him forget—until he felt a movement behind his seat.

Lenny froze. He thought he'd heard something earlier, but had put it down to the car being a little beaten down. This, though faint, was undeniable: someone was hiding on the floor in the back of the car. His first thought was to swerve the car into traffic; his second thought was a little less insane.

He turned down the radio. He figured that, whoever it was, if they wanted him dead, he'd be dead by now. "Who's there?" he said.

There was no response.

Lenny wondered for a second if he was losing his mind. "Hello?" he said. There was nothing. "I'm going to count to three, and then we're both going headfirst into that bus!" Lenny shouted.

"I'm sorry," came the voice from the back.

Lenny immediately knew the voice. "Jimmy?"

Lenny's younger son appeared in the rearview mirror. "I'm sorry," Jimmy repeated.

Lenny was at first relieved, but soon became enraged. "What the fuck—" He turned right on 29th Street and parked the car under the shadows of a huge, abandoned factory. "What the fuck do you think you're doing?" Lenny shouted. He got out of his seat, went around the back, and pulled Jimmy out of the car.

His son was instantly ready to go: he put up his hands, prepared to fight. He looked like he was terrified, but his fists were so tight that his knuckles were white. Lenny saw himself in his boy.

"What are you doing?" Lenny asked, trying to take his anger down a couple of notches. Jimmy didn't answer. He was shaking a little, but he hadn't dropped his guard.

"Jimmy?" Lenny said, trying to get his boy to calm down too. He walked toward his son, but Jimmy unloaded with his best right hand, which missed by a mile. The fright of throwing a punch scared Jimmy even more. He then turned and ran into traffic.

"Jimmy!" Lenny shouted, as he took after him.

Jimmy sprinted and tried to make it to the end of the block. Lenny cut him off by grabbing his boy around the waist. Immediately, Jimmy tried to bite, scratch, and punch his father. He was wild—almost uncontrollable. "I'll kill you!" the kid screamed over and over again.

"Hey, hey, hey, look at me," Lenny whispered into his ear as he held him tightly. He had his son wrapped securely enough in his arms that he couldn't hurt himself. Lenny had no idea what was going on, but Jimmy was terrified, and even though there was no danger, he was fighting for his life.

People were beginning to stare as they walked by. Lenny just sat on the edge of the sidewalk and held his shaking son. "I'm sorry," Lenny said over and over. "I'm sorry."

Jimmy's anger turned to tears and he struggled less. "You scared me," he said.

"I'm sorry. It's the car. It's seeing you in the car—" Lenny said. "I didn't know you were there." He began to sob. "I should have known you were in trouble. I'm sorry. I should have protected you and your brother."

Jimmy heard his father cry and knew that he was talking about now *and* before, all at the same time. They were the words of a man riddled with guilt, who had never gotten to say sorry.

"It wasn't your fault," Jimmy said.

His son's kind words only made Lenny sob harder. He released his grasp on Jimmy and hid his face in his hands.

"I was only in the car today because I thought you were leaving. I don't want you to go. I like having you around," Jimmy said. His eyes filled, too, but he didn't cry.

Lenny laughed and wiped his eyes. "You know crying is for girls, right?"

"You must be a big girl then," Jimmy said as he stood up.

"And you must be nearly a girl," Lenny replied.

"I'd rather be nearly a girl than a full girl," Jimmy said.

Lenny put his arm around his boy's shoulder. He felt like he'd made some real connection with his youngest, but his oldest was still up for grabs.

Babu lay in his darkened bedroom. It wasn't particularly late, and the noise of the keys in the tray by the door let him know that there was nothing to worry about. He heard his wife's footsteps as she walked directly to the room. She knew where he was.

"Hey, honey," she said as she opened the door and tried to let as little light from the hallway in as possible. She leaned in and gave her huge husband a kiss on his clammy forehead. "You're not doing so well?" she asked.

Babu's tired eyes watched as she kicked off her shoes, took off her earrings, unclipped her bra under her blouse, and let it slip to the floor. She got in the bed on the little piece of mattress that was left beside Babu, and snuggled.

She was a slight woman, and she was short, too. She had nothing to do with the wrestling business, and didn't want anything to do with it. He had met her on a break in Hawaii, where she'd worked the bar. Babu had spent three weeks sitting in front of her. She had smiled a beautiful smile, looked tanned and relaxed and happy with life. He went there to die, though—at least he had thought so. Doctors had been telling him for years that it was only a matter of time before his body gave out on him.

He lay there in pain, and wished that this was the night his body did give up. He was tired, constantly sore. He wasn't half as happy, or half as spry. He found it hard to complain, though, because the closer he got to dying the more he felt loved and wanted.

"I'm okay," he whispered.

She began to rub his chest and massage his huge fingers. She was used to this, and he was used to having her look after him. He was huge, and she wasn't; he was in the wrestling business, and she wasn't. He was dying, and she wasn't.

"Is it your back?" she asked.

He could only nod.

She kissed him on the cheek. "I'm sorry, honey."

"That's okay," he lied. "I'm feeling better now."

"Better?" she asked.

"Yeah."

"Can I get you anything?" She sat up a little.

"Can you wait just a little longer?" he asked.

"Of course."

His massive hand guided her head gently onto his chest. "Where does a politician go to check out books?" he asked.

She smiled—it was joke time. "I don't know."

"The lie-brary. Get it?"

Her head rose and fell in sync with the movement of his chest as he laughed at his own joke.

"Why did the Chinese male prostitute become a priest?" Babu couldn't see it, but she was crying now. It was such a shame; he was such a big, strong man.

"I don't know," she said, hiding her tears. "Why did he?"

"Because he was hoe-Lee?"

She laughed at that one; it was good. The more she laughed, the more he laughed.

"I want to go here, when it's my time," Babu said.

"Like this?" she asked.

"Just like this," he replied.

Ava squeezed her husband's huge hand. His talk wasn't dramatic, or over-the-top; it was practical, and that was what made it all the more heartbreaking.

"You promise?" she asked.

"Promise," he replied. "I will come home."

Lenny didn't have any money to treat Jimmy, but that didn't mean that Jimmy couldn't treat them both. Babu's ten-dollar gift bought them each a pair of new sunglasses and a candy bar. Jimmy felt cool as ice as he sat crammed in the driver's seat between his father's legs as they cruised slowly through the neighborhood in Edgar's car.

"Left a little," Lenny said. "The key here is not to park the car on anyone's back or head."

"Roger," Jimmy said.

"A tap more of the gas, and keep it left, here."

"Over and out."

Lenny leaned forward and checked out both sides for any signs of danger.

"How are we doing?" Jimmy asked.

"Coming up to Granddad's place soon. Maybe you should pull in and let me take over." Lenny took a quick peek in the rearview mirror. "Oh, fuck," he said.

Jimmy wobbled the car with fright. "What?"

"My parole officer is behind us," Lenny said. "What the fuck?"

Jimmy started to panic a little. His driving became more erratic. "What are we going to do?"

"I don't think he—can you slip over, if I take a sharp right here?" Lenny asked.

"What?"

Lenny didn't have time to repeat himself. He pulled down hard on the steering wheel and pushed down on the gas, taking the car on a tight right turn. "Now jump over," Lenny said.

Jimmy quickly slid over from driver's seat to the floor of the passenger side. Lenny looked behind him again, but there was no car there. They must have shaken their tail. Lenny put his foot down and took the next right, which put them behind the parole officer's car. Lenny watched as Tad slowly freewheeled past Edgar's house.

"What's he looking for?" Jimmy asked.

"Nothing, son," Lenny said. He parked and wondered, just as his son did, what the parole officer was looking for.

Edgar stood in his tiny front garden, in his dirt-stained white shirt. He watched as his son and grandson came walking down the street in unison. They had a matching walk, and matching sunglasses. He would have been ecstatic, if he wasn't plagued with the feeling that Lenny was bound to fuck it up again.

"Lenny?" whispered Donta from the dark. "Lenny?"

Lenny awoke suddenly to find a gloved hand over his mouth and a huge, shiny hunting knife an inch from his eyeball. "Wakey-wakey, Lenny," Donta said as he grabbed Lenny by the hair and pulled him out of bed.

Lenny slipped out of Donta's grasp and slid backward along the floor into the corner of the room.

"It's up to you whether we wake the others in the house or not," Donta said.

"Who sent you?" Lenny asked.

"Joe wants to have a talk. Are you free?" Donta replied.

Another player coming out of the bushes.

"Put the knife away," Lenny said.

Donta did just that.

Outside, Donta opened the passenger door for Lenny and got in himself on the driver's side. As he rode away from Edgar's house, Lenny heard the faint voice of someone shouting behind them. Lenny turned to see his father running behind them with his shotgun in his hand. Jimmy was standing in the doorway of the house in his pajamas.

Lenny tried to open the door to let them know he would be okay, but it was locked from the outside. Lenny pulled and pulled on the lever as Donta's car left Edgar's house behind.

Donta dragged Lenny from the car and muscled him towards Joe, who was standing alone on the promenade.

"How the fuck would you even know how to treat a gem like that?" Joe said, as he pointed to Manhattan. "Just look at it! Look! The greatest fucking city in the world, and you think that you can have it?" Joe grabbed Lenny by the throat. "I can't even remember the last time I grabbed another man by the throat. God in heaven, help me, I will fucking cut your head off and dump you in the river if I have to."

Lenny was calm. "We both know that you're not going to kill me, Joe."

Joe punched Lenny in the face. "You think you're going to outlast me?" Joe said. "You think your little magazine article is going to protect you? If you want to hide from me in plain sight, you better get yourself a *way* bigger spotlight than a fucking magazine article. You hear me?"

Lenny nodded. "I'm working on it."

"I spent ten years putting this territory back together," Joe said. "I bought a place and got to know the right people here. I nurtured New York back to her knees, when all the other bosses couldn't give a fuck about her. I put in the time and I put in the money."

Lenny was used to these types of negotiations. The ones where his face was beaten. But it was normally over much smaller stuff than a territory. "Neither of us deserves it," he said.

"But I fucking promise you, I'll end up with it," Joe replied. "You have nothing left to barter with. You have no leverage, no wrestlers, and that means no TV show to submit to your station. You're fucked." Joe looked back over the river at the city, all lit up. "You know the difference between me and those other fucking apes that came before me? I always knew that there was a way to get rid of people without blood or bodies—or attention."

Lenny watched Donta from the corner of his eye. He knew Joe wasn't the killing kind, but Donta gave out the vibe that he certainly was.

"Here's what's going to happen," Joe said. "You're going to announce a unification match with your champion against the other titleholder, Emmet Cash, from the Carolinas. We're going to do it ten days from now, which will fill your booking at the Garden. No more waiting, and no more risks for me. We will do this quickly, so no one has a chance to pull any fast ones. You're going to drop the belt there, take ten-fucking-percent of the door, and leave New York to me."

"Ten percent?" Lenny laughed. He had no idea what was making him so brave.

"You're lucky that I'm giving you anything, you ungrateful little prick. You own a shell—a thin approximation of what a territory should be. No one knows who your champion is, and you bring nothing to the gate. You have nothing to leverage your position—you earn no money. You are a nobody, and you'll be paid like a nobody. And fuck you for talking to me! Now you're getting two percent of the gate. You add no value to this match—zero. Do you want zero percent of the gate?" Joe spat in Lenny's face. "I didn't play patience up here for a decade so you could come along at the last second and fuck it up for me. Ten nights, and all of this ends—and I get what I've earned."

Donta hit Lenny in the gut, which folded Lenny over. He dropped to his knees, falling face-first at Donta's feet. Lenny saw the opportunity. "Don't ever come into my house again," Lenny said as he found enough flesh to bite into Donta's calf.

Joe laid in some kicks, and Donta laid in some stomps. Lenny was soon unconscious on the ground.

CHAPTER FOURTEEN

1984.
Five days after Lenny got out.
New York.

Lenny's wounds were all fresh and opened again thanks to his meeting with Joe. He couldn't move his neck, and he had a couple more loose teeth at the back of his mouth. He was alive, though, and back at his father's place. All he could think of was sleeping; he was nearly off his feet from exhaustion. Before he could open the front door, though, Edgar charged him, pushing Lenny toward the side of his house.

"How is Jimmy?" Lenny asked.

He knew the look—he remembered it from childhood. Edgar Long lifted his fist and punched his son in the face with it. There were no sounds, and no words. Edgar threw it, and Lenny took it. Both men let the moment sit for a minute.

"I want you out of here," Edgar said. "You can lie to that parole officer about being here, but I don't want you actually staying here and bringing all of this shit to my door."

With those words, Edgar left Lenny on his own. Lenny understood. What could he say? His father was right.

Edgar reappeared around the side of the house and hugged his son. "I'm very sorry for hitting you, Lenard. But I can't go through something else bad again. I've had my fill."

"I know. I'm sorry."

"I didn't know if you were dead or not. I didn't know whether to call the cops or not. I don't know what you're doing. I don't know what you're thinking."

"It's nearly finished," Lenny said.

"Well, it's not going to end here," Edgar said. "I wish you'd see that you're so very far out of your league with these people. You're not bad like they are. You don't have that streak in you that makes people nasty. You're a fucking driver who stumbled into a contract."

Lenny could see that his father's eyes were full when he broke from their embrace.

"Leave now. Please," Edgar said as he walked back into his house.

Lenny was tired, hurting, and without a plan. The players had all revealed themselves. The snakes were all out in the open, but Lenny was drifting. This wasn't the way it was supposed to go when he got out. He had no idea what was happening in the bigger picture, but he figured it might just be time to find out.

"You could always come home and stay with me and Mom," Jimmy said, his face pressed through the gate at the back of the house.

Lenny smiled. It was great to see his boy again. "Not yet, son."

"Why not?" Jimmy scaled the gate and half fell over it on Lenny's side. "Where are you going to go?"

"I've got a place."

"Can I come?" Jimmy asked.

Lenny put out his hand for Jimmy to slap; Jimmy obliged. "I've got some business to do," Lenny said. "It'll just take me a couple of days, and then I'll come back here for you, and we'll do something together. What do you think?"

Jimmy nodded. "Was that man going to kill you last night?"

Lenny knelt down in front of his son. "No one is going to kill me. Do you hear me?"

Jimmy tried to smile, but he wasn't convinced.

"There are a few people out there who are trying to—to bully me. They're trying to get me to do something that I don't want to do. And do you know what they can all do?"

"Fuck off?" Jimmy answered innocently.

Lenny laughed. "Exactly."

Jimmy hugged his father. "I can get us some money."

"Money?" Lenny said. He leaned back and looked his boy in the face.

"That's all we need to get out of here. No more problems," Jimmy replied.

Lenny knew his son was right. Jimmy's summation was simple, but correct. "I appreciate the offer, son. But I'm going to make this all better. I promise you that." Lenny stood, but his son wasn't done hugging yet.

"I'm going to help out too," Jimmy said.

Babu's wife opened the door with an air of suspicion. Lenny stood outside with Bree's old, faded garden gnome under his arm. "Oh, I'm sorry," he said. "I must have the wrong place."

"Lenny?" Ava asked.

"Yes?"

"I'm Ava," she said, as she opened her door wider for Lenny to come in. "Is the gnome sleeping here too?"

Lenny nodded and smiled as he walked in the door. The rooms were alive with the smells of food and baking. Ava was fixing her hair like someone who was in a hurry to go out. "I don't know where Chrissy is," she said. "But he said that you should hang out here for him."

Lenny stood silently and uncomfortably in the hallway. He really felt bad about going back to Babu's place.

"You're welcome to anything in this house. Just help yourself," she said as she disappeared up the stairs.

"Thank you very much. I really feel bad about . . . but it will only be for a couple of days," Lenny said loudly in her direction.

"How are the boys?" Ava shouted back down.

Lenny wasn't sure who she meant. In wrestling, "the Boys" were the wrestlers.

"I hear Luke—or Kid—is the champion, now, right?" she continued.

Lenny was surprised to hear a stranger talk about his boys. "Yes. That's what I hear."

Ava hurried back down the stairs and along the hallway.

"Did I make you late?" Lenny asked.

Ava was polite in shaking her head, but they both knew that her waiting for Lenny to get there had made her late for work. "I'm really sorry to be running out like this, but they're short-staffed and I—"

Lenny stood aside and smiled. "No, please. And thank you."

Ava had a kind face. "Any time." She left in a rush.

Lenny didn't know what to do, really. He thought about napping on the couch. Maybe see if they had any of that amazing soup left. As he tiptoed into the sitting room, the phone began to ring. He thought about answering it; maybe it was Babu checking in. On the other hand, it might be Ava's mom or something, and Lenny didn't want to have to explain his situation, so he let it ring. He lay on the couch, making sure to not put his feet up on the material.

The phone stopped ringing, but almost immediately started again.

Lenny closed his eyes and tried hard to sleep. His night with Joe hadn't been the most pleasant, and sleeping alone, after all his years of sharing with people he didn't trust, was a weird and hard thing to adjust to.

The phone stopped, but started up again.

"What the fuck?" Lenny covered his ears and crunched his eyelids closed. The phone kept ringing, and it was a bell phone, which made it all the more piercing.

Lenny sat and the phone rang.

Even though she had to rush, Ava made it to work with a couple of minutes to spare—just like always. She stopped in the dreary alley-way at the side of her job and lit her cigarette. She reached behind the stacked boxes and pulled out her trusty, rusty tin can that she used for her ashtray. New York might have been a shitty town, but Ava was going to do her bit to keep her part clean.

She thought about her husband and how she would love one more summer in Hawaii; one more great vacation together. She was sure that a month away from the city would rejuvenate Babu—but she also knew that might be asking too much. She tapped the butt of her cigarette into the can and watched a car pull up a few feet from her.

Donta Veal rolled down the driver's window. Ava didn't know him, but she could sense that he wasn't good news.

"Do your husband a favor. Tell him to pick up his phone," Donta said.

Ava walked away fast.

"Lenny, do you think my ass looks big in this?"

Lenny had found the spare room and closed the door. His tired and beaten body melted into the mattress. He was snoring.

"Lenny, do you think my ass looks big in this?"

Lenny woke up and tried to comprehend what he was seeing ten inches from his face.

"How cheeky am I?" Babu asked.

Lenny stared at Babu's bare ass hanging out of a homemade toga. "What the fuck?"

Babu turned around and began to wiggle his stomach and hips. "I think I've put on some weight—what do you think?"

Lenny flopped back to his sleeping position. "What time is it?"

"It's time to tell the truth."

"What? What the fuck are you talking about?"

"I need to know," Babu said.

"Need to know what?" Lenny asked.

"I need to know if you find me attractive," Babu said as he launched himself into a big splash across the bed. His gigantic body, even in slow motion and in jest, crushed Lenny and collapsed the bed on all sides, until the mattress hit the floor. Babu howled with laughter as Lenny struggled for air. His panic only made the giant laugh even more.

"I can't fucking breathe," Lenny tried to shout.

Babu lifted most of his girth off of Lenny so he could remain conscious, but just for a second. "How many times did this happen to you in prison?" Babu asked.

Lenny tried to push Babu off him, but only managed to fart from the strain. Both men laughed. Babu in a toga and Lenny with a giant man-boob pushing into his left eye. The more he laughed, the more Lenny farted.

"Jesus Christ," Babu said, as he tried to lift himself off Lenny. Lenny was gone: no sound, just completely silent convulsions of laughter. Babu could see tears run from Lenny's beaten eyes. It became infectious, until Babu was laughing at Lenny laughing. Both turned into fart-producing children.

"You know, I owe you an apology," Babu said.

"Oh yeah?" Lenny said, wiping his eyes.

Babu was suddenly more earnest. "I should have told you about your boy."

Lenny hugged what he could get his arms around. "Thank you for watching over them, and making sure that they were looked after."

Babu patted Lenny's arm. "I know you'll do the same for me."

Lenny looked at Babu's face: it was white and haggard. Enough to change the mood completely. The giant's eyes were shadowed, gray around the outside. Lenny knew what his friend was saying, and he could only nod.

With Lenny's acknowledgment, Babu became lighter, more free. "Thank you," said the failing giant.

"I have a confession, too," Lenny said.

"What?"

"Your phone rang on and off today for about four hours, and I didn't answer it once," Lenny said. "Sorry."

"That was Ricky," Babu said hopefully as he got up. "He always calls like that."

Unfortunately, Babu couldn't have been more wrong.

Jimmy tiptoed up to Babu's door. He was on a highly secretive mission, and he knew it. "Hello?" he said as he knocked on the door. "Pop?"

Inside, Lenny couldn't believe the voice he was hearing. "Jimmy?" he said to himself as he came to the door to investigate. Lenny opened Babu's door and saw his boy standing there. He looked up and down the alley for signs of anyone else, but Jimmy was alone. "What are you doing here?" Lenny asked.

"I have an important message," Jimmy said.

"You have what?" Lenny asked as he put on his jacket and closed the door behind him.

"What are you doing?" Jimmy said.

Lenny grabbed his son's arm and marched him up the alleyway. "I'm taking you back to Granddad's. How did you even get here?"

"I've been here a million times before," Jimmy replied.

"On your own?" Lenny asked.

"No, this is the first time on my own," Jimmy said. "But what am I supposed to do if I need you?"

"You call me here. I'll go to you. Understand?" Lenny said. Jimmy nodded. "I'll get you the number, hang on," Lenny said as he turned to walk back to Babu's.

"I already know it," Jimmy said. "And Ricky's. And Kid's, too."

Lenny knew that his father would be worried. "Okay, well, you call here, let it ring twice, then stop. Then call again. That way I know it's you and answer it. Okay?"

Jimmy got it. He loved this spy secret code stuff. "Twice, and stop, then call again."

"Does Granddad know where you are?" Lenny asked.

"No, I swore to not tell anyone, and I didn't," Jimmy said as he handed Lenny his note.

"You swore to who?" Lenny asked. Jimmy nodded at the note. Lenny opened the folded piece of paper and read the message.

"Where did you get this?" Lenny asked.

"He called me," Jimmy said. "Asked me to make sure you knew what was going on."

CHAPTER FIFTEEN

1984.
Six days after Lenny got out.
New York.

Everyone turned to watch the giant walk through the airport. He was Godzilla, or King Kong—something freakish. Babu hated people staring at him. He hated navigating crowds, turnstiles, and doorways. He just wanted a more normal life, but that was never in the cards for him; a man his size was always going to draw attention. A few deeper male voices booed him and told him how much he sucked as he walked toward arrivals with his head bowed. The giant knew the date was right, and the time was right; he and Ricky were both meticulous about such things. In all his years in wrestling, Babu's mind was a constant Rolodex of dates, times, venues, and flight numbers. It was the way he and all the other successful wrestlers lived their lives.

But when the Pan Am 747SP aircraft, flight number 801, arrived at JFK without Ricky on board, alarm bells began to ring in Babu's head. As much as he hated to be stared at, the giant needed to check for himself. Ricky didn't miss flights—not his style.

Babu saw with his own eyes that the gate was empty, and that everyone was long gone. He hoped that Ricky found his van outside or something. But Babu knew it was something more serious. It was more than a no-show. He knew that if someone had taken Ricky out of the equation, New York had no chance of stringing together a miracle fast enough to keep them afloat. If Ricky wasn't able to get home in time, then New York was ripe for the picking. Babu couldn't help but feel like it was all his fault; he needed to know if stringing Joe along had gotten his friend hurt, or worse.

CHAPTER SIXTEEN

Kid Devine sat in the front row of an empty Madison Square Garden. He thought about his match that was coming up, and how it would play out. He thought about his father, the wrestling business, the threats, and how all that would play out too.

He heard footsteps on the risers behind him.

"Let me smarten you up," said the voice in the darkness.

In wrestling, this phrase meant everything. A veteran saying those words to a rookie was a passing of the torch; a sign that you'd been truly accepted in the wrestling business. It involved a lot of trust—a lot of faith that the person learning would take on the old traditions, the proper way of doing things. That they would protect the secrets of the wrestling business.

On this night, the rookie knew the voice of the person that was sitting about twenty rows back. Only the ring was lit, so Kid could only make out a silhouette in the stands.

"Can we let the people in?" a staff member shouted. "They're starting to go crazy out there."

"No," the man in the stands replied. "A few more minutes."

Kid stood up and leaned against the apron of the twenty-by-twenty red, white, and blue ring. He tried to look beyond the lights. "Why don't you come down here and show me something, old man?" he said. "It's been a while."

The man in the stands struck a match for his cigarette, and Kid caught a glimpse of his pained, pale face. "You okay?" Kid asked.

"I'm fine," the man answered. He took a pull from his cigarette. "Now, there's only four basic parts to a wrestling match: the Shine, the Heat, the Comeback, and the Finish. The Shine is where our hero starts off well, and wins a couple of small, early victories to get the crowd excited. They paid good money, so give them what they want." He took another pull and continued.

"To start with."

Kid moved to jump the barrier. "You can stay where you are," the man in the stands said. Kid reluctantly stayed where he was, but he had no idea why he couldn't go see his mentor.

"The second part of the match is the Heat," the man said.

"I know this stuff," Kid replied.

The man continued regardless. "And the Heat is where it begins to go wrong for our hero," the man said. "The heel sees an opportunity to win, and he takes it. It's the part of the match where the audience decides whether the babyface hero is worth supporting or not."

"Seriously, man. What are you doing up there? I can't see you," Kid said.

"This part of the match is when bad things happen to good people." The man stood and walked very slowly and feebly down the steps toward the ring.

"What's the matter with you?" Kid asked.

"And, of course, the Comeback is when the babyface decides that he's not having any more," the man said. "He finds a reserve of strength, tenacity, and passion to lift himself off the ground, and fucking fights like a man. This should drive the crowd wild. It should lift them to somewhere higher—to some kind of belief that we can all do that, if we're pushed hard enough." The shadowy mentor dropped his cigarette on the floor and stomped it out with his foot.

"I'm going to start letting these people in now," the front-of-house manager shouted from the opening door.

"The hero can never give up during the Comeback phase," the man said. "Never."

Tad sat at his perfectly placed desk in a small, partitioned office. It was about twelve feet by twelve feet, but it was his kingdom. He particularly liked to boss women parolees around—it made him feel good. This morning, though, his first appointment was with Lenard Long. Tad looked at his diary and noticed he had treated himself to five women in a row after Lenny.

"Next," Tad shouted. Lenny pushed the door open a little to make sure it was okay to enter. "Come in, Mister Long."

Lenny did and sat down opposite the greasy-haired parole officer. Tad took out a form. He had a pen holder that was populated by fifty ballpoint pens, and all of them still had their caps attached.

"Did we do a piss test the last time we met?" Tad asked.

"No," Lenny replied.

Tick.

"Are you a homosexual?" Tad asked.

"What?"

Tad looked up from his form sternly, but broke into a smile. "Just kidding. See, this isn't so bad, is it? Parole doesn't have to be me all over your ass, and you, like, hating me doing that to you."

Lenny was just going to agree to whatever he had to, if it would get him the fuck out of there. "Okay," he said.

Tad dropped his pen and leaned back in his chair to prove that he had a rebellious streak. "Are you doing your bit, Lenard?"

"I don't know what that is," Lenny said.

"People always wonder what it is we do," Tad said. "Do we just look at people pissing all day, or are we checking up on people in Mexican restaurants? Neither. We give people the option to take from society, or to give back. If you're one of the ones who gives back, then you'll never have to worry about Tad Stolliday. However—"

"I have a job. I have a place to stay," Lenny replied. "I'm not doing any drugs, and I can even stay away from alcohol, if you want me to."

Tad looked hurt that he didn't get to finish his speech. "What job have you got?"

"I'm promoting matches," Lenny said.

Tad laughed a little. "No, a real job."

Lenny had thought his reply mightn't go that well. "I'm the owner of the New York Booking Agency."

"But my understanding is—that's not—that company is—how do you say? Finished."

Lenny looked confidently at Tad. "It's nowhere near finished. Not now that I'm out."

Tad saw a difference in Lenny—a knowing, something under the surface. "Spot checks are what works. That's what I do: I drop in on people, and make sure that they're keeping the promises they made to this great city. Just so you know."

"You can drop in on me anytime," Lenny replied.

With that, Tad packed up his rebel behavior and picked up his pen again. There was paperwork to be done.

With Babu on his way to see Joe, Lenny called Ade. She arranged to meet him on West 19th Street. It would be safe there, with not many people around, so they could talk.

"She's just gone in," Jimmy said to his father, who was hiding around the corner.

"Anyone with her?" Lenny asked.

"Nope."

Jimmy was a perfect human recon machine; he was small enough to go unnoticed. Lenny looked up and down the street for anyone who could do him harm. With Ricky out of the picture, he wasn't taking any chances.

"Okay, go in and scout the place. Make sure that it's just her,"

Lenny said to Jimmy. Jimmy nodded. He was only too thrilled to be helping out his father.

Lenny composed himself and went over his memorized script. This was the beginning of his play. Now that he had all the snakes out of the bushes, he needed to cash in quick and decisively. He weighed up the long list of things that could go wrong; he also thought about staying stuck where he was. A man with nothing. A man who couldn't even try to go home.

Lenny was more willing to roll the dice.

A couple of minutes later, Jimmy appeared and walked past Lenny like they'd never even met. "She's alone," the boy whispered.

Lenny walked left as Jimmy walked right.

It was a gallery: pure white, with various pieces of art on the walls. Ade seemed to be pulled in by the giant black-and-white picture of a hand. It held a card that said in red print: I SHOP, THEREFORE I AM.

"Do you like it?" Ade asked, as if she had sensed Lenny approaching.

"No," he replied.

She turned around. "Why not?"

"Why don't we grab some coffee?" Lenny asked.

"Tell me your idea first. Then we'll see if it's worth coffee or not," Ade replied.

Lenny took another look at the piece on the wall to buy himself that extra second so he could make sure that he was doing the right thing. She was the best angle he had; he might as well swing for the fences with it. He said, "Well, the other bosses have starved us of wrestlers, which kills our TV content, and Ricky didn't come back to town, either."

"He didn't?" she said.

Lenny shook his head. "I'm hoping he's okay."

Ade could see that Lenny was desperately trying to adjust to being the boss. "So, what are you thinking?"

"I've got no choice. I've got to do champion versus champion," Lenny said.

Ade was totally disappointed. This same idea had been shot down a hundred times in the last decade, and she knew that was what Joe Lapine had in mind. She wasn't going to go directly against the National Wrestling Council—she had already learned her lesson. "This is what you called me into the city for? They're not going to cut us in on that deal, no matter what we offer," she said.

"I don't want to do business with the other wrestling bosses, Ade. I'm talking about professional wrestling heavyweight champion versus boxing heavyweight champion," he said. "That's why I need you."

The idea was so out of left field that Ade had to check that he wasn't joking. "Are you serious?"

Lenny might never have run a wrestling company before, but he knew his wrestling history. He was like an encyclopedia of past matches, angles, winners, and losers. He knew what he liked as a fan, and he knew what had drawn the big numbers in the past. Wrestling and boxing had been linked since day one—and crossing both had always meant money. "They did it in Japan before," Lenny said. "Boxing champ versus wrestling champ. It created a ton of interest and tickets sales. It was a terrible match—most all wrestler versus boxer matches are—but we can make it better."

Ade began to think about it. It was genius, really. This was the way to put on a match that the world would be interested in, without relying on the NWC to supply the talent on the other side of the ring. "But your champion—"

"I'll talk to my champion," Lenny said.

Ade continued, "No, I mean your champ would have to lose. No one is going to put Jinky Keeves in the ring against a rookie wrestler and then let the wrestler win."

Lenny could sense they were on a roll. "I agree," he said. "But by losing, my champion has to become a star. We'll make him valiant and heroic; we'll give him no chance from the start. We'll set the story like David versus Goliath: in the end, the boxing Goliath wins, but our guy is seen and respected by millions who might want to see his next match."

"How do we even get this sanctioned?" she asked.

"We might have to go outside the US," Lenny replied. "All I need for now are headlines—exposure. I need my champion's face everywhere. He has to be introduced to America with a bang. Then we're going to have stadiums and international promoters kicking our doors in."

"Lenny." Ade was surprised—delighted, but surprised. "This is—I can make this work. I can make money from this. We can run the video packages on your TV."

Lenny put out his hand for Ade to shake. "I want a press conference—I want this to look legit. I want my New York territory to come across like the crown jewel again."

"Just one thing," Ade said before she shook hands.

"Yeah?"

She slipped a small stack of hundred dollar bills into Lenny's pocket. "You have to start looking like a boss if we're to do this. If we're going before the world, I want you to be believable."

Lenny nodded; there was no counterargument that he could make. "I'll repay you out of our take," he said as he took her money.

Ade was genuinely excited. "I could kiss you."

"Let's wait until this whole thing is over—then we'll see if you feel the same way."

Babu filled the hotel elevator like rising bread in a hot oven. A couple of other waiting patrons decided to wait for the next elevator when they saw who their company would be.

Not only was Babu huge, he looked pissed. He was pissed.

When he got to the sixth floor, he stooped and walked as fast as his legs would carry him to the door at the end of the hallway. The same door that Donta Veal was sitting in front of on the floor. Babu himself had visited this door many times over the years.

"What can I do for you?" Donta asked when he saw the giant approaching. Somewhere in his bored mind he hoped that Babu's wife had told him that he'd followed her to work.

"Where's Joe?" Babu asked.

Donta was slightly disappointed that Babu wasn't here to see him. "He's not in there."

Babu kept walking directly for the door until Donta simply had to move out of the way or be trampled. The giant shoved his shoulder into Joe's door and it immediately collapsed. "Joe?" he shouted. "We had a fucking deal, Joe." Babu checked every room in the suite but Joe wasn't there. "Where is he?" Babu asked Donta.

Donta was now standing in the doorway. "Don't know," he said. "Now, who am I going to say is paying for that door?"

"He'll have a lot more to worry about when I see him," Babu said.

Donta stood into Babu's range. "You making threats now?"

Babu took a step toward Donta. "You're fucking right I am. Where's Ricky Plick?"

Donta never flinched.

"I said, where's Ricky?" Babu shouted.

Donta stepped back. "Never heard of him."

Babu didn't believe him. "I saw you here with Joe before. I know you know who I'm talking about."

Donta lit himself a cigarette. "Did it ever cross your mind that maybe Ricky just stayed where he was?"

Babu didn't have time to argue. He didn't know if Ricky was dead or dying, but he knew in his gut that it was one or the other. If Ricky just didn't want anything to do with New York he would have called.

"Things would be safer for everyone if you'd just deliver New York back here—like you said you would," Donta said.

"I'm working on it." Babu lied. He was already sick to his stomach that he and Joe Lapine had a secret handshake. He needed to find out if Ricky had tried to make contact before starting a war with a boss.

Babu promised himself as he left that if Joe broke the terms of their long-standing deal, there wouldn't be a building in New York big enough or strong enough to keep Joe alive.

Or anyone else that tried to stand in front of him.

Atlanta, Georgia.

This was the meeting that Joe hoped nobody else in the business had heard about. This was the meeting that made New York so vital. This was the meeting that Joe Lapine had been angling for behind everyone's back.

This was the biggest opportunity of them all.

Joe laughed at the rise of anxiety in his stomach as he waited for his host's car to pull up and park. A driver came around to the back door, and Sean Peak exited the car.

"Joe Lapine," Sean said with his hand outstretched, as if they had known each other for twenty years. "A pleasure."

"Mr. Peak," Joe replied. "The pleasure is all mine."

Sean stopped him right there. "It's Sean. Let's continue as we mean to go on." Joe smiled and nodded in agreement.

"You see that?" Sean asked as he pointed high above Joe's head.

Joe looked up into the dark sky at the tall, red, skeletal structure that stood large above them.

"I've been admiring it for at least twenty minutes," Joe said with a huge smile.

"That's it," Sean said. "That transponder is what gets me from coast to coast, from state to state."

Joe had known about it and studied the power of a national broadcast, but he hadn't wanted to think of the potential until he saw it.

"Back in Florida," Sean said, "I ran a little station where Proctor King taped his weekly wrestling show. He was an asshole but his numbers were consistently huge. With all due respect, his piece-of-shit wrestling show outdrew everything we had there. Then one thing led to another, and Proctor never came home."

Joe pretended that he had no idea what Sean was talking about. "I'm not sure I ever met Proctor," he said.

Sean continued, "I'm thinking about putting professional wrestling on my station here. Making it national."

Joe could hardly contain his excitement; this didn't happen very often for a man who had seen all that he had seen. He knew that whoever got this chance was going to be the king of wrestling for a long, long time. Why own a piece of America when you could lay claim to it all?

"My concern is that, in the past, your business hasn't been a united front," Sean said. "I had some dealings with Danno Garland that damn nearly made me shit my pants."

"Those days are gone," Joe said. "As a matter of fact, we're having a heavyweight title unification match in about a week's time to solidify the whole country again. It will be one champion. One sport. And I'm the man who will be sitting on top of that promise, Sean. You can deal with me on this personally."

"Well, let's see how you get on, Joe," Sean said. "I'd love to put wrestling on WSPS, but I have no interest in the old fractured way. If you can bring me the best wrestling matches, with the glam and the glitter that you guys have, I would be more than interested to put it out there for the whole country to see."

"It's all in hand," Joe said with a smile. "It's all in hand."

"These people will buy you and sell you back to yourself," Maw Maw Vosbury said as he stepped off the elevator. He was accompanied by Jinky Keeves, the smartly dressed heavyweight boxing champion of the world.

"I know these guys," Jinky said. "We don't have anything to worry about."

Maw Maw stopped his client in his tracks. "You know the three cups scam?" Maw Maw asked. "Three cups: they mix them around, and you guess where the money is."

"Yeah?"

"Well, these guys' whole business plan is to pick your pocket while you're looking at the cups." Maw Maw started to walk again. Jinky followed.

"So what are we talking to them for?" Jinky asked.

"I attend a yearly event in Los Angeles with these people," Maw Maw replied. "And one thing that I've learned is that they attract money. Big fucking money. And we like money. Do you like money? I like money."

Jinky nodded. The men stood at the entrance of the restaurant and took in its majesty. One hundred and seven stories above the dark and twinkling Manhattan streets, Windows on the World was the place to impress. It had large glass windows intersected with white columns. There were immaculate booths and tables and freshly polished brass rails. There was soft lighting and the best view of Manhattan: the rivers and the bridges of New York City. This was a place where the world heavyweight boxing champion and his manager could talk some business, and look good doing it.

Maw Maw and Jinky walked the black-and-white checkered floor toward their table, which was set for four. The champ took a quick look around to see if anyone had noticed him. Maw Maw shot his wrist out from his sleeve and watched the minute hand move closer to their meeting time.

Both men sat.

"I used to do a lot of business here, when Terry Garland was the boss," Maw Maw said. "You never had to worry about anything with Terry. He made good payoffs—always on time. His son was supposedly good, too, until he got himself killed."

"He got killed?" Jinky asked.

"These fucking guys rub each other out regularly." Maw Maw flashed a little smile as he rubbed his hands together. Jinky could tell that something was off.

"What is it?" Jinky asked.

"Well—usually, we'd wait for another six months, or so, before considering this kind of offer," Maw Maw said.

"Why is that?" Jinky asked.

"Because these guys are all over the place right now," Maw Maw said.

"So why are we doing business with them?"

"We're not doing business with *them*."

The champ was confused, but Maw Maw didn't like talking about any deals until something was signed.

"We're doing business with someone we know. A friend of ours," Maw Maw said.

"What makes you think that these wrestling guys are going to do what your friend says?"

"Because my friend is the only shot they have left. It's perfect." Jinky smiled; Maw Maw nodded in return. "They're desperate, and there's no better time to do business with someone," Maw Maw said as he stood up.

"Exactly," Ade said, putting her hand on his shoulder.

Maw Maw hugged Ade. "You look beautiful."

Jinky stood too. "I didn't know you were coming today."

Maw Maw smiled. "This is our friend."

"Your wife?" Jinky asked.

"Thank you," Ade said, as she sat in the seat her husband pulled out for her. "And you're right: in the midst of desperation is the best time to do business."

Maw Maw and Jinky sat too. They could see from the smile on Ade's face that she had taken no offense at all. Rather, she looked like she was enjoying the fact that the wrestling business was in such bad shape in New York. "Lenny Long will be joining us soon," Ade said. "Just let him—you know, think that he knows what he's talking about. Then later, we'll do the actual deal."

Maw Maw kissed his wife on the cheek. He was so proud of her, he could barely compose himself.

Ginny managed the full outfit this time. Head to toe, he was ready: he was shaven, and his hair was brushed. It was nearing the best time in the world for him. Every footstep that went past his door and every car light that flashed past his window made him more excited. Ginny sat patiently, even though he could hardly sit still. It was his time of the day to be younger, and to not be afraid. He could remember himself as a boy along with the simple things that used to fascinate him.

He didn't care that the people who came into his room wanted him back in his leisurewear. He didn't even answer them—he didn't listen when they tried to talk to him. Ginny sat by the door and waited for days, but nothing came.

So he decided to wait some more.

Lenny pulled his chair up to the table. He was a little starstruck by the champ sitting across from him. He hid his fannishness as best as he could as he shook everyone's hand.

"Looks like you've gone a few rounds yourself, champ," Jinky said to Lenny.

Lenny smiled. "Yeah, I fell down my stairs."

"I love to make people fall down stairs," said Jinky to a round of laughs.

"I know you do," Lenny replied. "It's a pleasure."

"So, what have you got for us, Lenny?" Maw Maw asked.

Lenny took a sip of water and began to compose himself. "I want to do a piece of business with you guys. I want to put the wrestling champion of the world against the boxing champion of the world."

"Obviously this wrestling champion loses, whoever he is," Jinky replied.

"You beat him, yes," Lenny replied.

"How badly, is the question," Jinky said.

"Barely," Lenny said.

Jinky was offended, but Maw Maw held him back by placing a soothing hand on the champ's forearm.

"What Lenny means is that it has to be competitive to a point. That way both sides get something from it," Ade said.

Lenny agreed. "Our guy looks good in defeat—that's what I want. I want people to remember the heroics of our champ. I want him to be talked about and remembered. I don't care if he wins or loses."

"How do we do this?" Maw Maw asked.

Lenny struggled a little with his collar. He was hot. Anxious. "Here's the way I see it," Lenny said. "Each side puts in one hundred thousand. That way, if anyone fucks around, goes into business for themselves, or pulls out the other side, we will at least get paid. We'll bill it as the 'world's first superfight' or 'champion versus champion for pride and legacy.' 'Which is the better sport?'"

"Sport?" Jinky said, laughing, "You guys are calling yourselves a sport?" Jinky's attitude was starting to annoy Lenny. Maw Maw, on the other hand, smelled money—lots of it. With a planned finish, he could get his champ in and out with guaranteed money and no injuries or defeat.

"Have you got a hundred grand?" Ade asked.

Lenny nodded.

"'Cause the last time we met I had to give you money for that suit," she pointed out.

"Do you like it?" Lenny asked.

Ade nodded.

"I've got the money," Lenny reiterated. "And we plan on putting this on closed circuit; selling the rights across the country. Ticket sales alone would be huge," Lenny said.

Maw Maw liked the idea, but felt that he had to lay down the golden rule before anything more was discussed. "I'm just saying this to you now, Lenny: if you or any of your crew tries to go off script in the match, he will kill your boy. I mean it. Don't try to make yourself off the back of our champ."

Lenny replied, "You have my permission to destroy anyone, including *my* champion—if you can—if the match goes bad."

"If I can?" Jinky asked.

Lenny nodded. "If you can."

Jinky and Lenny stared at each other.

"Gentlemen, are we here to talk business, or not?" Ade asked.

"A good wrestler will always destroy a great boxer," Lenny said directly to Jinky's face.

Jinky slammed his fist on the table and stood up to strike. "Are you trying something, boy?"

"No," replied Lenny, calmly.

"You think the few bangs and scrapes you've got on your face make you a fighter?" Jinky asked.

Maw Maw stood in between both men; he could see the money going down the drain. He walked Jinky back a little, and Ade took the distance between both camps as an opportunity to talk to Lenny.

"What the fuck are you doing?" Ade asked.

"They're going to sign," Lenny said.

"Are you trying to get yourself killed?"

Lenny knew what he was doing; he just couldn't tell Ade that. "We need to announce this on our TV next week. Nobody inside the business can know, only us. We'll call a press conference with the boxing press and the wrestling magazines that morning. Our TV will film it."

"Why are you trying to annoy these guys?" Ade asked.

"They're going to sign," Lenny repeated.

"You need to go. I'll finish this off."

Lenny looked over Ade's shoulder. He could see that the meeting was over for him.

"Okay," Lenny said. He stood, fixed his new jacket, and walked away. He purposefully walked away like a man who was disappointed and dejected; but from the front, where he knew they couldn't see him, Lenny looked like a man who had just won the lottery.

"What the fuck was that?" Maw Maw asked Ade as he came back to the table.

"Sit," she said. She was aware that everyone was watching.

"I'm going to follow that jumped-up little prick and beat his ass," Jinky said.

"Listen to me, both of you," Ade said. "This is the measure of where they're at. They're there for the taking. Do you hear me?" Ade tried to get both men to focus.

"I don't know—" Maw Maw said.

"His champion is his own son. He has no experience—he's no problem to us. We can have New York. Do you hear me?" Ade said.

Maw Maw nodded.

"I don't give two fucks about New York," Jinky said. "There's too much to lose, here. We get in bed with these guys, and we look like bums—amateurs."

"Jinky," Ade said, "I found you. I brought you into our deal here, and you became the heavyweight champion of the world. That was for you. This—New York—is for me."

Maw Maw slid his hand over to his wife. "You're right; I'm sorry. Let's show these carnival fucks how to play the three-cup game."

CHAPTER SEVENTEEN

1984.
Thirteen days after Lenny got out.
New York.

Lenny was rolling the dice; he knew he was. He had no real choice, because Ricky wasn't there, the NWC had frozen every wrestler in the country, and his TV station was gone if they couldn't fill the slot.

He was rolling the dice, and he was using his son to do it.

"What are we going for here?" Lenny asked. He and Kid were standing backstage at Madison Square Garden, leaning on the white brick walls. Lenny was wearing the only suit he owned. Before Kid could answer, Lenny spoke again. "What do you say last?" he asked.

"I say, 'He talks too much,'" Kid replied.

"And then what do you do?"

"I've got this," Kid said, turning away.

Lenny spun his boy around by the arm. He was deadly serious. "What do you do after you say 'he talks too much'?"

Kid answered, "I walk off calm, like a killer."

Lenny nodded. "Perfect." He looked at his oldest son. He could tell that he was ready to step up and be champion—ready to make some money. "If this is too much, or too soon, then you let me know," Lenny said.

"What other options do we have?" Kid asked.

Lenny couldn't answer that. They didn't have any other options.

Kid walked to the curtain and waited for his introduction. As soon as Lenny could see that nobody was watching him, he steadied himself against the wall and drew in a long, considered breath.

On the other side of the curtain, Ade stood at a podium. "Ladies and gentlemen," she said. "Thank you for being here for this truly momentous occasion." Ade looked out into the sea of reporters, journalists, and TV cameras. "It is my pleasure, along with Vosbury Promotions and the New York Booking Agency, to present to you today the world's first superfight: boxing versus wrestling, heavyweight champion versus heavyweight champion." Ade's words set off a blanket of flashing lights and mumblings of consultation among the reporters. Several of the more serious boxing writers loudly left their seats in disgust. Everyone else seemed at least willing to find out more. "Let me bring out now, at this time," Ade continued, "Maw Maw Vosbury, the manager of boxing's heavyweight champion of the world."

Ade stepped down from the podium and took a seat to the left. Maw Maw got a polite round of applause when he took her place. "Thank you, thank you," he said, before raising his arms to quiet the room. "Now, I know what some of you are thinking, and I know what some of you have already written on your little pads. But this is going to be the real deal. Two men, at the top of their respective sports, will be looking to find out just who is the best."

Lenny stood behind his boy at the curtain. He wanted to put his hand on his shoulder just to let him know that he was there. "Are you doing okay?" Lenny whispered.

Kid silently nodded and Lenny knew not to press any further. Lenny took a step back and closed his eyes. His heart was beginning to race. His hands were sweaty. He needed to stop this. He couldn't put his son in so much danger.

"Hey," Lenny whispered. But he was distracted from finishing his sentence by the sight of his parole officer standing at the end of the hallway.

"I'll be right back," Lenny said to Kid as he walked off. Lenny wanted to shake off Tad, so he could do his business without being humiliated.

In front of the press, Maw Maw was in full flow. "If that child tries too hard to hurt or incapacitate the real world heavyweight champion on the night—then we'll soon find out just how fake wrestling is. 'Cause let me tell you one thing, ladies and gentlemen, Jinky Keeves ain't going to play games for no man. I hope these wrestling guys know that."

Without warning, Jinky entered from stage left and held his boxing world title above his head. He was supposed to wait to be introduced, but he was going off script. He leaned into Maw Maw's mic. "I feel like I need to apologize," Jinky said. "I need to come out here and say something before the headlines are written and this thing is cast in stone. They came to us and asked for this. I know what record they have and I know what you all think of what they do for a living. But if some guy—any guy—says that he's willing to put down a large amount of money to get beat up by me, the *real* world heavyweight champion, then I'm going to take him on."

Across the city, Joe shouted at his driver. "Cut through the traffic—go around." They were battling the New York congestion to get to the Garden before Lenny put his champion out in front of the world. Lenny made sure that Joe heard what was unfolding, but purposefully left Joe with no real time to be present.

"*Welcome, ladies and gentlemen,*" said the voice on the radio in the car, "*to the announcement of this most unique event. Champion versus champion, boxing versus wrestling.*"

The simplicity of the words coming though the speakers sickened Joe's stomach—but they also lit up the promoter's side of his brain. Joe really had underestimated New York's resolve, especially with

Ricky out of the picture. And he had outright overlooked Lenny. Now he was going to pay for his oversight.

In North Carolina, Tanner lay tubed-up, bruised, and bandaged, but listening intently to the same voice on the radio that Joe heard in his car. Tanner might have been nearly finished, but only a fool would think that a man of his experience playing the game didn't have something left to sting with.

In his small home in Long Island City, Edgar Long sat with his youngest grandson, also listening to the same radio report.

"Do you think Kid is going to win?" Jimmy asked.

"Shh . . ." Edgar replied.

"I'm going to be stronger than Kid when I'm his age," Jimmy said. "I'm going to be able to pick up an elephant and smash it off a Ferris wheel."

"Shh . . ."

Lenny was in the restroom, trying to figure out how to perform his piece of the press conference without Tad seeing him "getting involved."

Kid Devine made his entrance to the stage unannounced, too. Jinky was still running his mouth at the podium as Kid appeared behind him. The young wrestling champion stopped and posed for photographs. This was the first time that the world had taken a good look at him. He was handsome, and very young, but not any smaller than the boxing champ.

"That's right ladies and gentlemen, here's the so-called champion from their side," Jinky said. "Too bad he's going to—"

Kid quickly grabbed Jinky from the side in a head-and-arm choke. The boxer was tied up and couldn't use his fists. The gathered press seemed to collectively roll their eyes at what they thought was a stunt playing out in front of them, but Maw Maw immediately knew it was no stunt. He sprang from his seat. Jinky was struggling and trying to jerk the wrestler from him, but the boxer ultimately had no answer for the predicament that he was in. Kid took Jinky to the ground and Jinky's contorted face and gasps for air quickly made the press think there was something legitimately shocking unfolding in front of them. Maw Maw grabbed Kid by the hair and tried to yank him off of his meal ticket. Lenny appeared through the curtain and tackled Maw Maw to the floor. Lenny and Kid, father and son, collectively fucking over the boxing business side-by-side.

Jinky went limp and Kid released his prone body to the rising sound of cameras clicking and questions being fired from the floor.

"He talks too much," Kid said before leaving the stage.

Lenny followed right behind.

"What do we do now?" Kid asked.

"Run," Lenny said.

In the car, Joe listened with his mouth agape as the news came in live.

"There was an altercation on the stage. The world heavyweight champion of boxing, Jinky Keeves, has been immobilized by Kid Devine, the wrestling champion. The boxer was talking, and the wrestler had enough. This doesn't look to us like a staged wrestling altercation. Mr. Keeves's face turned blue, and when the wrestler released him, the champion boxer was struggling for air. In all my years of covering sports, and particularly the grand sport of boxing, I have never seen anything like it."

Joe conceded it was brilliant. Without money, without any wrestlers, without any help, Lenny Long had made his champion the most talked-about athlete in all of sports.

Jimmy Long sat outside his grandfather's house. He was just about fed up with being left out. He thought that it was time he showed his father just how useful he could be.

Backstage at the Garden, Lenny and Kid were making their way out of there as fast as they could. Not only did Lenny have to watch his back from within the wrestling world—he now had the boxing world looking for his scalp too, plus his parole officer had surely seen him get into a physical altercation in front of the world.

"Lenny!" shouted Ade.

Lenny stopped as she marched toward them. "Keep going," Lenny said to Kid.

Kid waited beside his father.

"He's going to kill your boy in the ring, come time, Lenny." Ade said. "You know that?"

"No he won't, Ade," Lenny replied. "There's no match."

"What?" she said. For every step that Ade took forward, Lenny balanced it out with a step backward.

"The boxer chickened out," Lenny said. "We did everything we could to get him to face our wrestling champion. Everything."

"What the fuck are you talking about?" Ade asked.

"Haven't you heard? The boxing heavyweight champion is scared of us." Lenny fired a magazine from his pocket toward Ade. She had no clue what was going on as she picked it up. On the cover was a full-sized picture of Kid, and a small picture in the bottom corner of Jinky Keeves looking over his shoulder. The headline read: THE KID WHO KILLED BOXING.

This was Lenny's long con. Ade knew that wrestling magazines needed at least a week to turn up on the shelves. This magazine edition was dated for the next day, and it couldn't have been more like wrestling if it tried. In the real world, the wrestler was literally running from the boxer. In the press, however, it was the boxer who, after being legitimately humiliated at the press conference, wouldn't fight.

Lenny knew that by getting to the press first, it meant their side of the story was the correct one. The boxing world was already on the defensive. There was nothing like a four-page story with quotes to get the narrative straight.

"Lenny?" Ade asked. Her face was riddled with confusion and sadness. "What are you doing?"

Lenny turned back. "Fuck you, Ade. Don't you think for a second that I don't know what you did to Ricky."

Lenny and his son left.

CHAPTER EIGHTEEN

1984.
Fourteen days after Lenny got out.
New York.

Lenny got his father to drop him off in midtown. He was embarrassed by the ride, so he asked to be let out a couple of blocks before Benson's. His press conference angle was everywhere, on every paper and every news report, but he still couldn't afford a cab into the city.

"So what you're doing makes you—what?" Edgar asked.

"What?" Lenny replied. He was off in thought and wasn't really tuned in to what Edgar was asking.

"Luke—or Kid—or whatever he calls himself, is your boy. I know that. And Jimmy idolizes you too. I'm asking you to put them first. Put them before this fucking business poisons this whole family top to bottom. Or worse."

Lenny put his hand on his father's shoulder. "I will put my family before anything. I promise. But I can make something for us all. I know I can."

Edgar pulled in where Lenny asked him to. "I can't not . . . be fond of you. You know what I mean. Love you, or whatever. You're my son."

Lenny leaned in and gave Edgar a hug. Edgar patted Lenny awkwardly on the head.

"Here," Edgar said. "Here's something till you have yourself—" Edgar reached into his pocket and gave Lenny a couple of fifty-dollar bills. Lenny thought about putting up a little fight, but he was desperate.

"Thank you, Pop," Lenny said as he took the money and got out of the car.

Edgar drove away and Lenny refocused on the task at hand. He walked two blocks until he saw the red canopy extending out over the sidewalk. Lenny knew of Ben Benson's, but he'd never been in there before. It had been the boss's favorite. And it was where Joe would be.

Lenny wanted to find Joe before Joe found Lenny.

He walked in and was met with a good lunchtime trade. He passed the large PRIME MEATS sign with the bull's head on it and walked to the nice corner table where Joe was sitting with Donta Veal. Before Joe could say anything, Lenny slapped the *New York Times* down on the table. "They're all the same. We got the cover in every newspaper in New York. Every carpenter, cop, postman, and firefighter in the city is talking about us again." Lenny sat down beside Donta, facing Joe. "Nice to see you both again. I now have the most talked-about champion in decades. We both know that he's money. Correct?"

Joe was being outplayed by a rookie boss. But what could he do? He considered his first words carefully. "You're a fucking cunt," Joe said. "And not smart enough to construct something like this yourself."

Donta snorted a little as he sliced up his steak.

"Those boxing guys were pawns to raise our profile," Lenny said. "I've done that. Now it's time to talk about *our* business. We need to do what Danno wanted done: we need to unify our two wrestling heavyweight titles back together tomorrow night."

"That's what I said the other night by the river," Joe replied.

"You make it sound like we had a nice stroll or something, Joe," Lenny said. "Do you mean when you sent this piece of shit to come drag me out of bed? The night that you threatened my life? You mean that night by the river?"

Joe knew that Lenny held all the cards this time; he'd just have to listen and try to get a fair deal for himself in this match. His potential for a national expansion hinged on Joe being able to present a united front.

"Well, things have changed since that night," Lenny said.

"Changed?" Joe asked.

Lenny answered. "Now *I* get eighty percent of the gate, and *my* champ goes over."

"You want eighty percent *and* the win?" Joe asked.

"I don't want anything; that's just what's going to happen," Lenny said. "Eighty percent my way and we get to leave with the unified heavyweight championship of the world."

Joe threw Donta a quick look, telling him to not react.

"Who the fuck do you think you are, all of a sudden?" Joe asked.

Lenny stood up. "It's up to you, Joe, to make sure that this match makes it to the Garden."

Joe popped up out of his seat, too. "Sit the fuck down," he said. He knew that this much interest, money, and—most importantly— publicity in the unification meant that nothing bad could happen. The world was watching New York wrestling once again, and that meant Joe's national TV partner, too. Joe Lapine was caught. Lenny knew it. Joe knew it.

Lenny nodded at Donta, and then at Joe, before leaving the table.

"Lenny, wait," Joe said, following Lenny through the restaurant. "Eighty percent is fine, but you can't have the win."

Lenny stopped and smiled. "I will pay you back every cent you put into New York while I was inside. I'd be grateful to you—if I didn't know you so well."

Lenny walked through the door out into the hectic New York

street. Joe followed. He said, "Lenny, you're willing to screw over Ade Schiller, Maw Maw Vosbury, Tanner Blackwell, and me all in the same move? Come back to the table, and I can protect you."

"You have no choice but to protect me," Lenny said. "Or your house of cards here in New York will all be for nothing. You made yourself the face of this territory when you had no right; now you have no choice but to make sure that it's the cleanest territory in America."

Lenny turned away, but stopped. "Hey Joe," he called back. "Is that spotlight I'm hiding under big enough for you now?"

Lenny was pulling off the greatest act in wrestling history. And Joe was actually starting to believe that he wasn't petrified. "See you in the Garden tomorrow night," Lenny said as he walked away.

Donta stood in the doorway of the restaurant. "Why don't you let me sort this out, once and for all?" he said to his boss.

Joe shook his head. Donta wasn't a finesse kind of guy. Joe needed subtlety, a plan, and more time. But Donta was beginning to get sick of these guys pushing Joe around.

Ginny was wavering badly. He didn't know why they had all his things packed up and by the door; where were they bringing him? Why couldn't he stay in his room?

Where was his ice cream?

"Hello? Where am I going?" he asked a couple of visitors who walked by his door. "Where am I going?" he asked some delivery guys who didn't even look in his direction.

Ginny began to panic; everything was changing. He remembered his suitcase beside him, and remembered having it on the road, going to all the matches and all the towns. He remembered all the great times he had as a proud, professional wrestler—as well as all the great times he'd had with Ricky. He remembered the life they had and how very much he missed him. Ginny cried and wiped his nose. In moments of clarity like this, he knew what was happening to him. There was nothing scarier than knowing that your whole life was being erased, day by day, minute by minute.

Ginny had gone from being a tough, strong, independent man to an old fool who people looked past whenever he spoke.

As quickly as his memories had come back to fill him up, they went away again. "Hello? Where am I going?"

"This way," said an orderly.

Ginny stood and put out his arm for the man to take. He wasn't too sure on his feet anymore and needed the help. The orderly just walked ahead. Ginny shuffled behind him.

"Hello? Where am I going?"

Upstairs, Ginny was shown to his new room, and his new roommates. His bill hadn't been paid, and the nursing home wanted Ginny's prime first-floor room for someone else. He was now on the fourth floor, where all the other forgotten and agitated old people went.

Ginny looked around and saw his future. It scared him. Made him turn. Made him walk as fast as he could back the way he came. He took the stairs down three flights before anyone even knew that he was gone. His heart beat strong in his chest, and as he burst through the front door, he saw that there was nothing or no one there for him. He couldn't see his father or his brother, and the outside didn't look like the street that Ginny had grown up on at all. He was totally confused. In his mind, he was a boy, and this was where he lived. He knew he was a man too, somewhere, though.

"Is Mr. Lennon still alive?" Ginny asked a passing person. Mr. Lennon had taught Ginny how to wrestle. He had taken him from the street, taught him manners, and showed him how to be a man. Ginny noticed that the large gate at the end of the drive was open. "You better mind that the dog doesn't run out under the milk cart. Do you hear me?" Ginny said to no one in particular.

"Hello!" Ginny shouted.

"Wait," came a voice from behind.

Ginny stood still, doing as he was told. He'd forgotten that he was going to bust out of there. He'd forgotten that he had good lungs still. He'd forgotten that he was going back to the fourth floor.

So he waited. And heard a musical horn play.

The Pagladoni's Ice Cream van pulled into a visitor's parking spot.

Ginny might have forgotten a lot of things, but ice cream was still his favorite. "Are you for me?" Ginny wondered to himself. He was overcome with the need to know. "Are you for me?" he said a little louder.

Ginny began to walk toward the van. "Are you for me?"

Carlo Pagladoni walked around the back of his van and pulled out Ginny's favorite ice cream medley.

"Are you for me?" Ginny shouted.

"Of course I am, Ginny," Carlo answered.

"Where I am going?" Ginny asked.

"We're going to get all of this fixed," Carlo said.

"Can I come too? I'll get one of Babu's neckties," Jimmy said, following his father around Babu's spare room.

"Not tonight, buddy," Lenny answered.

"But I want to be there too," Jimmy said.

Lenny slid on the suit jacket that Ade had given him money for. "I know, but you and I will do something tomorrow."

"How can you take one of your children out for dinner, and not the other one?" Jimmy asked. "Isn't that child abuse or something?"

Lenny put on some cologne. "It's business."

"Yeah, the family business, and I'm family."

Lenny stopped what he was doing and paid attention to his youngest son. He could see the frustration and hurt in his boy's face. "You're too young. And you don't need to be around this business—trust me."

"I'm not a child," Jimmy said.

"I'll drop you off at Granddad's before—"

"I don't want to go there," Jimmy said. "I want to go back to Mom's."

Lenny had never heard that from Jimmy before. "Okay."

"I want to go now," Jimmy said.

"You can't."

"I want you to bring me."

"I can't."

"Why not? 'Cause your stupid fucking plan isn't—"

"Hey!"

Jimmy shut his mouth quickly.

"Now, listen to me," Lenny said. "I understand that you're frustrated, Jimmy, but this is nearly all over. Your brother and I have to be seen out in the city," Lenny explained. "We've got a huge match coming up in the Garden tomorrow, and I still have to prove myself—"

Lenny sat on his bed, and patted the space beside him; Jimmy sat defiantly with his back to his father.

"I'm walking a wire here," Lenny said. "And I have to keep my eyes on the finish line for another few days. Then we get paid. Then we are going to do exactly what you want to do." Lenny put his hand on Jimmy's head. "You hear me, son?"

Jimmy reluctantly nodded, but he wasn't totally sold.

Lenny and Jimmy rolled up to Edgar's place in the back of a taxi. Lenny spotted his parole officer's car parked a few doors down from his father's house.

"You can let him out here," Lenny said to the driver.

Jimmy looked up ahead to see what the problem was; he immediately saw what Lenny saw.

"This fucking guy," Lenny said to himself as he looked for his money.

"We should handle him," Jimmy whispered.

Lenny knew that Jimmy was serious. "No, we don't deal with him—we avoid him," Lenny said.

"He's too tight around our necks, Pop," Jimmy said.

Lenny nodded in agreement and kissed his son on the forehead. "If he asks—"

"I know," Jimmy replied. "I know how to avoid an interrogation."

Lenny watched his son walk toward Edgar's house. "Okay," he said to the driver. "Let's go."

As he walked to the house, Jimmy listened for his father's taxi pulling away. When he heard it, he veered toward Tad's car. "Hello," Jimmy said, as he knocked on Tad's window. The parole officer had been making little cheese and cracker treats for himself that went flying at Jimmy's appearance out of nowhere. Jimmy opened the door and let himself into the passenger's seat.

"Can I do something for you?" Tad asked.

"You want to catch my dad, don't you?" Jimmy asked. Tad shook his head. "Then what are you doing here all the time?" Jimmy said.

"I have the right to be where I want to be. Do you understand that?" Tad asked, picking a little cheese square from his shirt.

"I know what he's doing that he shouldn't be doing," Jimmy said.

"Really?" Tad replied.

"Yeah," Jimmy said. "He doesn't flush after he takes a shit, you pig, bacon asshole," Jimmy said as he got out of the car laughing. He stopped, returned, and opened Tad's door again. "You come around here again, and I'll tell the chief of police that you stuck your little finger in my ass just now."

Tad couldn't hide the horror on his face. Jimmy slammed the door again. He decided that he couldn't have done a finer job.

The Holland Hotel on 42nd Street was where Babu and Danno used to eat. So it was where Lenny and Kid met. They needed to look like they owned the city—like they were at the top of the tree. The truth was that both of them could barely afford to be inside the doors. Lenny had some money his father had given him, and Kid had a few bucks saved that he'd wanted to bring home to his mom. In the wrestling business, though, perception was everything. If they wanted to be treated like somebodies, then they had to go where all the somebodies went.

"Do you think you'll want dessert?" Lenny asked, as he looked at the menu and ran some math in his head. They had just been seated, but Lenny was already afraid of the bill.

"I just want to hear what we have to talk about," Kid answered. Lenny understood; he couldn't expect things between them to turn around in under a couple of weeks.

"What way do you see this match going?" Lenny asked.

"Whatever way you tell me it goes," Kid replied.

"Well, we have a lot more freedom now because of the awesome job you did at the press conference."

"You really think these guys are going to let that slide?" Kid asked.

"You know what I was taught when I first started in this business? That the greatest shield you have against all the snipers in the long grass is success. You are kept around and alive as long as you can make money." Lenny put out his hand for his son to slap. Kid didn't move. "Well," Lenny said. "We're fucking money."

"Am I winning, or am I doing the job?" Kid asked.

"We make the call on that now," Lenny said. "I want you to keep your belt and get his, too. The money is in keeping you front and center. You're the one in the papers; you're the one who people are talking about. Did you hear that the Garden is sold out?"

Kid didn't seem to care one way or another. "Okay."

"I know it's going to take time for us to work out—" Lenny stopped and waited for Kid to finish the thought. He wanted a sign that they were on the same page.

Kid leaned into the conversation for the first time. "I don't hate you. I don't love you. I just know that I don't need you in my personal life. You're my boss, or whatever fucked-up thing this is. I don't even know what's happening."

Lenny was just glad that his son was at least talking, even if he was saying things that were hard to hear. "What do you mean you don't know what's happening?" Lenny asked.

Kid sipped his water and thought about whether he even wanted to talk this out or not. "One minute, Ricky and Babu are afraid of what you're going to do if you find me in the wrestling business, and now you're like a pushy stage mom with me."

Lenny smiled. "A stage mom?"

Kid tried not to smile back. "You heard me."

"Can I get you gentlemen started with some drinks?" asked the pretty waitress.

"I'll just have water," Lenny said.

"Whiskey sour, please," Kid said.

Lenny was going to intervene, but he kept his mouth shut. If the champ was anyone other than his son, he'd be encouraging him to drink like a man. He wasn't anyone else, though—he *was* his son. That was what made all of this so hard. "We're going to go twelve minutes, bell to bell," Lenny said. "You're going over. You're both going to get color."

Lenny could see on Kid's face he wasn't sure what that meant.

"You're going to win the match, and unify the titles. Both of you are going to *blade*," Lenny said running a pretend razor across his forehead. "You'll be the undisputed heavyweight wrestling champion of the world."

Kid looked annoyed at Lenny explaining the wrestling terms, as if he knew what he had meant the first time.

"I want you to meet Babu tomorrow in the Garden to run through your match before anyone else gets there," Lenny said. "He's going to take you through it."

Kid was totally fine with all of that; it was all that he needed to hear. Both of their drinks were left in front of them. "I'll be right back to take your order," said the smiling waitress.

"Thank you," Lenny and Kid said together.

Lenny raised his glass. "To family." His toast made Kid sick to his stomach.

"Are we done?" Kid asked, without joining the toast.

"Done?" Lenny said.

"I gotta go," Kid replied.

Lenny was confused as to what he had said or done to make his son want to leave. "I'm trying here—"

Kid buttoned up his coat at the table. "I don't need you to try," he said. "I don't need you, period. This is a match that I'm going to be allowed to win. They'll pay me, and I'll bring that home to Mom. That's it. You and I are only bound by a con—something that's not real. And that's very fitting." Kid got up from the table and threw a twenty down.

"Where are you going?" Lenny asked.

"To get drunk." Kid walked through the busy restaurant as the other diners tried to figure out if he was the young man from the papers.

Lenny looked at his watch and wondered if his backup was in town yet.

1984.
Five days after Lenny got out.
Tokyo.

Mr. Asai looked like an Asian movie star. He wore a perfectly pressed black suit with a red handkerchief in his top pocket. His white shirt was supplemented by a white silk scarf draped over his neck. He was followed by Masa Kido, the English-speaking referee, who struggled to keep up with his boss. Masa was covered in dried blood.

"Where is he?" Mr. Asai asked in Japanese.

"He's up on your right in a private room, sir," Masa answered him, also in Japanese.

"How did this happen?"

"I don't know, sir."

"Find me whoever did this," Mr. Asai demanded.

"We've got the person who did this," Masa replied.

They arrived at the room. Mr. Asai waited for Masa to open the door and escort him inside. It was a pretty simple affair with some monitors, a couple of tubes, and a semiconscious Ricky Plick.

"Is he able to speak yet?" Mr. Asai asked.

"Yes, sir."

Mr. Asai walked closer and looked intently at Ricky's eyes. He wanted them to open. "Does anyone know he's here?"

"No," Masa replied. "We brought him in under covers, and through the service elevator."

"Keep it this way," Mr. Asai said. "Only you and I know, until we figure out what's happening here."

Mr. Asai knew that this had been more than a random attack. Ricky had been just about to go back to the US to insert himself into the septic web that covered New York. This was a business hit, and Mr. Asai wanted to make sure that he was on the right side of that business. He respected Ricky and had enjoyed doing business with him for many, many years. Mr. Asai didn't want the stigma of having a big name in the business die in his territory—especially without his permission.

"Who dares to come here and involve me in this?" Mr. Asai asked.

Masa didn't know who had done it, but he felt sorry for whoever it was.

"*Kimi ni kono koto wo shita yatsu ga watashi ni mo onaji koto wo shita. Aitsu ha hoka no otoko no ryouiki ni kotowari nashi ni ippo fumiire, sara ni hito wo koroshita. Sono koto wo aitsu ni zettai koukai sasete yaru,*" Mr. Asai said, when he saw Ricky open his eyes.

Mr. Asai nodded to Ricky and left.

"What did he say?" Ricky asked Masa.

"He said: 'The person who did this to you did this to me, too. They will learn that you can't step into another man's territory and spill blood—not without asking, and not without permission.'"

Ricky couldn't help but smile. "I need you to contact someone for me."

"Certainly. Who is it?"

Ricky would usually be wary of answering such a question, but Masa had just saved him from dying. There was nothing for him to worry about.

"Lenny Long. We need to keep that territory alive."

"Hello?" Jimmy said into the phone.

"Hello," Ricky said. He was still weak, and his voice sounded weird to Jimmy.

Edgar stood up from watching the TV and looked over at his grandson. "Who is it?"

"It's Mom," Jimmy lied.

Edgar sat down and went back to his guilty pleasure on TV: *The Young and the Restless.*

"Jimmy, where's your father?" Ricky asked.

After everything that had happened, Ricky knew that Lenny was too new to have picked sides. Ricky wanted to call Babu, but he knew that Babu had made a deal with Joe Lapine. The only one who had power and seemed uncompromised was Lenny.

"He's not living here no more," Jimmy said.

"I want you to write this down for me, and take it to him. No one else can know, you hear me?" Ricky said.

"Yes, Uncle Ricky. I saw a frog today." Jimmy whispered.

"Did you?" Ricky replied.

"Yeah," Jimmy said.

"Did he have a lady pig with him?"

"What?"

Ricky was terrible with children. "Nothing. Get a pen. Now, I don't want you to ask any questions, just write exactly what I say, okay?"

"Okay," Jimmy said.

"Tell your father I'm dead, and I want him to go with Ade."

"What?"

"Just write it and give it to him. I'm going to give you a number, too," Ricky said.

"How are you dead?"

Ricky drew a sore breath. "Did you write it?"

"That rhymes," Jimmy said.

"What? What rhymes?"

"Oh, nothing," Jimmy replied, after reading it again to himself. "I thought 'dead' and 'Ade' rhymed."

"Just take it to him, and leave your father my number here. You got that?"

Jimmy nodded, even though Ricky couldn't see it.

There was booming bass, a disco ball, a soaring chorus, and a collection of people who were all feeling it as they danced and intertwined like a stew of denim jackets and shoulder pads. Synth pop and saxophone riffs could be heard, along with dance tracks and catchy ballads. They were in a brownstone building that was once a church but had been transformed. The Limelight was the hottest club in New York. And in the middle of the euphoria was world heavyweight wrestling champion Kid Devine. He started out cool, keeping to himself in the corner. As the drinks rolled in and the night wore on, Kid wanted some recognition. Half of the world thought that he was the toughest man on the planet, and the other half thought he was a sneaky fuck who took people down from behind.

Luke Long was neither of those things, but his wrestling persona, Kid Devine, might have been both.

With each song, and each hour, he moved closer to the center of the floor, where he was also becoming more recognizable. People around him began to wonder if he was the guy who had choked out Jinky Keeves the day before. Kid hardly noticed; he was now with a woman who refused to be ignored. She was beautiful and blonde, with a dancer's body. She was someone Kid had no hope of getting without his newfound fame. She was also the woman Donta Veal liked to use to soften up his kills. She was the same woman who had drugged Mickey Jack Crisp before he was killed. And she was all over Kid.

Donta wasn't listening to his boss; he was trying to end this his own way.

"Where do you live?" the blonde lady asked Kid.

"What?" he replied, trying to hear her over the music.

She nodded toward the doorway, and now Kid knew what she wanted. He smiled and took her outstretched hand. They walked to the exit, but the blonde woman was stopped just before they made it outside.

"Move it," Ade said to her.

"Excuse me?" Donta's blonde accomplice replied.

"Get the fuck out of here," Ade said, "before I have you separated into ten different trash bags."

The blonde woman knew enough to not draw attention to herself. She let go of Kid's hand and slipped out before anything else happened.

"What do you want?" Kid asked Ade. She slapped him across his face and ushered him into a corner.

"That was fair," Kid said. Ade slapped him again. "And give that one to your father, when you see him."

"Now, two free ones are all you get," Kid said with a drunken smile.

"You think I'm flirting with you?" Ade asked. "You've got a lot to learn about this business." She opened the exit door with her foot. Kid shook his head. "No thanks," he told her. Ade looked around. No one in the whole building cared about what they were doing in the corner, and the deafening music made sure that no one could hear, even if they wanted to.

"Okay, so whose idea was it?" she asked.

Kid just shrugged. "I don't come up with the plans. I don't know what to say to you."

"I do—I know what you can say to me," she said.

"Oh yeah? What's that?"

"That you're going to bring the belt to me in Madison Square Garden tomorrow night."

Kid laughed at her suggestion. "And why would I do that?" he asked.

"Because you know that your father hasn't got what it takes to make it to the end of this without fucking it up. When he does fuck it up, that just means that you and your family will go back to square one."

Kid took a big drink before replying. "With everything I've been told about this business, if I was in trouble I'd never even know about it."

"So you think Lenny can take this huge deal all the way to the finish?" Ade asked.

Kid couldn't answer her question.

"Didn't think so. Let's go," Ade said.

"Why?"

"You're the goddamn champion of the world. Don't you think that when some half-drunk gorilla in here hears that, he'll be looking to smash your head in for a high-five from his pals?" Ade said.

"I can look after myself," Kid replied.

"No, that's your gimmick. Your wrestling persona is very well able to handle himself, but right now, you're a drunk fool who's too exposed out here."

"What do you care?" he asked.

Ade leaned into his ear. "One way or another, I'm going to make my money back off you. Let's go."

Kid accepted her invitation.

CHAPTER NINETEEN

1984.
Fifteen days after Lenny got out.
New York.

Babu looked around and soaked in the memories. He had once been the reigning champion and had sold out that same building month after month. Now the torch had truly been passed. He knew this would be his last time standing in that ring. He just wished that he knew where Ricky was, so he could see it, too.

"Tonight's the night, Kid." Babu said, as he stood in the ring in Madison Square Garden. Kid rolled under the bottom rope and stood in the middle of the ring too. "A champion doesn't roll his way into the ring," Babu said. "A champion takes the steps, wipes his feet on the apron, and enters through the ropes—slowly. Make your opponent wait tonight. Fuck him; you're the real champion."

Kid didn't look so good. Babu saw the roughness around his eyes, the paleness in his face. "You doing okay?" he asked.

Kid nodded.

"Any shit in your bag today?" Babu asked.

"Not yet."

Babu was happy to hear it. "That's progress," he said. "The more they see that it's not having an effect on you, the sooner they'll stop dumping on your stuff."

"I just want to be one of the Boys," Kid said.

His energy levels weren't exactly inspiring Babu. "Well," the giant said. "The whole business will be looking at you tonight. Do well, and they'll open their arms to you. They already begrudgingly like you for the way you handled the press conference."

Kid was shifty; something was wrong. Babu thought it was nerves. "When the rest of the boys come back," Babu said, "you shake every one of their hands and look them in the eyes. Even though you're on top. I want to hear you in the dressing room asking about the house and the payoffs."

Kid understood some of what Babu was saying, but not all. The giant explained, "Asking about the house is asking how many tickets have been sold, and the payoffs are going to be what they are, but it's nice for the champ to ask that for the boys who don't have that political clout back there, okay?"

"Yes, sir," Kid replied. By now he was actively avoiding eye contact with Babu.

"Now we don't have much time," Babu said. "So I want to get you off on the right foot." He circled the young champion. "Now, lock up with me," he said.

Kid snapped out his arms and grabbed Babu's giant shoulder on one side and his elbow on the other.

Babu broke away. "Are you trying to dance?"

"No."

"When you lock up, you grab," Babu said. "Let me see the struggle on your face; dig your feet into the ground, snap those arms out, and get into it. Don't let any daylight in—snug is good."

Babu and Kid locked up again.

"Much better," Babu said. "Now, I want you to listen to the ref tonight. You're the heel, so you're supposed to lead the match.

Leave that to Emmet, though: he'll tell you what spot to do next. If he doesn't call any spots that make you look good, then he's trying to fuck you over." Kid bounced up and down. His juices were starting to flow.

"What's your finish?" Babu asked.

"I—I don't have one. All I know is that I'm down to win."

"You need a finishing move that will pop the audience—something young and flashy, like you are. Actually, you already have one."

"The choke?"

"Exactly," Babu said. "The audience has already seen you use it, and win with it, too. They know it's devastating."

Babu noticed that Kid's eyes were suddenly distracted by someone walking in from the darkness of the arena. The giant turned to look and saw his wife standing there. Her presence made his stomach churn. He knew by her face that something was wrong.

"I'll be right back," he said. He slowly left the ring and limped over to his wife.

"You okay?" he asked her.

"Yeah, I'm fine. Just—"

"What is it?" Babu asked.

"Just—it's nothing," she said. "I don't even like saying it, but there's this guy who came around to work last week. He's kind of creepy. Well, he followed me home today, too."

Babu noticed blood on Ava's leg. "What happened?" he asked her.

"I—can you bring me home? He—"

"He what?" the giant asked.

"It's—nothing. I had to jump out of this guy's way. He said that he wanted you to know he was around."

Babu got the message loud and clear.

After Babu left, Kid Devine sat in the front row of an empty Madison Square Garden. He thought about his match that was coming up, and how it would play out. He thought about his father, the wrestling business, the threats, and how all that would play out too.

He heard footsteps on the risers behind him.

"Let me smarten you up," said the voice in the darkness.

In wrestling, this phrase meant everything. A veteran saying those words to a rookie was a passing of the torch; a sign that you'd been truly accepted in the wrestling business. It involved a lot of trust—a lot of faith that the person learning would take on the old traditions, the proper way of doing things. That they would protect the secrets of the wrestling business.

On this night, the rookie knew the voice of the person that was sitting about twenty rows back. Only the ring was lit, so Kid could only make out a silhouette in the stands.

"Can we let the people in?" a staff member shouted. "They're starting to go crazy out there."

"No," the man in the stands replied. "A few more minutes."

Kid stood up and leaned against the apron of the twenty-by-twenty red, white, and blue ring. He tried to look beyond the lights. "Why don't you come down here and show me something, old man?" he said. "It's been a while."

The man in the stands struck a match for his cigarette, and Kid caught a glimpse of his pained, pale face. "You okay?" Kid asked.

"I'm fine," the man answered. He took a pull from his cigarette. "Now, there's only four basic parts to a wrestling match: the Shine, the Heat, the Comeback, and the Finish. The Shine is where our hero starts off well, and wins a couple of small, early victories to get the crowd excited. They paid good money, so give them what they want." He took another pull and continued.

"To start with."

Kid moved to jump the barrier. "You can stay where you are," the man in the stands said. Kid reluctantly stayed where he was, but he had no idea why he couldn't go see his mentor.

"The second part of the match is the Heat," the man said.

"I know this stuff," Kid replied.

The man continued regardless. "And the Heat is where it begins to go wrong for our hero," the man said. "The heel sees an opportunity to win, and he takes it. It's the part of the match that the audience decides whether the babyface hero is worth supporting or not."

"Seriously, man. What are you doing up there? I can't see you," Kid said.

"This part of the match is when bad things happen to good people." The man stood and walked very slowly and feebly down the steps toward the ring.

"What's the matter with you?" Kid asked.

"And, of course, the Comeback is when the babyface decides that he's not having any more," the man said. "He finds a reserve of strength, tenacity, and passion to lift himself off the ground and fucking fight like a man. This should drive the crowd wild. It should lift them to somewhere higher—to some kind of belief that we can all do that, if we're pushed hard enough." The shadowy mentor dropped his cigarette on the floor and stomped it out with his foot.

"I'm going to start letting these people in now," the front-of-house manager shouted from the opening door.

"The hero can never give up during the Comeback phase," the man said. "Never."

The man in the stands stood in the light. It was Ricky Plick, sore, beaten up, and severely weakened.

"What happened to you?" Kid asked as he hopped the railing.

"The Finish can happen out of anywhere," Ricky said. "And our finish is happening now."

Kid was at his side now. Ricky could see that the boy was preoccupied by his frail condition, that he wasn't really listening. "I'm fine, Kid," Ricky said. "Someone nearly got me, is all. Now, I want you to listen to me." Ricky grabbed Kid by both sides of his head. "The finish can happen suddenly," he said. "If not, it can be seen from a mile away. Whatever finish you have lined up for tonight, change the fucking thing back."

"What?" Kid said. Ricky and the young champion could hear the stampede of excited fans enter the arena doors.

"You change the finish back to what you and your father discussed," Ricky said. "And then you keep yourself one hundred fucking miles away from Ade. You hear me?"

Kid wanted to make his own mind up. He knew what he wanted to do—he knew what was right for business.

"You see that world heavyweight title on your shoulder? I once picked that out of a grave," Ricky whispered. "People have done awful things to each other for that title. Don't make yourself one of them."

Jimmy dialed, let the phone ring twice, and hung up. Then he called again; just like Lenny had asked him to do. Lenny immediately answered, just like he said he would.

"Jimmy?" Lenny said.

"Pop?"

"Jimmy, what's wrong?" Lenny asked. He could tell straight away that his boy sounded scared.

"I need your help," Jimmy said.

Lenny Long was standing in Babu's hallway, just about ready to go to Madison Square Garden. He was dressed in his one suit and nice leather shoes that Ava had found him in a thrift store.

Jimmy Long was standing in Pizza Pizza, just about ready to get out of there—except he couldn't. The place was locked up and Jimmy wasn't exactly in there as a customer. He was dressed in black and wearing a ski mask.

"I'm in big trouble, Pop." Jimmy said.

Lenny looked at his watch as he quickly closed Babu's door. He was going to be late for his own card. He had to somehow get to Long Island City and back to the Garden again in time for the matches.

He began to run up the alley until he saw Tad Stolliday parked up ahead. Lenny looked behind him. There were no other real choices. If Lenny didn't face Tad now, he knew he would have to face him in the Garden in front of everyone.

Tad saw Lenny approach his car from the alley. He quickly got out of his car, even though Lenny was walking directly toward him.

"What do you want?" Lenny asked.

"Do you want me to conduct a piss test?" Tad replied.

Lenny knew he'd be clean, but he was more than aware of the time it would take to clear his name. Time he didn't have. "No," Lenny said, then with a little more softness in his voice, "I'm sorry."

Tad looked Lenny up and down. "You going somewhere nice?"

Lenny could see that Tad was willing to wait all night. He had some sandwiches packed, and a tall flask. "You know where I'm going," Lenny said. "I even called your office today to make sure that it was cool."

Tad pretended not to know what Lenny was talking about. "Oh, the wrestling match in the Garden?"

Lenny was losing time and patience. "Yes."

"Oh," Tad said, leaving a huge pause. "Okay, then." Lenny wasn't sure if that was his cue to leave. "Why don't you hop in, and I'll drive you there?" Tad said.

"Eh—I have to go to—my old man's house, first. I want to walk into the Garden with him," Lenny said. He had no intention of going to Edgar's, but he wanted to shake his parole officer off so he could get to Jimmy.

Tad said, "Jump in. You can have a sandwich and some peach tea."

Lenny couldn't believe his fucking luck. He knew there was no point in trying to argue. No point in trying to run. He got in and watched as Tad drove at precisely the speed limit in the direction of his father's house. Lenny knew time was ticking. His youngest son was in real trouble, and his oldest son was on the verge of the biggest match of his life.

Kid opened his gear bag slowly. There was nothing unexpected waiting for him. It seemed that he had earned enough respect from the returning roster to at least have his gear shit-free. As he stripped down and took out his boots, Kid ran through all the scenarios in his head. He knew that Ricky was out there, and so was Ade. Lenny promised him that he'd be in the crowd, too. But what would make the most impact, and the most money? He could go with the script, and become the undisputed champion—and the face of wrestling. But was that what he wanted? He could also call an audible in the ring, changing the script. He could lose, slink away from the business, and live his life. He was sure that he'd be well compensated by the other side for doing so.

As Ade said, did Kid think that Lenny had it in him to run the play all the way to the finish?

As Kid put on his gear, he didn't know.

Lenny knew that as soon as he was dropped off at his father's place, Tad would simply follow him. They were getting close, and Lenny needed to get his boy out of trouble and then speed his way to the Garden. By his watch, he knew the card had already started.

Tad was still obeying every light and every speed limit. Lenny sat in the passenger seat holding Tad's peach tea and an uneaten sandwich, at Tad's insistence.

"How do you think I should react to the shit you pulled at the press conference the other day?" Tad asked.

"You follow all your case load around this much?" Lenny asked.

"Are you getting lippy with me?"

Lenny knew he had to back down, figure another way to get himself away from Tad. "It was an act," Lenny said.

"An act?"

"Yeah, I know you won't tell anyone this but, what we do sometimes is for show. Like a play."

Tad enjoyed having power over someone who was now in power.

He saw Lenny's face everywhere in the press, and got off on the fact that he could make Lenny jump as high as Tad wanted him to jump.

"So it's fake?" Tad asked.

"You know, I said that once too," Lenny said. "And a good man slapped the living shit out of me for it."

"Sounds like a threat," Tad said.

Lenny shook his head. They pulled onto Edgar's street.

"Did you try it?" Tad asked.

Lenny wasn't listening; he was too busy planning how he was going to get out of there.

"Did you try my hospitality?" Tad asked again, elbowing Lenny back to the present. "Eat. Drink something."

Lenny unscrewed the flask and watched whatever was in there slosh around as they came closer to Lenny's father's house. As the car brushed the curb, Lenny dropped the flask into Tad's lap.

"What the hell?" Tad said.

"I'm sorry; butterfingers," Lenny replied.

Tad's crotch and torso were soaked: a perfect reason for Tad to go home, Lenny thought.

"Your father won't mind if I—" Tad got out of his car.

Lenny knew that Edgar had no idea they were coming. "Hey," Lenny said as he followed Tad toward Edgar's house. "I have to get—to the Garden. I just noticed the time."

"We've got time," Tad said.

We? Lenny thought.

Tad opened Edgar's front door, like he lived there. Lenny wanted to crack Tad's fucking head open right there and then.

Tad waddled down the hallway. "Is the bathroom this way?"

Lenny could only nod and go into the house himself. He entered the living room to look for Edgar as Tad took his pants off in the bathroom. Edgar entered his kitchen from the back door, visibly a little shaken.

"What's the matter, Pop?" Lenny asked.

"I—Jimmy is—I can't find him," Edgar said. "He was right here about an hour or so ago. Then he said that he was going down to Mrs. Cullimore's house to clean her windows. He's been doing that—for pocket money."

"Dad," Lenny said, "I know where he is."

"He's with you?" Edgar asked.

"Not exactly."

Edgar heard a noise coming from his bathroom. "Is that him?"

Lenny shook his head. "You have to help me."

Edgar's fear turned to anger. "What did you do?"

"I need your help," Lenny said. "Jimmy is in trouble."

Edgar stopped. So did Lenny.

"What kind of trouble?" Edgar asked.

"He got himself into something, but I'm going to get him out of it. Now, listen to me: my fucking parole officer is following me every-where. He can't see where I'm about to go, or what I'm about to do."

Edgar looked weak as he heard more.

"Pop, Jimmy is fine," Lenny said, not knowing if that was the truth or not. "I just need to help him now. Can you contain this asshole?"

Edgar needed a second to think. "I don't know who's in my house."

Lenny answered, "It's—"

Edgar interrupted his son. "*I don't know who's in my house.*"

Lenny thought for a second, until it hit him. "Perfect," he said, with a big grin on his face.

"Lenny," Edgar added. "Don't let anything happen to the boy."

Lenny gave his father an assuring nod as he raced out of his house. Jimmy was a couple of blocks away; it would be faster to run. Edgar took his shotgun out of his cupboard. He would use it to contain his home invader. After all, Edgar hadn't given anyone permission to enter his house.

It would at least take a while to clean up any confusion. Time enough for Lenny to do what he needed to do.

Lenny ran around the block in his leather shoes. He kept to the shadows—he didn't want anyone to explain to the cops that they saw a man in a suit right about the time a crime was committed. Lenny ran as fast as he could, but he had no idea what he was running toward. When he came face to face with Pizza Pizza, he slowed down and composed himself a little. Better to take a second and figure out a clean plan than to rush in and make matters worse.

He looked at his watch. He had less than an hour until the main event.

Lenny walked up to the front windows and could see what he presumed was his son, still wearing a ski mask, crouched down under a table. Jimmy could hardly contain his joy at seeing his father.

Lenny took another quick look around before pointing to the door and shrugging. Jimmy had no clue what Lenny was doing.

"Where?" Lenny mouthed.

Jimmy cupped his ear. Lenny knew that this was a bad idea. If he was even caught looking in the window of a place that had been broken into, Lenny knew that he would be heading back inside.

"Fucking where?" Lenny mouthed a little more clearly this time.

Jimmy put up his hands in question.

"Where did you get in?!" Lenny shouted.

Jimmy pointed up, and Lenny pointed up to clarify. Jimmy nodded. Lenny walked away from the window toward the alley at the side of the restaurant. He listened carefully for any squad cars or beat cops that might have been called out already. As he walked down the lane a little further, he could see the ladder that Jimmy was "cleaning windows" with, perched against the wall. Lenny used it, as his son had used it, to climb up onto the flat roof of the pizza place below. He stooped low and ran toward the skylight, which was smashed through with a brick.

From the roof, Lenny could see Jimmy's eyes through the ski mask looking back at him.

"Pop!" Jimmy shouted.

Lenny shushed him. "I'm going to get you out," he whispered.

Jimmy froze and looked to his left, toward the main window where Lenny had just been. "Pop?"

"What is it?" Lenny asked.

Jimmy paused. "A cop."

"What?" Lenny said.

Jimmy whispered. "There's a cop looking at me through the window." Just as Jimmy spoke, his head became illuminated by the cop's flashlight.

"Pop?" said the boy as he ran to hide somewhere else.

Lenny could then hear the rattle of the front door as the officer tried to gain access to the restaurant.

"Police! Stay where you are," the cop shouted.

Lenny ran, grabbed the ladder, and pulled it up onto the roof with him. He marched the ladder over to the broken skylight.

"I don't want to go away," Jimmy said. His voice was shaking with fear.

"You're not going anywhere," Lenny said. "Where is he?"

"I don't know," Jimmy replied.

"Can you see him outside?" Lenny asked.

"No."

Lenny needed to know for sure before he dropped the ladder into the building. He carefully went to the roof's edge that overlooked the alley. He could hear the nasal sound of a police radio just below him.

"I need backup, over," the cop said below.

They had no more time to fuck around. Lenny sprinted back to the skylight and slid the ladder down to his son.

"Go! Now, now, now," Lenny said. But there was nothing below; no eyes looking back at him. All Lenny could hear was the crying sounds of a trapped boy.

"Jimmy?" Lenny called.

There was no answer.

"Jimmy, I will whup you for the first time in your life if I have to call you again."

The boy was frozen in fear. Lenny wasn't sure where the cop was, but he knew he needed to act now. "Fuck it," Lenny said as he clambered down into the building. He pulled his suit jacket over his head as his new shoes touched down on the floor below. He waved Jimmy out from under the table where he was crouched.

Seeing his father's face jolted a terrified Jimmy to run toward him. Lenny lifted his boy and placed him as high up the ladder as he could. Lenny's heart was thumping. He knew he had so much to lose. As he put his own foot on the bottom rung, the cop from outside began to bang on the glass.

"Hey," he shouted. "Police!"

Jimmy wasn't up and out yet, but Lenny had to start climbing anyway. The cop kicked the door a couple of times before firing a shot through the glass that actually made Jimmy scream. "Hurry!" Lenny shouted as Jimmy dragged himself up the last few rungs. Lenny made it about halfway before the cop grabbed his foot. His shoe popped off and Lenny made another three or four rungs before the tenacious cop grabbed his other ankle. Lenny looked down and tried to cover his face with his arm; he needed to see the police officer to land a good, stiff kick. Both men's eyes locked, and the cop began taking the rungs one by one. He was not giving up in the struggle. Lenny could feel his arms weakening under the weight and the struggle of both men. He looked up and saw the panic in Jimmy's eyes. They both knew that below Lenny was at the end of the road. The last time they'd see each other with Lenny being a free man. The cop had made his way to Lenny's waist now and both son and father could tell the fight was coming to an end.

"Fight," Jimmy shouted. "Fight back."

Lenny instinctively threw a back elbow that hit something. The cop stumbled down a few rungs.

"Keep fighting," Jimmy roared. He could see the cop reaching for his gun with one hand and holding onto his father with the other.

"Now!" Jimmy shouted.

Lenny stomped down and his shoeless foot slid off the mark a couple of times before Lenny landed a good solid shot to the police officer's face that knocked him flat to the ground. Lenny threw his hand up to the highest rung he could grab and pulled himself hand-over-fist toward his boy. He powered himself to the roof and hoisted the ladder up in time to get out of there.

As Lenny and Jimmy stumbled away, Lenny wondered how much of his face the cop had seen, and if they could get anything on him from the shoe he lost in the struggle.

Lenny carried the ladder on his shoulder as they moved across the neighborhood by rooftop. He was now pretty sure that he had been seen—but not a hundred percent sure. Jimmy suddenly stopped and hugged Lenny tighter than Lenny had ever been hugged before.

"I'm sorry," Jimmy said.

"It's okay, son," Lenny replied.

"I've messed everything up," Jimmy said. "I was trying to make some money, too, like you and Kid are doing. He owed us. But when I jumped down, I hurt myself and I couldn't find anything to get back up again. I thought I was going to jail. I don't want to go to jail."

Lenny looked back to make sure that no one was coming up on them. "It's okay, son," Lenny said as he kissed his son's head. He had just enough time to get to the city and take his place in the front row at the Garden.

Lenny had come a long way since he'd started in the wrestling business as a green kid selling programs.

Lenny and Jimmy used the ladder to get back to the street. Lenny took off his other shoe and buried it in a trash pile. They could both hear the sounds of patrol cars in the distance as Lenny looked once more at his watch. He ditched the ladder over a hedge, took his son by the hand, and hailed a cab.

"What are you doing?" Jimmy asked.

Lenny didn't know what he was doing. He couldn't send Jimmy back to Edgar's because he didn't know what was happening there.

He couldn't take him to the Garden with him because he had no idea just how safe it might or might not be.

"How far is your house?" Lenny asked.

"My actual house?" Jimmy said.

"Can you get there by taxi?" Lenny asked.

"Will you come with me?" Jimmy said.

Lenny put out his hand to get the next cab.

On the sixth floor, at the end of the corridor, Babu was ready to go through the door again if he had to. Joe must have known that too, because the newly fitted door had been left open.

"Come in," Joe said when he saw the raging giant in his doorway.

Babu walked into the room where Joe was sitting in his plush chair. The matches were on the TV in the corner of the room.

"You owe me for the door," Joe said. "And for the fucking territory, too."

"Are you threatening my wife?" Babu asked.

"What?"

"Your little servant—" Babu grabbed Joe by his collar and hoisted him out of his chair. The pain of lifting Joe stunned Babu for a second, but the giant didn't have the patience for a cat-and-mouse scenario. "Are you trying to tell me something, Joe?"

"I didn't send him to do any such thing," Joe replied.

Babu sensed that Joe was telling the truth. He loosened his hold.

"You're the one who's been lying and stalling me—treating me like a fucking mark instead of the chairman," Joe said. "If you had delivered what you said at the beginning of all of this, you wouldn't have to be worrying about anyone, you giant-sized fuckup." Joe removed Babu's hands from his collar. "You would have all had a job here, and you would have all been well paid. Now look at the place. Falling apart. Again!" Joe had a great view of the city from his window. He could almost see all of the angles in which the territory could be taken.

"You said that no one would get hurt," Babu said.

"And I meant it."

"So what about Ricky?" Babu shouted.

Joe was so incensed that he rushed Babu this time. "He's fucking dead! It happened in some dirty, shitty road in Tokyo."

Babu grabbed Joe with more force than before, but this time he grabbed him around his neck. Within seconds, Joe was about at his breaking point: his eyes were bulging. Behind Babu, Donta sneaked in from the adjoining room with a baseball bat cocked over his shoulder.

"Why did you do it?" Babu asked, tears sliding down his face. Babu knew Ricky's attack was on his huge hands, too. He had been the one who broke the deal with Joe. "You should have taken it out on me. It was my deal—I fucked you around. Do you hear me? Do you hear me?" Babu shouted.

Donta smashed Babu across the right Achilles with such force that he was sure he'd broken Babu's leg and torn up his ankle. The giant roared in pain as he hit the ground. Joe collapsed. Donta came down across Babu's head and face twice more with the bat. Bones crunched. Donta then hammerfisted down onto Babu's huge skull, causing thick, dark red blood to stream from the comatose giant. Joe watched the carnage as he tried to catch his breath. Donta stood and stomped the heel of his shoe down around Babu's eyes over and over until Babu was motionless. "I fucking warned you," Donta shouted at the limp body under him. "Don't fucking make me do something!" Donta kicked Babu's head over and over again—even though there wasn't a breath, a sound, or any signs of life left. "Marching around this place for years, like you're someone. Fuck you!" Donta spat on the body of the giant. In his continued rage, he straddled him and began choking his huge neck.

Babu was already unrecognizable: his face was broken, swollen, and contorted.

"Stop," Joe managed to say.

Donta continued to shout. "You're all tough men when you're allowed to be with your fake fucking—" Like a mechanical piston, Babu's right fist came alive and drove Donta backward, toward the huge windows. Babu struggled to get up; he knew that he was close to dying. He needed to make it out of there so he could get home to his wife—he wasn't going to do her the disservice of dying at the hands of a cunt. He had a promise to keep.

Donta's face was covered in blood. He lifted himself to all fours before Babu kicked him in the ribcage as hard as he could—which lifted him from the ground. Babu collapsed in agony. His leg was in real bad shape. He dragged himself toward his attacker on sheer shock and adrenaline. He caught Donta by both sides of his head and lifted him clean off the ground. Babu then drove his own horribly disfigured head into Donta's face, which destroyed Donta's features completely. Babu ran his attacker's rag-doll body toward the wall, where Donta was crushed between bricks and the furious giant.

Joe tried to crawl out of the room.

Babu picked Donta up above his head and launched him as far as he could across the room before collapsing again himself. Donta landed like he'd been launched through the windshield of a crashing car. Babu dragged himself toward Joe. The chairman curled up in the corner of the room. Babu stood on one leg, grabbed Joe by his hair, and hoisted him to eye level. Joe couldn't look Babu in the face.

"Please," Joe begged.

"He's dead," Babu said of Donta.

Joe looked at the damage that had been done to Babu. "I'm sorry, Chrissy."

Babu punched the wall beside Joe's head with such power that it made Joe panic. "None of us can explain this away, Joe," Babu said. "Clean it up, and make it go away."

Joe nodded rapidly. "Yes, yes. Of course." Babu released him. "Why did you go after Ricky?" the giant asked.

The chairman looked at the blood that had been spilled and the lives that had been ruined again for New York. "You think I got to Ricky?" Joe said. "Look a little closer to home."

North Carolina.
Tanner knew that it must have been bad. He felt like he was carrying around a lead balloon in his stomach. His body was failing him. He was surrounded by machines and tubes. All his money couldn't buy his way out of this situation. He was alone, in a hospital bed, getting ready to die. He wanted to leave and at least spend his last night in his own home. It looked like he wasn't going to get that wish. He was, however, at least going to have time enough to fuck with his old colleagues.

Tanner picked up the pen and signed his territory over to Ade Schiller. She had always been working in the background. Always laying the groundwork. Among all the men, all the alpha bullshit, she was most dangerous of them all.

New York.
"Ladies and gentlemen, this contest is scheduled for one fall, with a twenty-minute time limit," said the ring announcer with the struggling comb-over. "This is for the undisputed heavyweight championship of the world."

The crowd rose to their feet; they knew that they were seeing history in the making. The Garden was packed, dark, loud, and ready to see the Kid Who Killed Boxing.

"Coming into the ring at this time, and weighing in at two hundred and ninety-seven pounds, from North Carolina, the NWC World Heavyweight Champion, the Prince of Panache: Emmet Cash!"

The crowd booed as Ricky watched in agony. He knew that Ade was also in the unlit crowd somewhere. Emmet Cash made his way to the ring and stood on the ropes to argue with the fans. Even though he was a champion, they had come to see the other guy.

"And his opponent, weighing in at two hundred and thirty-three pounds, from right here in New York City . . ." The crowd roared their approval. "The Kid Who Killed Boxing, and also the NWC World Heavyweight Champion: Kid Devine!"

The wall of sound hit Kid in the face as he made the short walk to the ring. He had never felt or seen anything like this before in his life. He was nervous, and adrenaline was flowing, but at least now he knew which way to go. He looked into the crowd to see who was looking back at him. He almost immediately saw the face he wanted to see. The person he knew he could make the most money with.

Kid Devine was ready to become his own man.

Outside, the cab screeched to a halt. Lenny and Jimmy were both stuck to the window of the taxi as it stopped. The Garden was an awesome sight, even though Lenny had seen it a thousand times before. He imagined what it was like in there now. Were they cheering for his boy? Would he make it through the match alright? Lenny had grown up wanting to be champion, and now his own son was doing just that.

"You got the money I gave you?" Lenny asked his son.

Jimmy couldn't look his father in the eye. He was afraid he might cry again if he did. He could only nod. "I got it."

"OK," Lenny said. He saw a boy lost beside him on the seat. Something told Lenny that sending that boy off home alone probably wasn't a good idea.

Both Lenny and Jimmy could hear the roar of the crowd inside. Jimmy leaned into his father. He didn't want him to go.

"You ready to go home?" Lenny asked Jimmy. He tried to lift his son's head so he could look him in the eye. Jimmy wasn't having it.

"You ready to go home, son?" Lenny asked again. Jimmy didn't want to but he knew he didn't have much choice.

"Yeah, I'm ready," Jimmy said.

"Let's go, then," Lenny said to his son.

"What?" Jimmy asked.

"Let's take you home," Lenny replied.

If the cop had seen Lenny, or if they had found some evidence on him, there was only one place he wanted to spend his last night. As tempting as the match at the Garden was, and as tempting as New York was, he couldn't risk not seeing her while he was free.

Lenny knew where he'd spend his last night, and it wasn't in the thick of the wrestling business. "I just need to collect something first," Lenny said.

Kid reached out to the crowd, and they began to chant his name. Emmet Cash pulled the young wrestler off the canvas by his hair, and the ref gave Cash a five count to let go. Cash, being a heel, blocked the ref's view, and raked Kid's eyes for good measure.

Edgar lay on his hallway floor with the lights off. He had a flashlight and a shotgun pointed at Tad, who was facing away from Edgar. Tad was in his underwear, on his knees with his hands behind his head.

"I will blow your fucking head off, you pervert," Edgar shouted.

"It's me, I swear! It's Tad Stolliday," Tad shouted.

He was terrified. Edgar continued to pretend he didn't know who his invader was. He did, however, take a few Polaroid pictures to show to the cops.

Babu lay on his bed, facing away from the light that came in through the door. He waited for his wife to join him and snuggle into him one last time, like he had promised.

Joe Lapine had just come back from the window, where he had seriously considered ending it all. The New York skyline had talked him out of it, though. The city was too alluring—too close to let go. Joe rolled Donta's body up in the giant rug in the middle of his room.

Ade watched the match from the fourth row. She didn't care that her marriage was in tatters. She didn't care that her home was smashed to pieces. She didn't care that her husband's career was over. Thanks to Tanner, she had her place back in the wrestling world; she also had one of the world champions. Ade was hoping that Kid was going to do what was right, and bring the belts back to her, too.

Ricky sat behind Ade. She had no idea that the man she'd tried to have murdered in Japan was only an arm's length away from her.

Ginny Ortiz sat in his first-floor corner room, with his pants unbuttoned to give his belly some more space. He would never have to worry about ice cream or moving again—not now that Ricky was back in town for good.

"Are you alright?" the ref shouted, so the crowd could hear. "Kid, are you alright?"

Kid was unresponsive. His opponent, the Prince of Panache, had him in a bear hug. The ref ran around the other side to get a better look, and to whisper to Kid, "Go home."

Kid had been waiting for those words, which in wrestling meant the end of the match was coming. The ref lifted Kid's hand into the air and dropped it. If it fell three times, then it meant that Kid was unconscious, unable to continue. The ref raised it a second time, and the crowd shouted and pleaded for Kid to fight back.

His hand fell again.

The referee looked almost nervous as he lifted the hand straight up in the air for a third time, where he again let it go. Kid's hand fell, but only halfway. The crowd cheered, screamed, and screeched collectively, as Kid's hand rose slowly back into the air by itself. His eyes opened. Cash looked like he had seen a ghost; he tried to squeeze harder, but Kid punched his way out of the hold. Emmet threw himself off the ropes, but Kid ducked under his clothesline attempt and tied him in the same chokehold that had rendered the world heavyweight boxing champion unconscious.

Madison Square Garden rumbled with a collective chaos. They knew: this was the move that killed boxing.

With the terrifying, exciting, and freeing sense of not knowing, Lenny sat in the taxi with no shoes, a faded garden gnome, and the happiest son in the world. As city turned to country, and buildings turned to trees, Lenny waited for their stop to come. Jimmy watched the road signs like a hawk.

"We're nearly there," he informed his father every three or four minutes.

Lenny wondered about the Garden, and he wondered about Ricky. He knew that no matter how the match went, he—or his family, if he wasn't around—would never have to worry about Ricky stiffing them. Even that one match would set them up comfortably for a long, long time.

Lenny tried to remember if he had touched anything other than the ladder. What about Jimmy using the phone from inside the pizza place? Surely they could trace that. Lenny tossed all the scenarios around in his head for the two-hour trip. He was ready for anything, especially now that he'd get to see Bree.

"We're here," Jimmy said excitedly. The boy paid the driver and told him to keep the change.

Lenny and Jimmy got out of the cab, and Lenny took a second to straighten himself. They both walked down the street to Jimmy's house. It was a quiet night, punctured here and there by sirens and the occasional truck rushing by on the small road behind the house.

"Her car is there, and the light is on," Jimmy said.

Lenny's heart began to beat like a hopeful teenager's. Jimmy stopped his father and straightened his hair.

"You go ahead," Jimmy said as he hung back a little.

All of the years that Lenny had been trying to survive, all of the stupid things he'd done and the trouble he'd made, all of the jobs he'd taken and the chaos he'd brought, from crashing the van, to hiding the money, to getting beat up at Danno's anniversary, to being educated by Ricky Plick and threatened by Proctor King, to leaving the business for his family, returning to New York, and pulling the trigger—it had all been because Lenny Long was trying to go home. And even though he wasn't sure if he'd be welcomed or hated, he needed to know. If it was just for one visit—even if the cops arrived to take him away—Lenny just wanted to go home.

He stood on an unfamiliar street, in front of a strange house, but he knew exactly where he was.

He knocked at the door and waited.